NEW PENGUIN SHAKESPEARE

GENERAL EDITOR: T. J. B. SPENCER

ASSOCIATE EDITOR: STANLEY WELLS

WILLIAM SHAKESPEARE

*

ALL'S WELL THAT ENDS WELL

EDITED BY
BARBARA EVERETT

PENGUIN BOOKS

PENGUIN BOOKS

Published by the Penguin Group
27 Wrights Lane, London w8 5tz England
Viking Penguin Inc., 40 West 23rd Street, New York, New York 10010, USA
Penguin Books Australia Ltd, Ringwood, Victoria, Australia
Penguin Books Canada Ltd, 2801 John Street, Markham, Ontario, Canada l3r 1b4
Penguin Books (NZ) Ltd, 182–190 Wairau Road, Auckland 10, New Zealand

Penguin Books Ltd, Registered Offices: Harmondsworth, Middlesex, England

This edition first published in Penguin Books 1970
Reprinted 1978, 1981, 1982, 1984, 1988

This edition copyright © Penguin Books, 1970
Introduction and notes copyright © Barbara Everett, 1970
All rights reserved

Made and printed in Great Britain by
Richard Clay Ltd, Bungay, Suffolk
Set in Monotype Ehrhardt

CONTENTS

INTRODUCTION

All's Well That Ends Well is not one of the more popular of Shakespeare's plays. This is regrettable, since it is a distinguished work: mature, subtle, and haunting. But certainly, there are real difficulties in the way of appreciation. One of the most difficult problems concerns its tone – the level and kind of seriousness with which the writer is presenting his materials. *All's Well That Ends Well* is usually thought of as a 'dark comedy' or 'problem play'. It is clearly a serious comedy, in that it is full of issues which can tax and vex the mind; moreover, the issues are explicit – the characters argue, think, debate, and doubt. It is characteristic that the first climax of the action, the rejection of Helena by Bertram on the grounds of her inferior social class, is marked by the King's passionate yet fully rational argument for the superiority of Merit over Birth. The play is a serious one, moreover, in a rather different sense from this. It contains no crimes and its only death is illusory – the very absurdity of Bertram's being arrested on a charge of wife-murder in the last scene serves to define the milieu here as one where 'such things do not happen' – yet it shows things grave enough: the sadness, defeat, and decline of the old, and the natural egoism of the young. In its appeal to the mind, then, and in the gravity of its vision, *All's Well That Ends Well* is a sober work, elegiac rather than saturnalian. And yet it is also, and truly, a romantic comedy. Coleridge spoke of it as 'not an agreeable story, but still full of love', and his emphasis on the quality of feeling in the play is just. The main action in it is a love story; and though happiness is not one of the things this play directly concerns itself with (there are other goods, even for comedy) nevertheless the love story ends as happily as it can. Now, the combination of all these – a romantic love story, an astringent intellectuality of presentation, and a grey vision of things – does not promise, at first sight, an easy and harmonious literary experience. Certainly this particular blend of materials is unique in Shakespeare, and the elusive and suggestive style which it produces is so original as to be frequently missed or under-rated.

For such diverse materials to fall into relationship with each other, and communicate what they have to communicate, demands an especially receptive and flexible sympathy in the reader. But here another problem arises. The play seems to rebut the sympathy it needs by the very nature of the story it tells. Shakespeare has found an edgy and affronting tale, and has left it more difficult than when he found it. He must have been looking for a story that was romantic, that told of a happy and fulfilled love, and yet that did so in a striking and startling way: such that the 'romance' could work on freshened perceptions and a livelier sense of fact. He found in Boccaccio (or his translator) a story whose pursuant heroine loved – so its first paragraph tells us – 'more than was meet for a maiden of her age', and Shakespeare perhaps saw here the element of the extreme, the surprising, the intensely individual, that he wanted for his heroine and for his comedy. Nothing in the rest of Boccaccio's story matches this hinted-at extremity, least of all the 'sage lady' who is his heroine. Boccaccio's narrative has a suavity, a grace, and a control that almost entirely conceal the fierce and archaic lineaments of the older stories within it. For within *his* story there are others. Boccaccio's tale of a young woman, a doctor's daughter, who manages at last to win, by the bed-trick, the man who has rejected her because of her inferior birth – this is in fact his deft interweaving of two very old folk tales, a tale of the Curing of the King and a tale of a Clever Wench. Except for the extraordinariness of the incident (mainly, in fact, the bed-trick) we should scarcely guess at these sources in Boccaccio. But we can hardly fail to guess at them in Shakespeare: who has, most interest-ingly, revived the buried folk-tale elements and brought them into bold and disturbing prominence. Helena enters the Court of France like a saviour-knight in the Waste Land of the Fisher King; the beginning of her cure is an archaic ritual, announced in stumbling and 'primitive' verse. But this account is, of course, partial; if Shakespeare had only made the story *more* like folk tale, the play would present fewer difficulties. He has in fact made the story more up-to-date as well as more archaic – given it a striking modernity as well as barbarous depths. If France in this play is sometimes reminiscent of a feudal Waste Land, its *genius loci* (so to speak) is the great creator of an intensely modern sceptical self-consciousness, Shake-speare's contemporary Montaigne. Treated in this way, an already slightly uncomfortable story becomes twice as un-comfortable, and infinitely more strange.

The treatment of the bed-trick, an aspect of the play it is hard to ignore, affords one of the best examples of the richly affronting strangeness Shakespeare achieves in his conversion of the original story. The bed-trick (a fictional convention for the most part, although there seem to have been a few occurrences of it in real life) was an unavoidable part of the story Shakespeare had chosen. His heroine achieves nominal marriage with the man she loves by curing his guardian, the King; but Bertram angrily imposes apparently impossible conditions – that he will consummate the marriage only *after* she has conceived a child by him. This riddling impossibility is soluble, like many ancient riddles, by a small intellectual adjustment: Bertram must be tricked into making love with Helena in ignorance of her identity, Helena must 'become' someone else, the mistress Bertram desires. This situation Boccaccio passes over with a calm speed, motivated, one presumes, not so much by the indelicacy of the arrangement as by its unlikelihood. Shakespeare brings it well to the fore in the second half of his play, coolly exploring its possibilities. What makes this remarkable is that in the earlier part of the play Shakespeare has managed to create the sense of living in precisely that 'modern' world to which this archaic convention is most offensive. He has created, mainly through his heroine, the sense of a world which counts sexual experience as vital: vital in that it may be a focus of that fusion of sensations and experiences which makes up the consciousness of a person. It is Helena's love that makes her a person, and she longs to express her love. This longing takes her unerringly, in the course of the action, to the bed-trick – that expression of the impersonal in sexuality, only acceptable in some archaic folk-tale world that regards persons as *things*, and bodies as chattels of the spirit. It is the collocation of these two opposed aspects of sexuality that is disturbing, and not the mere use of the bed-trick in itself. That Helena's deep and inward consciousness should resolve itself in the frank device of the bed-trick; that the subtle and ambitious exploration of the first part of the play should descend to a mere unravelling of plot in the second movement – this tends to cause a shock to the mind, as when Hamlet says with a comparable achievement of the outrageous: 'The King is a *thing*'.

There are many such contrasts and collocations in *All's*

Well That Ends Well. And the play does not always resolve its paradoxes very explicitly. Unlike a good deal of the satirical and realistic writing with which it has affinities, this is a work which does not give us much clear direction as to how we should judge and what we should think; it makes its 'points', diverse and sometimes contradictory as they are, and leaves us alone with them. It has a quality, in short, summed up by the figure of Diana, whom we see perplexing and irritating the King in the play's last scene, as she enumerates all the riddles and impossibilities of the action; and many readers may well feel like echoing the King's exasperated response:

> *Take her away, I do not like her now.*   V.3.279

Diana resolves her riddles only by pointing to the loving Helena, now visibly pregnant, who remains as enigmatic but in one sense as simple as she has always been. It may equally be said that the play's paradoxes as a whole serve simply to turn a more intensive and questioning attention to familiar things, which we see more clearly than usual because from strange and various angles. Though 'romantic', the play is strikingly unfantastic: when we move from France to Italy, we move merely from Court to Camp, and find them much what they always were. The strangeness lies, not (as in true romance) in new places, but in new light thrown on familiar ground.

The play's verbal style works to the same end. At first it can seem both difficult and puzzlingly diverse; but on better acquaintance it may be more justly found lucid and expressive. The diversity of style is so marked indeed that it has been used as evidence for dating the play within almost every period of Shakespeare's career, from the early 1590s to 'after 1608'. But a single play will often contain passages written in very various modes. Here the stylistic variations are far from random; they are dictated by literary purpose. They communicate mood, tone, and character. Helena's primitive and oracular couplets, for instance, at her meeting with the King –

> He that of greatest works is finisher
> Oft does them by the weakest minister –
>
> II.1.136–7

are merely a way of conveying, but with critical detachment, her ambiguous innocence and its impact on the court (for the King uses the same mode of speech). Similarly expressive, though different in kind, are the couplets of the King's long speech on Honour:

> Good alone
> Is good, without a name: vileness is so;
> The property by what it is should go,
> Not by the title. . . .
>
> II.3.127–30

These impressive though fine-drawn aphorisms prove, ironically, far less persuasive than the royal blast of rage which follows them. Or, for a last example, there is Bertram's smoothly diplomatic apologia, spoken before he is exposed:

> At first
> I stuck my choice upon her, ere my heart
> Durst make too bold a herald of my tongue;
> Where, the impression of mine eye infixing,
> Contempt his scornful perspective did lend me. . . .
>
> V.3.44–8

There is something self-betraying in his easy and conventional abstractions.

In the light of its dramatic functions, the play's stylistic diversity grows transparent, ceasing to give trouble. Similarly, an aspect of the style which is sometimes found disappointing, its low-keyed formality, becomes a virtue when we recognize its power to capture real and complex tones of voice. *All's Well That Ends Well* has its big speeches, but is perhaps more remarkable for its subtleties of intonation. The King's memories of his friend the dead Count, for instance ('I, after him, do after him wish too'), hauntingly trace the inward involutions of mood. Those special indices of expressive speech, the broken sentence and abrupt pregnant phrase, are a characteristic of the play. Exclamations like the Countess's 'O that "had"', how sad a passage 'tis!', or the young courtiers' exchange, 'what things are we!' – 'Merely our own traitors', have a powerful suggestiveness. Only a medium at once so diverse in its modes and so reticently formal in its language could have given rise to this tonal complexity and power of implication.

The competing centres of dramatic interest in the comedy give perhaps even more trouble than its apparent conflict of verbal styles. It seems no accident that during the two centuries before our own there were two markedly different stage texts of the play, each fashioned as a setting for one of the chief characters. The eighteenth-century version of *All's Well That Ends Well* is represented by the text prepared for the stage by Garrick in the 1750s. The play has become a farce, with Parolles as the leading character. During the last decade of the eighteenth century Kemble reconstructed the text, and a simplified, idealized Helena moved to the centre of a play now turned sentimental romance; she held this position for something like a hundred years, infrequently staged though the play was. And during the present century, most productions still seem to have had difficulty in doing justice to both centres of interest. On or off the stage it is not easy to reconcile the two characters and all they represent. Whatever one thinks of the homage Helena received from some nineteenth-century critics (Coleridge called her Shakespeare's 'loveliest character'), she is undeniably a remarkable study of intense feeling. But with all her complication and inner reserve, she is probably more effective in the study than on the stage. Parolles, on the other hand, is a type from social comedy, whom no one has ever venerated – though Johnson seems, from his comparison of Parolles with Falstaff, to be prepared to feel at least some affection for him. He is essentially a product of the theatre, fashioned out of comic routines and ancient, yet always fresh, stage business. With his shabbiness, his treachery, and his pompous vulgarity, he is an odd companion for the young heroine of a romantic comedy. Yet Shakespeare emphatic-ally places them in relationship at an early point in the play. Their encounter, with its effect of paradox, expresses in little some part of the play's meaning. Shakespeare's design may become clearer if we look more closely at Helena and Parolles, both separately and in their involve-ment with each other.

*

We have already noted part of Helena's 'ancestry' as a character: she is a folk-tale heroine derived from, or rather glimpsed through, Boccaccio's story and perhaps a number of analogous stories and ballads known to Shake-speare. The bold outlines of her character are given her by her narrative function; and it is from such narrative sources that she takes her purity, intensity, and primitive angularity. It is largely the folk-tale origins of her character that have caused her to be regarded by many (especially in the nineteenth century) as the Providence of the play, a saving force, Shakespeare's best woman; and that have caused some more modern readers to feel an equally strong repugnance. But this is only one side of Helena's ancestry, for there are aspects of the character which relate her closely to some of Shakespeare's earlier heroines (though not all would agree that they are chronologically earlier), and these have very little to do with folk tales. In what may be Shakespeare's first comedy, *The Two Gentlemen of Verona*, Julia pursues a faithless and unloving love with a devotion equal to Helena's. Another Helena, who very possibly gave the later heroine her name, bewails her unrequited love in language strikingly close to our Helena's analyses of her situation:

> only give me leave,
> Unworthy as I am, to follow you. . . .
>   The story shall be changed:
> Apollo flies, and Daphne holds the chase;
> The dove pursues the griffin; the mild hind
> Makes speed to catch the tiger. . . .
> A Midsummer Night's Dream, II.i.206-7, 230-33

In *Venus and Adonis* Venus woos Adonis with all the passion, and something of the perversity, with which Helena yearns after Bertram. And, in her special quality of steadfastness, of patient holding-on, Helena is closest of all to Viola, the heroine of *Twelfth Night*, the comedy which *All's Well That Ends Well* probably succeeded. In fact, Helena has qualities which have developed from preceding heroines, and if she differs from them, it is by an extension and intensification of qualities they share.

There is something, however, which distinguishes Helena (and hence her play), and which makes her transcend both her comic ancestry and her folk-tale origins. Helena is the only one of Shakespeare's comic heroines who is given – and who needs, in order to define herself – genuinely introspective soliloquies. The intensity and extremity which have come to her from folk tale, from loving 'more than was meet', combine with the quality of female self-containedness with which Shakespeare seems to have been more and more concerned in the mature comedies. And from the fusion of these two things there emerges a radically new comic heroine. For Helena is *inward*. There is nothing which we do not know about the earlier heroines, in so far as we need to know anything; and the fact is that we do not need to know much. There is a good deal we need to know about Helena, and we never know it all. The earlier heroines keep no secrets from the audience, least of all when they are disguised and prevaricating. When they are, like Rosalind, 'fathom deep in love', the water is clear all the way down. Essentially they are transparent, and the transparency is a part of their value. This is not true of Helena. She is much given to secrecies and reticences. And this interesting technical feature has made some critics and readers, who are not among Helena's admirers, discuss her in unnecessarily rancorous terms. It needs to be said simply that Helena is rare among the heroines of romantic comedy in that she does not assume disguise (unless her pilgrim's robe of penitence, or the device of the bed-trick, can be counted as disguise) and yet she is opaque to us throughout the play.

In dramatic terms, there is a reason for this opacity. With a character like Rosalind, Shakespeare was exploring something relatively constant; Rosalind is a carefully charted-out area, which does not essentially change in the course of the play. We can, therefore, become deeply familiar with her, and the *rapport* between character and audience is complete. But Helena is by no means a 'steady-state' character. Like all the young people in this play, she is in process of evolution – although after the bed-trick she seems to 'steady' dramatically and remain constant for the rest of the play. And it is interesting that she ceases to appear so opaque at this point; she begins to become familiar. In all the early part of the play, Helena is coming into being as a character, just as – in naturalistic terms – she is coming into being as a person. As a result, we cannot 'know' her; we can only watch, with a greater or lesser degree of sympathetic involvement, a dynamic process of change called Helena.

This fact is most relevant in the long first scene of the play, which is, surely, an unacknowledged *tour de force* of dramatic artistry. It is a difficult scene, from the point of view of Helena's characterization, because so much is left implicit; but it is also a brilliant one. We see a person who is, at first, in some kind of stasis, locked up in herself and unable to advance. Her first and for some time only speech is a riddle: 'I do affect a sorrow indeed, but I have it too'. Her second is a paradox in soliloquy: she expounds an impossible love. She impatiently disclaims affection for her dead father –

> *What was he like?*
> *I have forgot him –*

and owns to a passion that she contemplates with sharp and self-mocking truth:

> *now he's gone, and my idolatrous fancy*
> *Must sanctify his relics.*

This is more like the voice, not of a romantic heroine, but of Hamlet; even of Edmund in *King Lear*. Both riddle and paradox give her a curious free-standing dignity and isolation, and put her askance of the audience as well as of the other on-stage characters. This is a person who seems incapable of advancing into the *engagement* of comedy; the verse that Helena speaks in this early part of the play is heavy with some kind of strange inhibition, a sense of total impossibility or failure. It is all the more striking, then, that by the end of this first scene Shakespeare has made Helena convincingly advance into the out-going decisiveness and certainty of her last soliloquy here:

> *Our remedies oft in ourselves do lie,*
> *Which we ascribe to heaven.*

The stress falls on 'ourselves'; it is to this discovery that the whole scene has been proceeding. Helena has discovered energies in herself to initiate the long advance into activity that is her propulsion of the plot, until she becomes (some would say) *mere* activity, capable of managing the plot and of nothing else.

Whether or not this is a just criticism can be left to emerge in due course. It is enough to notice, for the moment, the remarkable impression Shakespeare gives in this first scene of a person who *has* an inward life to come to terms with, and to take strength from. In part it is done by Helena's indirectness – by the fact that we are often left to guess or work out what connexions she is making between things, what underlies a certain question or a certain answer. It is done partly by stressing her social isolation – which gives her only companions such as Parolles, with whom there is no question of her fully communicating. But it is done most powerfully as well as most economically by giving her a speech such as the following: which is saying, in simple paraphrasable terms, something like 'It's a pity that low-born people like

me can do little more to achieve what they want than
wanting it' – but which suggests a great deal more:

> 'Tis pity –
> *That wishing well had not a body in't*
> *Which might be felt, that we, the poorer born,*
> *Whose baser stars do shut us up in wishes,*
> *Might with effects of them follow our friends,*
> *And show what we alone must think, which never*
> *Returns us thanks.*   I.1.176, 178–83

This difficult but brilliantly expressive passage seems to
reveal the depths of a mind caught in a tortuous frustra-
tion; the over-riding impression is of isolation and
abstraction, both summed up in the ambiguous phrase
'show what we alone must think'. It is no wonder that
Parolles, to whom she is talking, is plainly dazed and
confused by her replies. Plainly, too, it will take a powerful
force to release Helena from this unpromising state of
mind. It is the force of 'nature' which she invokes in the
last soliloquy of this scene that is largely responsible for
doing so:

> *The mightiest space in fortune nature brings*
> *To join like likes, and kiss like native things.*

The 'nature' that Helena turns to here, with a sudden
certainty and confidence, is not a thing easy to interpret in
a phrase: its area of reference is immense. But one limited
aspect of 'nature' can be mentioned as relevant, since
Shakespeare's purpose in the scene of the curing of the
King may be clarified as a result.

What first and perhaps most draws the attention about
Helena is her appearance of taut rationality, her ability to
analyse herself. But this impression is rapidly succeeded by
the recognition that the self that she is analysing is not at

all rational and clear: it is the self of a folk-tale heroine, driven into activity by strong and deep instincts and impulses – what Helena herself calls 'wishes', in fact. This self is far from being simply sexual, but sexual it certainly is. Hence the fact that when she first appears in the King's court, Lafew twice makes marked reference to her beauty and sexual vitality, and twice describes the King himself, after his cure, as one who has specifically gained in 'lustiness'; moreover, Helena herself speaks as though the cure incurred the risk of indelicate imputations being made against her. She sincerely claims to be moved by 'grace' when she begins the cure of the King. It would be a mistake to question her claim: grace too is far from the rationality and personality (in a narrow sense) that she exhibits at the start of the play. But it would be an equal mistake to lose sight of the 'nature' that animates her. As a character, Helena has *power*; and there are moments in the play when this power is clearly recognizable as a more attractive and benign form of that which Shakespeare gives (in the work which was probably his last) to the strange and terrible Venus invoked there:

> *Hail, sovereign queen of secrets, who hast power*
> *To call the fiercest tyrant from his rage*
> *And weep unto a girl; that hast the might*
> *Even with an eye-glance to choke Mars's drum*
> *And turn th'alarm to whispers; that canst make*
> *A cripple flourish with his crutch, and cure him*
> *Before Apollo; that mayst force the king*
> *To be his subject's vassal, and induce*
> *Stale gravity to dance. . . .*
>
> The Two Noble Kinsmen, V.i.77–85

*

Helena may be compared to Venus; but she is also a waiting-gentlewoman. For Shakespeare has given considerable social realism to the original situation, and has widened and deepened the statement made by Beltramo, Boccaccio's hero and the original of Shakespeare's Bertram, that he will not marry this doctor's daughter, so far beneath him in rank. Helena's exact social position in the play may be clarified by remembering that she holds much the same position as Maria in *Twelfth Night*. In fact, the Countess Olivia's household in that play, with its clown, steward, and waiting-gentlewoman Maria, seems to be the model for the Countess of Rossillion's – despite the great difference in the age of the two Countesses. It must also be noted that both Helena and Maria are gentlewomen, and not menials; and that Helena's upbringing by the Countess gives her almost the status of a daughter. Nevertheless we feel sharply the full weight of the words 'patronage' and 'condescension' as we watch the Countess and Lafew – kind and wise as they are – discuss Helena and her prospects in the first scene of the play. It is not impossible that there is unconscious irony in Lafew's remark 'Your commendations, madam, get from her tears'. At any rate, there is a very obvious distinction made between Helena and Bertram, which gives point and weight to the fact that in the course of the action the Countess comes to regard Helena as a truer child, on moral grounds, than her own son.

The difference in social class between the hero and heroine is not, of course, left as an isolated fact in the play. There is in *All's Well That Ends Well* a more exact and pressing sense of an actual society – a lived-in, firmly imagined, and clearly stratified social world – than in any other of Shakespeare's comedies. Correspondingly, one of the things that give it its unique tone is the gravity and intensity with which it focuses (and makes us focus) on *behaviour*, the way a man appears to his fellows, and the consonance (or lack of it) between the outward and inward man. To this whole side of the play Parolles is the clue. Parolles must, it seems, have come into being as a dramatic counterpoise and antithesis to Helena. Bertram needs a strong reason to make him withstand a force like Helena's 'nature', and Parolles embodies it. In the language of the folk-tale world, Parolles is the Tempter, Bertram's Evil Angel; and the older people in the play, the Countess and Lafew, do steadily and stoutly speak of Parolles in these terms (though Shakespeare is quite happy to make, in addition, the more realistic suggestion that on the whole Bertram needs no tempter). There is a real sense, moreover, in which Parolles is for Bertram a true moral alternative to Helena. The ambush of Parolles and the bed-trick take place on the same night. And though the two events are dissociated in terms of plot (indeed it can be said that the Parolles incident is built up to compensate for the thinness of the main plot) the immediate juxtaposition of the two 'tricks' or ambushes, as Bertram moves casually from one to another, makes its own bold point. Two parallel tests are taking place, and the humiliation which Helena chooses to undergo has a beauty and fruitfulness which the enforced humiliation of Parolles lacks. In addition, the young Count is himself being tested and found wanting in both situations: as his judgement (in having trusted Parolles) will be proved shallow in the ambush scene, so will the outcome of the bed-trick prove his honour false. Bertram believes himself the master in both situations, and yet it is the commoners, Helena and Parolles, who finally put him in his place.

The moral alternative that Parolles presents to Helena's at first more inward graces is the charm of the external, the superficial. He is, as stage type, a 'swaggerer', and, as social type, a climbing would-be courtier. In making Parolles a follower of perverted courtly values Shakespeare is treating a topic so familiar to his audience that he could afford to be casually allusive; but modern audiences probably need some information. It can be said that the great ambition of a courtly code such as dominated Elizabethan society was to identify morals and manners, beliefs and behaviour. ('Manners maketh man'.) The weak point of such an ideal is that it can appear to exalt mere manners and mere behaviour, using viciously superficial forms and affectations as a cover for brutish misbehaviour. Early in *All's Well That Ends Well* (I.2.24 onwards) we are told by the King that the late Count of Rossillion, Bertram's father, embodied true courtesy: not only was he well born, but he was kind and good, especially to those lower than himself in birth. But now the Count is remembered only by the King. He has been succeeded by men who approach the old ideal only in their fondness for fine surfaces, smart appearances: the young are men (says the King)

> *whose constancies*
> *Expire before their fashions.*

Courtesy has dwindled into an ethos in which a sense of 'ends' is lost in a world of 'means'. Of this world, Parolles, whose name means 'mere words', 'a faithless word of honour', and whose tawdry clothes are perpetually trailing gaudy scarfs, is the human embodiment. On his first appearance Helena sums up the (real) appeal of his shoddy brightness, perhaps in contrast to her own bare and inward intensity:

> *these fixed evils sit so fit in him*
> *That they take place when virtue's steely bones*
> *Looks bleak i'th'cold wind.* I.1.101-3

But Parolles is not the only embodiment of this world of external social forms in the play. Shakespeare manages to suggest, by brief and telling touches, a milieu more pervasive. The Clown has some vivid reports on court life. Its language he crystallizes (II.2) into the ludicrous and mannered catch-phrase 'O Lord, sir!' (which Parolles himself faithfully produces in a critical context later: 'O Lord, sir, let me live!'). He reduces to its essentials the sophistication of court love (III.2.14–16): 'The brains of my Cupid's knocked out, and I begin to love as an old man loves money, with no stomach'. And finally there is his vignette of the home-coming heroes, courtiers to a man, arriving at Rossillion (IV.5.101–3): 'Faith, there's a dozen of 'em with delicate fine hats, and most courteous feathers which bow the head and nod at every man'.

Shakespeare brings this 'most courteous feather', Parolles, into the play early on – at a point, in fact, at which we might have expected a dialogue between the hero and heroine. Instead, we have the notorious discussion of virginity which takes place between Helena and Parolles (I.1.105–211). To understand more of the significance of Parolles – halfway, one might say, between the Elizabethan 'false courtier' and the fop of Restoration comedy – is to see more clearly Shakespeare's purpose in this much-disliked debate. For, however hidden Helena's state of mind here, the exchange between them is vital to the play and to the heroine's future role in it. On his entry Parolles confronts the introspective and passionate Helena with the external milieu with which she must come to terms if she is to prove herself fit for Rossillion: as she says of this friend of Bertram's, 'I love him for his sake'. She is going to have to achieve the life that 'nature' directs her to in what is in certain senses the most unnatural world in the world. (And it is a part of the ironical point that Parolles defends a mechanically aggressive sexual activity in the name of 'nature'.) Without the somewhat unrealistic resource of, say, Viola in *Twelfth Night*, to disguise herself as a boy and hope for the best, Helena finds herself in a position much closer to Ophelia's, for whom, as Polonius tells her, 'Lord Hamlet is a prince out of thy star'. That is to say, Helena exists in a social world whose presuppositions are those which face virgins in the tough and cruel court of *Hamlet*. First, there seems no hope of marriage to the Count; on rational grounds – and before the King marvellously alters the situation – she must presume herself simply 'not in his sphere'. Shakespeare makes evident and significant this gap in social class: if Helena were Bertram's equal, she would never be allowed her unguarded dialogue with the raffish Parolles, calmly discussing sexual life, nor would she be spied on and reported to the Countess by a steward, as she is later. Secondly, in so far as she has any prospect of a relationship with Bertram at all, the only hope would be an affair such as he later undertakes (or thinks he does) with Diana.

It is the function of this curious – yet, in the end, remarkably informative – little scene with Parolles to make all this quite clear, both to Helena and to the audience. The gracious, kindly, and very slightly formidable elders have left the stage, taking Bertram with them; and in place of their real, if demanding, courtesies, Helena faces the momentarily more relevant 'courtesy' of someone of her own class and generation. To her question, concerning virginity, 'How might one do, sir, to lose it to her own liking?', Parolles has the bleakest of answers: 'Marry, ill, to like him that ne'er it likes'. This hard cynicism is to govern Bertram's behaviour, at least: when he has had, as he thinks, Diana's virginity, he cares neither for it nor for her. It is in a world marked by such exchanges of courtesy that Helena, with her voracious but natural idealism, must find herself. After all, there is really no alternative to the life of 'courtesy' in this extremely worldly play. Helena can hardly elect for the barren alternative offered by the Clown, in whom the dolour of mere sexuality meets the dour (though sometimes haunting) wit of a world-hating theology. Lavatch is introduced, at some length (I.3), shortly after Helena's encounter with Parolles, and underlines many of Parolles's points. If Helena is proposing to be the 'One good woman in ten' in the treacherous, lecherous world Lavatch lives in, she has her work cut out. And yet the encounter with Parolles seems so to have invigorated her as to have made her willing to try. It is his presentation of the shallow externals of a court code that seemingly sharpens her sense of herself; she is *defined* by this dramatic – though oblique – encounter with so appallingly unpromising a milieu. 'Our remedies oft in ourselves do lie'. Parolles has unwittingly pushed Helena into a discovery of her 'nature', and, with the thought of the King's disease, she is in action.

Helena becomes so much a person of action, indeed, that we are never again so close to her as in this first scene. She reveals her feelings in the beautiful scene with the Countess, but already we are seeing her somewhat from the outside – in part, with the eyes of the Countess; hence, it is with an effect of naturalness (rather than of deceit) that Helena is perceived to be giving a slightly different account of herself from the one we have heard. She does have one later soliloquy, that which marks her departure from the scene at the close of the first part of the action (III.2.99–129). This speech, though highly praised (it is often spoken of as the only strongly Shakespearian passage

26

in the play; which is perhaps imperceptive), is in fact a very formal piece of writing, in which Helena is probably acting Chorus rather than thinking aloud. We come closer to her again in the second part of the play; but her appearances are so few and brief that they merely counterbalance, rather than contradict, the general movement of the play. The impasse at the beginning, which is profoundly personal as well as social, is resolved by a movement into impersonal activity. When we arrive with Helena at Florence (in Act III, scene 5), there is a real sense that we are starting things all over again, but in an infinitely simpler world. The worthy Widow and Mariana discuss, as did the aristocratic Countess and Lafew, the proper upbringing of the young and the importance of decent behaviour. Helena has to hear from them news of Bertram as deflating as was Parolles's brisk picture of meaningless sexuality. The difference lies in the simplicity of the reactions and the pleasant crudity of the solutions. There is a refreshing directness, for instance, in Diana's thoughts on Bertram and Parolles that balances, and in a sense dissolves, the self-defeating complexities of Helena's love:

> *'Tis pity he is not honest. Yond's that same knave*
> *That leads him to these places. Were I his lady*
> *I would poison that vile rascal.* III.5.81–3

Similarly, the Widow and Mariana have a brisk way with the graces of a would-be courtier. 'Marry, hang you!' – 'And your courtesy, for a ring-carrier!' they retort, as Parolles salutes them (III.5.90–91).

Helena allows Diana to take her place, nominally, at the forefront of the action. She herself disappears into, and disguises herself as, this apparently simple physical creature whom Bertram desires (though Diana is, of course, far from stupid; in fact she is probably the cleverest person in the play). But the change certainly entails the disappearance from near the centre of the action of the former unhappy, inward Helena, whose complex problems are so absorbing to the attention. The play has, that is, a rhythm not unlike that which appears in some other plays by Shakespeare (in *Measure for Measure* and *The Winter's Tale*, for instance). The writer demands a flexible responsiveness in the audience: the play moves to the new centre of action, and attention shifts away from Helena, who can look after herself in the background, to those who are the focal points of the solution, as she was of the problem.

Before that solution can be achieved, Parolles must be exposed. The long scene of the ambush, which plays so important a part in the second movement of the play, is remarkable for two reasons. The first is that it magnificently fulfils its function, in that Parolles shows himself as he really is. The young courtiers who are supposedly his friends trick him into believing that he is among enemies, and in danger of instant death unless he betrays his cause. This he does with a promptitude and thoroughness that finally destroy any claims he has to honour or minimal decency, and in the process indict the shallowness of the young Bertram who has trusted in him. But the scene does more than this: its power, in fact, lies in the way it transforms something merely functional into another dimension. In dramaturgical terms this is merely a 'gulling' scene: a scene in which a fool is shown up and humiliated. The unpleasant power of such scenes, outside Shakespeare, lies almost invariably in their cheerful cruelty; they are a substitute for bear- or cock-baiting. But Shakespeare's scene is as far from sadism as it is from sentimentality. It quite lacks, moreover, the mechanical

28

quality often present in these gulling scenes; the situation
has been given life and significance. The young men's
trick is not a mere device. Seen clearly, it is a translation
into external terms of precisely those ideas which inform
the 'courtesy' of Parolles. He has always been, we may
say, fighting for his life among enemies; his civilities are
mere defence and evasion. When the young men persuade
him that he is now cornered indeed, he becomes – for the
first time in the play – completely natural. It is a scene of
betrayal in more senses than one: Parolles betrays himself, Bertram, and the young men, and they assist him.
The epigraph of this painfully funny scene might be the
gravely serious exchange between the young Dumaines
which immediately precedes it: 'As we are ourselves, what
things are we!' – 'Merely our own traitors' (IV.3.18–20).

With ludicrous alacrity Parolles first pours out all the
military information he has. Then, with a furious desire to
placate, he augments this with fantasies about the private
lives and personal habits of his comrades-in-arms. These
comrades, who are of course the young courtiers sur-
rounding him, are deeply stung as well as amused by the
lies Parolles tells, far more than by the military secrets he
betrays. For his fantasies have an exactness of social detail
and a cruel eye for characteristic behaviour which have a
peculiar power to hurt those who live by a courtly code of
manners. The blindfolded and bound Parolles is, all in all,
more than a match for the young men who surround him.
His only motive is an animal urge to save his skin; but his
complete irresponsibility and lack of scruple put his
tormentors in need of protection from *him*.

The second transformation of the gulling scene is still
to come. When the officers have left their victim to consider his dishonoured life, Parolles is alone on stage for the
first time in the play. We should hardly have expected the

shallow swaggerer of the earlier scenes to be shown communing with himself in soliloquy. But Parolles has changed in this scene, as Helena changed and developed in the first scene of the play. Both find themselves in some kind of trap, and the struggle to get out changes their nature and gives them, as characters, a new dimension. Lafew's tart assessment of Parolles, 'The soul of this man is his clothes', turns out to be true, but not quite adequate. For, stripped of his gaudy superficies of manners, he reveals another and truer self:

> Yet am I thankful. If my heart were great
> 'Twould burst at this. Captain I'll be no more,
> But I will eat and drink and sleep as soft
> As captain shall. Simply the thing I am
> Shall make me live.   IV.3.320–24

Diana, even more tersely than Lafew, has called Parolles 'That jackanapes with scarfs', and, now that the scarfs are off, there *is* something of the tame ape in him. After this, he may try with Lavatch a slightly humbler form of his old swaggering style, but it is no use. The Clown is prompt to tell him that he smells – with the rank smell of a *thing* (an object or creature), not a man. Parolles has been abased, and nothing abases him more than his readiness to accept indignity: 'being fooled, by foolery thrive'. His fate is to become a Fool in the service of Lafew, to whom he had once talked indignantly of his rights as a man. Lafew's tolerant, contemptuous acceptance of him (V.2.52–3) – 'Though you are a fool and a knave you shall eat. Go to, follow' – makes for Parolles a happy ending that is ironical indeed.

*

Helena and Parolles are associated in a way as yet only touched on. Their common link is Bertram; and the story of each is set in the context of the story of the house of Rossillion.

There is a real sense in which the comedy has been Bertram's story from the beginning. We open with the Countess's grave and moving sentence 'In delivering my son from me, I bury a second husband'. Yet here, in the early part of the play, Bertram hardly emerges as a person; he is 'my son', the Count of Rossillion whom the elders are deeply concerned with because he is the continuity of the line itself. (It is a memorable moment in the play when Helena herself contributes to this view, addressing Bertram as 'Rossillion' at the end of the first movement, before she leaves in penitential dress to start again as Bertram's wife, and one who cares for his house and line more than for her own personal pride.) The relation of the two generations is extremely important in *All's Well That Ends Well*; and what the elders think of Bertram is to be taken with some (though not total) seriousness. They are an important enough group to need a brief consideration on their own account, before we turn to him.

The Countess and Lafew are (like Parolles and Lavatch) Shakespeare's addition to his source; and the King of France has had so much added to him as to count substantially as Shakespeare's creation. These elders are, in their realism and humanity, reminiscent of the senior generation in *Hamlet*, or the King in *Henry IV* (especially in his relation to his grown son); but with this marked difference – they are entirely benignant. The Countess is wise, poised, kind; Lafew is shrewd and tough; and the King, with his conscientiousness, his irony, and his moments of asperity, is the most likeable monarch in Shakespeare. Their charm is real, as is their goodness. But their authority has a natural limitation which is best illustrated by the King's fine speech in the first Act. He

evokes in it the memory of his friend, Bertram's father, a
great soldier, a wit, and a good man: and the speech ends
with a haunting cadence in which the King, quoting the
late Count's wish not to live 'After my flame lacks oil',
goes on:

> *This he wished.*
> *I, after him, do after him wish too,*
> *Since I nor wax nor honey can bring home,*
> *I quickly were dissolvèd from my hive*
> *To give some labourers room.*   I.2.63–7

It is an elegiac, even nostalgic, spirit which animates this
speech; the cadence is beautiful but it is, all the same, a
dying fall. The same dying fall – if perhaps in a more
sinewy, more colloquial form – shapes the Countess's
brief 'O that "had", how sad a passage 'tis!' and her light
phrase to the Clown: 'To be young again, if we could!' In
a crisper form still, it is to be heard in Lafew's dry 'for
doing I am past'. These sad cadences have their appropriateness. For the King is gravely ill, until he is cured
by young Helena; the Countess has just buried her
husband; and Lafew's name probably derives from *le feu*
and means 'the late'. In fact the comedy opens with
everyone dressed in black. We can certainly speak of these
elderly personages as nearly perfect, but it is to the point
that one of the meanings of 'perfect' is 'finished'. They
give vital support to the activity of the young (the Countess
blesses, Lafew judges, the King dispenses bounty and
threatens 'revenge and hate') but they do not and cannot
act themselves. Indeed, it is their peculiarly static quality
which gives the play something of its tone and character –
its withdrawn, contemplative, and reflective note. The
elders even impose this quality on those in relation to them:
the oddly still, frozen quality of Lavatch, for instance,

with his sometimes beautiful rhetoric and his complete ineffectuality, derives from the fact that he is the Countess's Clown. When they are together, they stand like two figures in a frieze.

Now, the young are very far from perfect, but on the other hand they are only just beginning; and in this beginning is a large part of the hope of the old, whom they balance in a larger perspective of mutual need. 'In delivering my son from me . . .' says the Countess, and the play turns on – its very structure is governed by – this son's departure from home and his coming home again.

Shakespeare presents Bertram as one who has not yet formed his character, a youth not yet come of age. To the extent that he is at all interesting as a person, he is unpleasant: he has, indeed, a kind of well-bred loutishness fitted to his age and standing. And yet he too is moved, as Helena is, by 'nature'. He is called to the court of Paris by his surrogate father, the King (and watched over by his second surrogate father, Lafew), although he regards his relationship to the King as an existence 'evermore in subjection' (I.1.5). And long before the issue of marriage to Helena gives him a further motive, he is eager to assert his independence and take his leave:

> *I shall stay here the forehorse to a smock,*
> *Creaking my shoes on the plain masonry,*
> *Till honour be bought up, and no sword worn*
> *But one to dance with. By heaven, I'll steal away!*
>
> II.1.30–33

Where he goes is not really material. He goes *away*; as it happens, to the convenient wars in the South. The incessant pressure of the senior generation has become such

that France is to Bertram a 'dark house' (as he calls it),
not so unlike what Hamlet calls the 'prison' of Denmark.

Before he goes, Bertram is faced by his first moment of
choice: when Helena unexpectedly chooses *him*. In this
important scene (II.3) Bertram first begins to show
marked character (in a personal as well as dramatic sense):
he begins to move into the centre of the action. His
attempted refusal of Helena is, in rational motivation,
snobbish and boorish. Yet Shakespeare has treated it so
that there is something real in it, above the question of
social class: some saving recalcitrance, some live obstinacy
that stands up to and answers this benevolent despot, the
philosopher King. For there is, of course, a momentary
breath of the sinister, as the happy, elderly King surveys
the obedient young lords ranged for Helena's delectation,
and tells her (II.3.55):

Thou hast power to choose, and they none to forsake.

Bertram's tart refusal gives us the great comic pleasure of
anticlimax (as does the undoubtedly sympathetic Diana's
cool teasing of the King in the last scene of the play). But
it does more than this. It would be foolish to propose too
seriously a comparison with Cordelia, but in Bertram's
refusal to co-operate with the plans of his King-father
there are points prefiguring her defiance. It is, at any rate, a
gesture of freedom, always an exhilarating thing. And the
Helena who also cured the King in the name of freedom
('Health shall live free and sickness freely die') can
hardly complain if her husband demands the same freedom. All she can do, she does: she frees him further by
ceasing to exist to him in her own identity. She dies to
him, moving first into the austerely sexless and un-
individuated garb of a pilgrim, then into the 'person' of

34

the woman he desires. She lets him, that is, this time initiate things freely and for himself, contenting herself with a patient and dutiful regularizing function: Bertram can take pride in thinking he is conducting a romantic and illicit affair, whereas he is in fact consummating his marriage and getting himself an heir. What he has done, he has done freely; and if that freedom is an illusion, he has yet to find it out.

The finding-out takes place (as is proper for a denouement) in the long and very fine last scene of the comedy, which deserves some attention in its own right. Shakespeare has given great care to this scene, in which Bertram comes home, and things come home to Bertram: nothing could be further from the truth than the supposition that Shakespeare is hastily huddling his drama to an end. The style of much of it is bare, but with the intentionality that marks all stylistic changes in this intensely stylish work: the interest is now strongly situational, and the situation is certainly enough to carry the interest. Shakespeare has gathered all his characters to meet the returning hero. The Countess is there, of course; Lafew has made a special request to witness the coming interview; Shakespeare has sent the King out on progress so as to bring him within range of Rossillion; Helena, Diana, and the Widow are on the last stages of their weary journey across Europe, and will shortly arrive; even Parolles will be called. There is, in fact, a very grand, formal, and forgiving reception committee to meet the young man who has triumphantly proceeded home; free (as he thinks) of his desire by satisfaction and his unwanted wife by death, free of his surrogate fathers by manly prowess in the wars and of his out-grown and ill-chosen friend by virtue of having seen him degraded. Bertram thinks himself, in short, what is often called mature. Since he has (unknown to himself) fathered a child and is on the way to becoming an elder on his own account, this notion is not wholly unfounded; moreover a process is beginning which will prove ageing to him.

The process of reception and forgiveness is crystallized by the fact that a new wife is to be found for Bertram: he is to *start again* in a way somewhat different from Helena's painful and plodding journey. The unseen young woman in question is one Maudlin, daughter of Lafew: named after Mary Magdalen, the Saint of Penitence, and so especially suitable for a nominally penitent hero. Bertram produces the ring, and is about to become freely engaged, explaining romantically that Maudlin is the one whom he has loved all along, when things begin to come alive. Bertram is finding out about the nature of freedom. This first part of the scene has witnessed a fine and formal burial of the dead: Helena is treated much like the late Count of Rossillion at the opening of the play. Even Bertram finds he can allow that he has loved his wife, now that she is, as everyone thinks, safely dead. 'And now forget her', adds the King, turning to the future. But future love can only be pledged by the ring; and when Bertram readily produces it, it turns out to be (useful symbolic property that it is) as loaded with an undismissible past as any elder's memory. For it is the ring which Helena–Diana gave him in bed, a pledge of love in return for the ring he gave her, bearing the honour of his house. When Bertram is (farcically but in some sense justifiably) about to be carried off to prison on a charge of having murdered the owner of the ring, he is interrupted by the appearance of Diana, come to say that whether or not Bertram has a dead wife, he certainly has a living one: herself. That is to say, Bertram's freedom has now very nearly landed him with three wives: Maudlin, withdrawn in disgust by Lafew on account of the question of the other two; Helena, for whose murder he is about to be incarcerated; and Diana, whom he believes himself to have spent one hour with, doesn't care for now, and is going to have to dishonour himself telling lies about in order to get out of marrying. And this situation the audience are, of course, free to find farce, but it contains also – as does much good farce – the lineaments of the blackest comedy. Bertram's ordinary vices are following him home with the logic of nightmare, and the humiliation is a good deal worse, given his aristocratic pretensions, than anything endured by Helena or Parolles. The end of freedom, for the Count of Rossillion, is to have made plain to him the defining boundaries thrown up by his own past and his own nature.

But Bertram in a sense stays free to the end. The close of this final scene, and the presentation of Bertram with it, have probably caused even more bewilderment than the scene in its entirety. And yet the close is vital to the play. Bertram's nightmare is ended by the return of Helena. Diana, who has pursued Bertram like a prim and pretty member of the Eumenides, can now relinquish her prey in favour of the more loving Helena. 'Guilty and ... not guilty' as he is, Diana quits him, handing him over to Helena's judgement and mercy. Bertram, of course, asks for pardon. What is he to say now? He and Helena, in this comedy of individuals, are deeply familiar and yet they have hardly met; they have made love but scarcely achieved conversation. Helena's unexpected reply to the King gives him his cue. To the King's delighted exclamation (which hardly expects an answer):

> *Is there no exorcist*
> *Beguiles the truer office of mine eyes?*
> *Is't real that I see?*

she replies, with an echo of Bertram's blunt truth in the proposal scene:

> *No, my good lord,*
> *'Tis but the shadow of a wife you see,*
> *The name and not the thing.*

And when Bertram now asks for pardon, she answers him with courtesy but also with the same richly ambiguous independence:

> *O my good lord, when I was like this maid*
> *I found you wondrous kind.*

Her genuinely courteous attribution of all the *kindness* to him, and the sharp truthfulness of the irony that lies inside the courtesy, leave him free now *not* to be kind. He bravely asks, as he asked before, to judge for himself; and he makes the request formally to his and her surrogate father, the King:

> *If she, my liege, can make me know this clearly*
> *I'll love her dearly, ever, ever dearly.*

It is an outrageous answer, of course; it is monstrous for a penitent hero to take the heroine on terms. But Bertram's 'If' is repeated, first by Helena, who echoes Bertram's; then three times by the King, first with regard to Diana (if she is a virgin he will find her a husband), then with regard to the whole action ('if it end so meet . . .'), and finally in the Epilogue:

> *All is well ended if this suit be won,*
> *That you express content.*

Bertram's 'If' starts a chain of conditions, that lead us out of the play; so that *All's Well That Ends Well* is (as its title half ironically promises) an open-ended work indeed. With a pregnant heroine on stage at the end of it, the gesture to futurity is in place. Whether this ending (which has so often been taken as a symptom of an author's doubt or cynicism) makes a convincing and true close for the comedy can only be judged by considering the effect of the whole.

*

If Cressida were restored to Troilus at the end of their play, we should not, probably, feel much hope for their future. When Helena and Bertram come together at the end of theirs, it is possible to feel (though not everyone does) a good deal of hope in the future. For the whole of the rest of the play prepares a ground which makes such hope feasible. This is partly a matter of their being the most signal case of what the rest of the play richly illustrates, that unlikes (even opposites) may come together in mutual need and reciprocal help. The whole strong and fertile relation of old and young in the play (Helena curing the King, the King directing Bertram, and so on) lies behind Helena and Bertram as a pattern of relationship.

But there is another reason why a sense of hopefulness at the end of the play may be well grounded. The world which *All's Well That Ends Well* portrays is a tough one, but not one without a sense of value; and hope in the future is a vital part of that sense of value. This is, of course, a very old comic morality (if it can be called such); all Shakespeare's comedies inculcate a cheerful trust in Time to do what present persons cannot. But they do it, on the whole, casually and peripherally. The very title of our play declares the prominence in it of a forward-looking rhythm of feeling, a stress on the relation of present and future. It is this, perhaps, that Helena means by 'wishing well' (I.1.178) and Diana by 'vowed true' (IV.2.22). Such a value operates naturally in a play that deals so directly, as this does, with the relation of old and young, of the dead and the as yet unborn. To say this is to see the need to extend the word 'hope' to something more comprehensive, and speak rather of the operation in the play of memory and hope together. For the play calls up a sense of a true relation not only of present and future, but of present and past as well. Memory is, with some naturalness, the vivid and enriching force which characterizes the old, hope the steady drive that activates the young, and the two interlock and exchange: at the end of the play the old look forward, the young look back. These things are not mere moods affecting persons: memory and hope are rather energizing forces in the play, and give the present moment a peculiar charge of significance and potentiality. The King's evocation of his friend the late Count of Rossillion gives him as haunting and as judicial a presence in the play as Hamlet Senior has in his; and Bertram tells the King – ambiguously enough for the remark to escape offence – that nothing about his dead father was as beautiful as the living King's memory of him. Like the King's memories of the past, Helena's hopes for the future realize themselves in a sufficiently present form: 'she feels her young one kick', Diana tells the assembly.

The profundity and peculiar character of *All's Well That Ends Well* are to be found here: that it manages to give so strong a sense of past and future, ends and beginnings, within a world of fine-surfaced present moments. We could perhaps say that the play deals with the powerful workings of nature *within* the civilized, the 'courtly'. Hence the 'open' ending of the play – which is in some sense the mere beginning, as well as a simple moment of pause for actors and audience. Hence, too, some of the strange but fine stylistic achievements of the play. An exquisitely mannered prose, or a markedly dry and sober verse, will suddenly take on submerged dimensions and show the pressure of grave, vivid, and powerfully 'natural' meaning. The two courtiers, the Dumaines, discuss Bertram's scandalous behaviour in mannered chit-chat; but what they say deepens out of charm into sobriety: 'As we are ourselves, what things are we!' Lafew, encountering Parolles and Bertram after the King's cure, discourses to them in an instructive and more elderly form of the same courtly prose; and a window suddenly and smoothly opens out of his balanced clauses, on to a wide view:

> *They say miracles are past, and we have our philosophical persons to make modern and familiar, things supernatural and causeless. Hence is it that we make trifles of terrors, ensconcing ourselves into seeming knowledge when we should submit ourselves to an unknown fear.* II.3.1–6

One of the finest and yet most reticent of these effects, occurring, like many of them, at an 'unnoticeable' and essentially understated point of the action, comes in the little scene where Helena, Diana, and the Widow set out on their long journey in pursuit of the King, and homeward bound. The women are trustful but Helena warns them that more hardship is yet to come: a warning met by an abstract fervour on Diana's part reminiscent of the earlier and younger Helena:

HELENA
                    You, Diana,
Under my poor instructions yet must suffer
Something in my behalf.
DIANA   *Let death and honesty*
Go with your impositions, I am yours,
Upon your will to suffer.   IV.4.26–30

Helena meets this with words so enigmatic, in their densely suggestive plainness, as to have caused difficulty. She simply repeats her word 'Yet', letting it carry all its punning senses – 'Wait a little: still more: not now: nevertheless –'. She adds that Time also uses the same word, with all its different meanings – many of them painful to accept – when moving slowly to the crown of the year, summer:

> Yet, I pray you.
> *But with the word the time will bring on summer,*
> *When briars shall have leaves as well as thorns*
> *And be as sweet as sharp. We must away;*
> *Our wagon is prepared, and time revives us.*
> *All's well that ends well. . . .*   IV.4.30–35

The fineness here is of an unusual kind, hardly present elsewhere in Shakespeare. The nearest thing to it is perhaps not in Shakespeare at all, but in an unlike spirit, Milton: who speaks, in one of his sonnets, of winter pleasures:

> *what may be won*
> *From the hard season gaining.*

This is, similarly, poetry of a 'hard season'. The dry rigour of the context throws into startling depth the image of the 'sweet briar', happiness. *All's Well That Ends Well* is a wintry play, but this image of high summer happiness – out of sight but real, and only to be reached by holding on to a *yetness* of things – is as strong and spare as anything to be found in Shakespeare's comedies.

FURTHER READING

Textual and Editorial

THE best recent edition of *All's Well That Ends Well* is the new Arden (1959), by G. K. Hunter. His substantial Introduction is well worth consulting on any aspect of the play. There are valuable notes and a stimulating discussion of the text by John Dover Wilson in the New Cambridge edition (1929), which also has a summary of the stage history, by Harold Child. W. W. Greg's *The Shakespeare First Folio* (Oxford, 1955) should be consulted for its authoritative and succinct exposition of the peculiarities and probable history of the text. C. J. Sisson's *New Readings in Shakespeare* (Cambridge, 1956) is of interest in what it has to say of the major textual cruces.

Sources

The sources, and the use Shakespeare makes of them, are admirably discussed by Geoffrey Bullough in *Narrative and Dramatic Sources of Shakespeare*, Volume 2 (1958); he also reprints the major source, Novel 38 in William Painter's *The Palace of Pleasure* (1575 edition). A modernized version of Painter's novel (1566 edition) is included in T. J. B. Spencer's *Elizabethan Love Stories* (Penguin Shakespeare Library, 1968, pages 41–50).

Criticism

There are some good isolated things in earlier critics: Johnson's contemptuous description of a Bertram 'dismissed to happiness', Coleridge's sympathetic defence of Bertram, and Shaw's tribute to a play 'rooted in my deeper affections' (largely because of the 'Ibsenite' character of the heroine). Modern English criticism of the play gets under way with Edward

Dowden's remarks in *Shakspere: A critical study of His Mind and Art* (1875). Dowden finds it a 'dark' comedy on a serious subject: 'dark' in being the product of a troubled and depressed period in Shakespeare's life, serious in its presentation of a good woman who must act 'providence', carrying out a 'healing of the body of the French King, healing of the spirit of the man she loves'. Dowden shows himself aware of the difficulties inherent in the subject: in the presentation of Helena herself and above all in the indelicacy of the 'bed-trick'. A bold and influential attempt to meet these difficulties was made by W. W. Lawrence (*Shakespeare's Problem Comedies*, 1931; Penguin Shakespeare Library, 1969). He called attention to the nature of the play's source-materials: popular and primitive tales of a 'Clever Wench' who cunningly, and wholly laudably, wins (or wins back) a husband who would evade her if he could. Lawrence's study did not, of course, finally settle the question of the play's relation to its source-materials: subsequent critics have reopened it by developing a point he had himself made – the difference between the 'realism' of Shakespeare's 'problem comedies' and the 'genial' spirit of the romances. The play's critics frequently point to the difference between the romance source-materials and the 'realism' of the dramatic treatment as contributing to the peculiar character of the play or even to its peculiar failure. E. M. W. Tillyard (*Shakespeare's Problem Plays*, 1950; Penguin Books, 1965) laid a good deal of stress on the play's failure: the 'feebleness in execution', 'lack of imaginative warmth', and 'defective poetical style' arise, he argued, from the problem of reconciling an improbable romantic plot with realistic characters. He followed Dowden in his basic reading of the play, finding 'heavenly grace' in Helena and 'unredeemed man' in Bertram. Harold S. Wilson argued ('Dramatic Emphasis in *All's Well That Ends Well*', *Huntington Library Quarterly* 13, 1950) that the play's difficulties are deliberate: Shakespeare is intent on transforming his source into a very different study of character. The romance–realism formulation received an original and striking variant in M. C. Bradbrook's 'Virtue is the True

Nobility' (*Review of English Studies*, N.S. 1, 1950), which suggested that 'the dramatist and poet in Shakespeare were pulling different ways'. The dramatist, she argued, wrote a play on the old debate theme of Birth and Merit, while the poet's play dealt with unrequited love with a depth and intensity which recall the Sonnets. Clifford Leech ('The Theme of Ambition in *All's Well That Ends Well*', *ELH: A Journal of English Literary History* 21, 1954) found that the play lacks a 'sense of fusion' such as would help us see its disparate elements in clearer focus. For example, its heroine is presented as having both attractive and more questionable qualities: she is 'sick' with love, and her determination to succeed in her private purpose may remind us even of such a character as Edmund in *King Lear*. A. H. Carter ('In Defense of Bertram', *Shakespeare Quarterly* 7, 1956) also combats the idea of a flawless Helena: everyone in this comedy of character has natural faults. Bertrand Evans (*Shakespeare's Comedies*, Oxford, 1960) has some acute observations on Shakespeare's unusual dramaturgical procedure in this play, especially on Helena's relationship with the audience: now intimate, now aloof. He is less convincing when he proceeds to character criticism and offers us a Helena 'hard-eyed beneath her pilgrim's hood'. Walter N. King ('Shakespeare's "Mingled Yarn"', *Modern Language Quarterly* 21, 1960) concedes the play's angularities and oddities of treatment, but maintains that its very peculiarities are vital to a 'psychological study' that deeply and realistically portrays the 'virtues and faults of ordinary human nature'. In his lively chapter in *Angel with Horns* (1961), A. P. Rossiter also stresses the degree of realism in Helena, Bertram, and Parolles, which makes them transcend their moralistic schema. James L. Calderwood ('Styles of Knowing in *All's Well*', *Modern Language Quarterly* 25, 1964) finds that, despite the disparity and disharmony of the play's elements, it coheres as a study of the attainment of maturity through knowledge: knowledge of the self and of others. Jay L. Halio's '*All's Well That Ends Well*' (*Shakespeare Quarterly* 15, 1964) has some apt things to say on the more melancholy characteristics of the King, the Countess, and Lafew, and the play's presentation of the theme of age, decline, and death. In an excellent short article, 'The Life of Shame: Parolles and *All's Well*' (*Essays in Criticism* 15, 1965), Robert Hapgood demonstrates how shameful are the ordeals undergone by all those in the play who hunger for life and in the end happily enjoy it. R. G. Hunter includes an excellent chapter on the play in his *Shakespeare and the Comedy of Forgiveness* (New York, 1965); Roger Warren has some interesting things to say about Bertram and Helena in 'Why Does It End Well? Helena, Bertram and the *Sonnets*', *Shakespeare Survey 22* (Cambridge, 1969).

There is one full-length study of *All's Well That Ends Well*: Joseph G. Price's *The Unfortunate Comedy* (Liverpool, 1968), the bulk of which is a balanced and informative survey of the play's history on the stage and at the hands of critics. Mr Price shows how the play's chief problem is its variousness: it has seemed by turns 'farcical comedy, sentimental romance, romantic fable, serious drama, cynical satire, and a thematic dramatization'. He concludes with a brief but eminently sane defence of 'this very human play'.

The style of *All's Well That Ends Well* is a subject of considerable interest, but not much that is illuminating has been written on it. There are one or two brief but highly perceptive comments in John Arthos's essay 'The Comedy of Generation' (*Essays in Criticism* 10, 1955). G. Wilson Knight writes brilliantly on the play's prose in his long essay in *The Sovereign Flower* (1958). (This very personal study, which sees the play as essentially concerned with 'the miraculous', has an admirable exposition of its 'ethic of honour'.) Lastly, Una Ellis-Fermor has a short but very suggestive discussion of the play's 'word music' in *Shakespeare the Dramatist* (1961).

ALL'S WELL THAT ENDS WELL

THE CHARACTERS IN THE PLAY

BERTRAM, Count of Rossillion, a ward of the King of France
The COUNTESS of Rossillion, Bertram's mother
HELENA, a young girl brought up by the Countess
PAROLLES, Bertram's friend
Rynaldo, STEWARD in the Countess's household
Lavatch, CLOWN in the Countess's household
A Page in the Countess's household

The KING of France
LAFEW, an old Lord
The brothers Dumaine, two French LORDS: later Captains serving the Duke of Florence
Other LORDS
Two French SOLDIERS
A GENTLEMAN, Astringer to the Court of France
A Messenger

The DUKE of Florence
WIDOW Capilet of Florence
DIANA, the Widow's daughter
MARIANA, a friend of the Widow

Lords, Attendants, Soldiers, Citizens

Enter young Bertram, Count of Rossillion, his mother
the Countess, Helena, and Lord Lafew; all in black

COUNTESS In delivering my son from me, I bury a second
husband.

BERTRAM And I in going, madam, weep o'er my father's
death anew; but I must attend his majesty's command,
to whom I am now in ward, evermore in subjection.

LAFEW You shall find of the King a husband, madam;
you, sir, a father. He that so generally is at all times good
must of necessity hold his virtue to you, whose worthiness would stir it up where it wanted, rather than lack it
where there is such abundance.   10

COUNTESS What hope is there of his majesty's amend-
ment?

LAFEW He hath abandoned his physicians, madam, under
whose practices he hath persecuted time with hope, and
finds no other advantage in the process but only the
losing of hope by time.

COUNTESS This young gentlewoman had a father – O
that 'had', how sad a passage 'tis! – whose skill was
almost as great as his honesty; had it stretched so far,
would have made nature immortal, and death should   20
have play for lack of work. Would for the King's sake he
were living! I think it would be the death of the King's
disease.

LAFEW How called you the man you speak of, madam?

COUNTESS He was famous, sir, in his profession, and it
was his great right to be so: Gerard de Narbon.

LAFEW He was excellent indeed, madam. The King very
lately spoke of him admiringly, and mourningly. He
was skilful enough to have lived still, if knowledge could
30 be set up against mortality.

BERTRAM What is it, my good lord, the King languishes
of?

LAFEW A fistula, my lord.

BERTRAM I heard not of it before.

LAFEW I would it were not notorious. Was this gentlewoman the daughter of Gerard de Narbon?

COUNTESS His sole child, my lord, and bequeathed to my
overlooking. I have those hopes of her good, that her
education promises her dispositions she inherits – which
40 makes fair gifts fairer; for where an unclean mind
carries virtuous qualities, there commendations go with
pity: they are virtues and traitors too. In her they are the
better for their simpleness. She derives her honesty and
achieves her goodness.

LAFEW Your commendations, madam, get from her tears.

COUNTESS 'Tis the best brine a maiden can season her
praise in. The remembrance of her father never
approaches her heart but the tyranny of her sorrows
takes all livelihood from her cheek. No more of this,
50 Helena; go to, no more, lest it be rather thought you
affect a sorrow than to have't.

HELENA I do affect a sorrow indeed, but I have it too.

LAFEW Moderate lamentation is the right of the dead,
excessive grief the enemy to the living.

COUNTESS If the living be enemy to the grief, the excess
makes it soon mortal.

BERTRAM Madam, I desire your holy wishes.

LAFEW How understand we that?

COUNTESS
Be thou blessed, Bertram, and succeed thy father

In manners as in shape! Thy blood and virtue 60
Contend for empire in thee, and thy goodness
Share with thy birthright! Love all, trust a few,
Do wrong to none. Be able for thine enemy
Rather in power than use, and keep thy friend
Under thy own life's key. Be checked for silence,
But never taxed for speech. What heaven more will,
That thee may furnish and my prayers pluck down,
Fall on thy head! Farewell. – My lord,
'Tis an unseasoned courtier: good my lord,
Advise him.

LAFEW   He cannot want the best 70
That shall attend his love.

COUNTESS Heaven bless him! Farewell, Bertram. *Exit*

BERTRAM The best wishes that can be forged in your
thoughts be servants to you! (*To Helena*) Be comfortable
to my mother, your mistress, and make much of her.

LAFEW Farewell, pretty lady. You must hold the credit of
your father.   *Exeunt Bertram and Lafew*

HELENA
O, were that all! I think not on my father,
And these great tears grace his remembrance more
Than those I shed for him. What was he like? 80
I have forgot him. My imagination
Carries no favour in't but Bertram's.
I am undone: there is no living, none,
If Bertram be away. 'Twere all one
That I should love a bright particular star
And think to wed it, he is so above me.
In his bright radiance and collateral light
Must I be comforted, not in his sphere.
Th'ambition in my love thus plagues itself:
The hind that would be mated by the lion 90
Must die for love. 'Twas pretty, though a plague,

To see him every hour, to sit and draw
His archèd brows, his hawking eye, his curls,
In our heart's table – heart too capable
Of every line and trick of his sweet favour.
But now he's gone, and my idolatrous fancy
Must sanctify his relics. Who comes here?

Enter Parolles

One that goes with him. I love him for his sake,
And yet I know him a notorious liar,
100 Think him a great way fool, solely a coward,
Yet these fixed evils sit so fit in him
That they take place when virtue's steely bones
Looks bleak i'th'cold wind. Withal, full oft we see
Cold wisdom waiting on superfluous folly.

PAROLLES Save you, fair queen!

HELENA And you, monarch!

PAROLLES No.

HELENA And no.

PAROLLES Are you meditating on virginity?

110 HELENA Ay. You have some stain of soldier in you: let me
ask you a question. Man is enemy to virginity; how may
we barricado it against him?

PAROLLES Keep him out.

HELENA But he assails, and our virginity, though valiant,
in the defence yet is weak. Unfold to us some warlike
resistance.

PAROLLES There is none. Man setting down before you
will undermine you and blow you up.

HELENA Bless our poor virginity from underminers and
120 blowers-up! Is there no military policy how virgins
might blow up men?

PAROLLES Virginity being blown down, man will quick-
lier be blown up; marry, in blowing him down again,
with the breach yourselves made you lose your city. It

is not politic in the commonwealth of nature to preserve virginity. Loss of virginity is rational increase, and there was never virgin got till virginity was first lost. That you were made of is mettle to make virgins. Virginity, by being once lost, may be ten times found; by being ever kept it is ever lost. 'Tis too cold a companion. Away with't! 130

HELENA I will stand for't a little, though therefore I die a virgin.

PAROLLES There's little can be said in't; 'tis against the rule of nature. To speak on the part of virginity is to accuse your mothers, which is most infallible disobedience. He that hangs himself is a virgin; virginity murders itself, and should be buried in highways out of all sanctified limit, as a desperate offendress against nature. Virginity breeds mites, much like a cheese, consumes itself to the very paring, and so dies with feeding his own stomach. Besides, virginity is peevish, proud, idle, made of self-love which is the most inhibited sin in the canon. Keep it not; you cannot choose but lose by't. Out with't! Within ten year it will make itself two, which is a goodly increase, and the principal itself not much the worse. Away with't! 140

HELENA How might one do, sir, to lose it to her own liking?

PAROLLES Let me see. Marry, ill, to like him that ne'er it likes. 'Tis a commodity will lose the gloss with lying; the longer kept, the less worth. Off with't while 'tis vendible; answer the time of request. Virginity, like an old courtier, wears her cap out of fashion, richly suited but unsuitable, just like the brooch and the toothpick, which wear not now. Your date is better in your pie and your porridge than in your cheek; and your virginity, your old virginity, is like one of our French withered 150

160 pears: it looks ill, it eats drily; marry, 'tis a withered
pear; it was formerly better; marry, yet 'tis a withered
pear. Will you anything with it?

HELENA
Not my virginity, yet . . .
There shall your master have a thousand loves,
A mother, and a mistress, and a friend,
A phoenix, captain, and an enemy,
A guide, a goddess, and a sovereign,
A counsellor, a traitress, and a dear;
His humble ambition, proud humility,
His jarring concord, and his discord dulcet,
170 His faith, his sweet disaster; with a world
Of pretty, fond, adoptious christendoms
That blinking Cupid gossips. Now shall he –
I know not what he shall. God send him well!
The court's a learning-place, and he is one –

PAROLLES
What one, i'faith?

HELENA
That I wish well. 'Tis pity –

PAROLLES
What's pity?

HELENA
That wishing well had not a body in't
Which might be felt, that we, the poorer born,
180 Whose baser stars do shut us up in wishes,
Might with effects of them follow our friends,
And show what we alone must think, which never
Returns us thanks.

Enter Page

PAGE Monsieur Parolles, my lord calls for you.   *Exit*
PAROLLES Little Helen, farewell. If I can remember thee
I will think of thee at court.

HELENA Monsieur Parolles, you were born under a charitable star.

PAROLLES Under Mars, I.

HELENA I especially think under Mars. 190

PAROLLES Why under Mars?

HELENA The wars hath so kept you under that you must needs be born under Mars.

PAROLLES When he was predominant.

HELENA When he was retrograde, I think rather.

PAROLLES Why think you so?

HELENA You go so much backward when you fight.

PAROLLES That's for advantage.

HELENA So is running away, when fear proposes the safety. But the composition that your valour and fear 200 makes in you is a virtue of a good wing, and I like the wear well.

PAROLLES I am so full of businesses I cannot answer thee acutely. I will return perfect courtier, in the which my instruction shall serve to naturalize thee, so thou wilt be capable of a courtier's counsel, and understand what advice shall thrust upon thee; else thou diest in thine unthankfulness, and thine ignorance makes thee away. Farewell. When thou hast leisure, say thy prayers; when thou hast none, remember thy friends. Get thee a good 210 husband, and use him as he uses thee. So, farewell. *Exit*

HELENA

Our remedies oft in ourselves do lie,
Which we ascribe to heaven. The fated sky
Gives us free scope, only doth backward pull
Our slow designs when we ourselves are dull.
What power is it which mounts my love so high,
That makes me see, and cannot feed mine eye?
The mightiest space in fortune nature brings
To join like likes, and kiss like native things.

220   Impossible be strange attempts to those
That weigh their pains in sense, and do suppose
What hath been cannot be. Who ever strove
To show her merit that did miss her love?
The King's disease – my project may deceive me,
But my intents are fixed, and will not leave me.   *Exit*

I.2   *Flourish of cornets. Enter the King of France with*
        letters, and divers attendants

KING

The Florentines and Senoys are by th'ears,
Have fought with equal fortune, and continue
A braving war.

FIRST LORD   So 'tis reported, sir.

KING

Nay, 'tis most credible. We here receive it
A certainty, vouched from our cousin Austria,
With caution that the Florentine will move us
For speedy aid; wherein our dearest friend
Prejudicates the business, and would seem
To have us make denial.

FIRST LORD   His love and wisdom,
10   Approved so to your majesty, may plead
For amplest credence.

KING   He hath armed our answer,
And Florence is denied before he comes;
Yet, for our gentlemen that mean to see
The Tuscan service, freely have they leave
To stand on either part.

SECOND LORD   It well may serve
A nursery to our gentry, who are sick
For breathing and exploit.

KING   What's he comes here?

Enter Bertram, Lafew, and Parolles

FIRST LORD

It is the Count Rossillion, my good lord,
Young Bertram.

KING   Youth, thou bearest thy father's face;
Frank nature, rather curious than in haste,   20
Hath well composed thee. Thy father's moral parts
Mayst thou inherit too! Welcome to Paris.

BERTRAM

My thanks and duty are your majesty's.

KING

I would I had that corporal soundness now,
As when thy father and myself in friendship
First tried our soldiership. He did look far
Into the service of the time, and was
Discipled of the bravest. He lasted long,
But on us both did haggish age steal on,
And wore us out of act. It much repairs me   30
To talk of your good father. In his youth
He had the wit which I can well observe
Today in our young lords, but they may jest
Till their own scorn return to them unnoted
Ere they can hide their levity in honour.
So like a courtier, contempt nor bitterness
Were in his pride or sharpness; if they were,
His equal had awaked them, and his honour,
Clock to itself, knew the true minute when
Exception bid him speak, and at this time   40
His tongue obeyed his hand. Who were below him
He used as creatures of another place,
And bowed his eminent top to their low ranks,
Making them proud of his humility,
In their poor praise he humbled. Such a man
Might be a copy to these younger times;

Which, followed well, would demonstrate them now
But goers backward.

BERTRAM His good remembrance, sir,
Lies richer in your thoughts than on his tomb;
50 So in approof lives not his epitaph
As in your royal speech.

KING
Would I were with him! He would always say –
Methinks I hear him now; his plausive words
He scattered not in ears, but grafted them
To grow there and to bear – 'Let me not live',
This his good melancholy oft began
On the catastrophe and heel of pastime,
When it was out, 'Let me not live', quoth he,
'After my flame lacks oil, to be the snuff
60 Of younger spirits, whose apprehensive senses
All but new things disdain; whose judgements are
Mere fathers of their garments; whose constancies
Expire before their fashions.' This he wished.
I, after him, do after him wish too,
Since I nor wax nor honey can bring home,
I quickly were dissolvèd from my hive
To give some labourers room.

SECOND LORD You're loved, sir;
They that least lend it you shall lack you first.

KING
I fill a place, I know't. How long is't, Count,
70 Since the physician at your father's died?
He was much famed.

BERTRAM Some six months since, my lord.

KING
If he were living I would try him yet.
Lend me an arm. – The rest have worn me out
With several applications; nature and sickness

Debate it at their leisure. Welcome, Count,
My son's no dearer.

BERTRAM   Thank your majesty.

Exeunt. Flourish

Enter the Countess, Rynaldo her Steward, and I.3
Lavatch her Clown

COUNTESS I will now hear. What say you of this gentlewoman?

STEWARD Madam, the care I have had to even your
content I wish might be found in the calendar of my
past endeavours, for then we wound our modesty, and
make foul the clearness of our deservings, when of ourselves we publish them.

COUNTESS What does this knave here? Get you gone,
sirrah. The complaints I have heard of you I do not all
believe; 'tis my slowness that I do not, for I know you   10
lack not folly to commit them, and have ability enough
to make such knaveries yours.

CLOWN 'Tis not unknown to you, madam, I am a poor
fellow.

COUNTESS Well, sir.

CLOWN No, madam, 'tis not so well that I am poor,
though many of the rich are damned; but if I may have
your ladyship's good will to go to the world, Isbel the
woman and I will do as we may.

COUNTESS Wilt thou needs be a beggar?   20

CLOWN I do beg your good will in this case.

COUNTESS In what case?

CLOWN In Isbel's case and mine own. Service is no
heritage, and I think I shall never have the blessing of
God till I have issue o'my body; for they say barnes are
blessings.

61

COUNTESS Tell me thy reason why thou wilt marry.

CLOWN My poor body, madam, requires it. I am driven
30   on by the flesh, and he must needs go that the devil
drives.

COUNTESS Is this all your worship's reason?

CLOWN Faith, madam, I have other holy reasons, such as
they are.

COUNTESS May the world know them?

CLOWN I have been, madam, a wicked creature, as you
and all flesh and blood are, and indeed I do marry that I
may repent.

COUNTESS Thy marriage, sooner than thy wickedness.

CLOWN I am out o'friends, madam, and I hope to have
40   friends for my wife's sake.

COUNTESS Such friends are thine enemies, knave.

CLOWN Y'are shallow, madam; e'en great friends, for the
knaves come to do that for me which I am aweary of.
He that ears my land spares my team, and gives me
leave to in the crop. If I be his cuckold, he's my drudge.
He that comforts my wife is the cherisher of my flesh
and blood; he that cherishes my flesh and blood loves
my flesh and blood; he that loves my flesh and blood is
my friend; *ergo*, he that kisses my wife is my friend. If
50   men could be contented to be what they are, there were
no fear in marriage; for young Charbon the puritan and
old Poysam the papist, howsome'er their hearts are
severed in religion, their heads are both one: they may
jowl horns together like any deer i'th'herd.

COUNTESS Wilt thou ever be a foul-mouthed and
calumnious knave?

CLOWN A prophet I, madam, and I speak the truth the
next way:

For I the ballad will repeat
60   Which men full true shall find:

62

       Your marriage comes by destiny,
         Your cuckoo sings by kind.

COUNTESS Get you gone, sir. I'll talk with you more anon.

STEWARD May it please you, madam, that he bid Helen
  come to you: of her I am to speak.

COUNTESS Sirrah, tell my gentlewoman I would speak
  with her – Helen, I mean.

CLOWN
       Was this fair face the cause, quoth she,
         Why the Grecians sackèd Troy?
       Fond done, done fond,   70
         Was this King Priam's joy?
       With that she sighèd as she stood,
       With that she sighèd as she stood,
         And gave this sentence then:
       Among nine bad if one be good,
       Among nine bad if one be good,
         There's yet one good in ten.

COUNTESS What, one good in ten? You corrupt the song,
  sirrah.

CLOWN One good woman in ten, madam, which is a   80
  purifying o'th'song. Would God would serve the world
  so all the year! We'd find no fault with the tithe-woman
  if I were the parson. One in ten, quoth 'a! An we might
  have a good woman born but one every blazing star or
  at an earthquake, 'twould mend the lottery well; a man
  may draw his heart out ere 'a pluck one.

COUNTESS You'll be gone, sir knave, and do as I command you!

CLOWN That man should be at woman's command, and
  yet no hurt done! Though honesty be no puritan, yet it   90
  will do no hurt. It will wear the surplice of humility over
  the black gown of a big heart. I am going, forsooth. The
  business is for Helen to come hither.   *Exit*

COUNTESS Well, now.

STEWARD I know, madam, you love your gentlewoman entirely.

COUNTESS Faith, I do. Her father bequeathed her to me, and she herself, without other advantage, may lawfully make title to as much love as she finds. There is more
100 owing her than is paid, and more shall be paid her than she'll demand.

STEWARD Madam, I was very late more near her than I think she wished me. Alone she was, and did communicate to herself her own words to her own ears; she thought, I dare vow for her, they touched not any stranger sense. Her matter was, she loved your son. Fortune, she said, was no goddess, that had put such difference betwixt their two estates; Love no god, that would not extend his might only where qualities were
110 level; Dian no queen of virgins, that would suffer her poor knight surprised without rescue in the first assault or ransom afterward. This she delivered in the most bitter touch of sorrow that e'er I heard virgin exclaim in, which I held my duty speedily to acquaint you withal, sithence, in the loss that may happen, it concerns you something to know it.

COUNTESS You have discharged this honestly; keep it to yourself. Many likelihoods informed me of this before, which hung so tottering in the balance that I could
120 neither believe nor misdoubt. Pray you leave me. Stall this in your bosom, and I thank you for your honest care. I will speak with you further anon.   *Exit Steward*
        Enter Helena

COUNTESS

Even so it was with me when I was young.

If ever we are nature's, these are ours; this thorn
Doth to our rose of youth rightly belong;

Our blood to us, this to our blood is born.
It is the show and seal of nature's truth,
Where love's strong passion is impressed in youth.
By our remembrances of days foregone,
Such were our faults, or then we thought them none. 130
Her eye is sick on't; I observe her now.

HELENA

What is your pleasure, madam?

COUNTESS   You know, Helen,
I am a mother to you.

HELENA

Mine honourable mistress.

COUNTESS   Nay, a mother
Why not a mother? When I said 'a mother',
Methought you saw a serpent. What's in 'mother'
That you start at it? I say I am your mother,
And put you in the catalogue of those
That were enwombèd mine. 'Tis often seen
Adoption strives with nature, and choice breeds 140
A native slip to us from foreign seeds.
You ne'er oppressed me with a mother's groan,
Yet I express to you a mother's care.
God's mercy, maiden! Does it curd thy blood
To say I am thy mother? What's the matter,
That this distempered messenger of wet,
The many-coloured Iris, rounds thine eye?
Why, that you are my daughter?

HELENA   That I am not.

COUNTESS

I say I am your mother.

HELENA   Pardon, madam.
The Count Rossillion cannot be my brother.   150
I am from humble, he from honoured name;
No note upon my parents, his all noble.

65

My master, my dear lord he is, and I
His servant live, and will his vassal die.
He must not be my brother.

COUNTESS   Nor I your mother?

HELENA

You are my mother, madam; would you were –
So that my lord your son were not my brother –
Indeed my mother! Or were you both our mothers
I care no more for than I do for heaven,
160 So I were not his sister. Can't no other
But, I your daughter, he must be my brother?

COUNTESS

Yes, Helen, you might be my daughter-in-law.
God shield you mean it not! 'Daughter' and 'mother'
So strive upon your pulse. What, pale again?
My fear hath catched your fondness. Now I see
The mystery of your loneliness, and find
Your salt tears' head. Now to all sense 'tis gross:
You love my son. Invention is ashamed
Against the proclamation of thy passion
170 To say thou dost not. Therefore tell me true;
But tell me then, 'tis so; for, look, thy cheeks
Confess it t'one to th'other, and thine eyes
See it so grossly shown in thy behaviours
That in their kind they speak it; only sin
And hellish obstinacy tie thy tongue,
That truth should be suspected. Speak, is't so?
If it be so, you have wound a goodly clew;
If it be not, forswear't; howe'er, I charge thee,
As heaven shall work in me for thine avail,
180 To tell me truly.

HELENA   Good madam, pardon me.

COUNTESS

Do you love my son?

66

HELENA   Your pardon, noble mistress.

COUNTESS

  Love you my son?

HELENA   Do not you love him, madam?

COUNTESS

  Go not about; my love hath in't a bond
  Whereof the world takes note. Come, come, disclose
  The state of your affection, for your passions
  Have to the full appeached.

HELENA   Then I confess,
  Here on my knee, before high heaven and you,
  That before you, and next unto high heaven,
  I love your son.
  My friends were poor, but honest; so's my love.   190
  Be not offended, for it hurts not him
  That he is loved of me. I follow him not
  By any token of presumptuous suit,
  Nor would I have him till I do deserve him,
  Yet never know how that desert should be.
  I know I love in vain, strive against hope,
  Yet in this captious and intenable sieve
  I still pour in the waters of my love
  And lack not to lose still. Thus, Indian-like,
  Religious in mine error, I adore   200
  The sun that looks upon his worshipper
  But knows of him no more. My dearest madam,
  Let not your hate encounter with my love,
  For loving where you do; but if yourself,
  Whose aged honour cites a virtuous youth,
  Did ever, in so true a flame of liking,
  Wish chastely and love dearly, that your Dian
  Was both herself and love – O then, give pity
  To her whose state is such that cannot choose
  But lend and give where she is sure to lose;   210

That seeks not to find that her search implies,
But riddle-like lives sweetly where she dies.

COUNTESS
Had you not lately an intent – speak truly –
To go to Paris?

HELENA   Madam, I had.

COUNTESS   Wherefore? tell true.

HELENA
I will tell truth, by grace itself I swear.
You know my father left me some prescriptions
Of rare and proved effects, such as his reading
And manifest experience had collected
For general sovereignty; and that he willed me
In heedfullest reservation to bestow them,
As notes whose faculties inclusive were
More than they were in note. Amongst the rest
There is a remedy, approved, set down,
To cure the desperate languishings whereof
The King is rendered lost.

COUNTESS   This was your motive
For Paris, was it? Speak.

HELENA
My lord your son made me to think of this,
Else Paris and the medicine and the King
Had from the conversation of my thoughts
Haply been absent then.

COUNTESS   But think you, Helen,
If you should tender your supposèd aid,
He would receive it? He and his physicians
Are of a mind: he, that they cannot help him;
They, that they cannot help. How shall they credit
A poor unlearnèd virgin, when the schools,
Embowelled of their doctrine, have left off
The danger to itself?

HELENA   There's something in't
More than my father's skill, which was the greatest
Of his profession, that his good receipt
Shall for my legacy be sanctified   240
By th'luckiest stars in heaven; and would your honour
But give me leave to try success, I'd venture
The well-lost life of mine on his grace's cure
By such a day, an hour.
COUNTESS   Dost thou believe't?
HELENA
Ay, madam, knowingly.
COUNTESS
Why, Helen, thou shalt have my leave and love,
Means and attendants, and my loving greetings
To those of mine in court. I'll stay at home
And pray God's blessing into thy attempt.
Be gone tomorrow, and be sure of this,   250
What I can help thee to, thou shalt not miss.   *Exeunt*

*

Enter the King with divers young Lords taking leave II.1
for the Florentine war; Bertram and Parolles;
attendants. Flourish of cornets

KING
Farewell, young lords; these warlike principles
Do not throw from you; and you, my lords, farewell.
Share the advice betwixt you; if both gain all,
The gift doth stretch itself as 'tis received,
And is enough for both.
FIRST LORD   'Tis our hope, sir,
After well-entered soldiers, to return
And find your grace in health.

KING

No, no, it cannot be; and yet my heart
Will not confess he owes the malady
That doth my life besiege. Farewell, young lords.
Whether I live or die, be you the sons
Of worthy Frenchmen. Let higher Italy –
Those bated that inherit but the fall
Of the last monarchy – see that you come
Not to woo honour, but to wed it. When
The bravest questant shrinks, find what you seek,
That fame may cry you loud. I say farewell.

FIRST LORD

Health at your bidding serve your majesty!

KING

Those girls of Italy, take heed of them:
They say our French lack language to deny
If they demand. Beware of being captives
Before you serve.

BOTH LORDS   Our hearts receive your warnings.

KING

Farewell. (*To some attendants*) Come hither to me.
          He withdraws

FIRST LORD

O my sweet lord, that you will stay behind us!

PAROLLES

'Tis not his fault, the spark.

SECOND LORD   O, 'tis brave wars!

PAROLLES

Most admirable! I have seen those wars.

BERTRAM

I am commanded here, and kept a coil with
'Too young', and 'The next year', and ''Tis too early'.

PAROLLES

An thy mind stand to't, boy, steal away bravely.

BERTRAM

  I shall stay here the forehorse to a smock,   30
  Creaking my shoes on the plain masonry,
  Till honour be bought up, and no sword worn
  But one to dance with. By heaven, I'll steal away!

FIRST LORD

  There's honour in the theft.

PAROLLES   Commit it, Count.

SECOND LORD I am your accessary; and so farewell.

BERTRAM I grow to you, and our parting is a tortured body.

FIRST LORD Farewell, captain.

SECOND LORD Sweet Monsieur Parolles!

PAROLLES Noble heroes, my sword and yours are kin. 40 Good sparks and lustrous, a word, good metals. You shall find in the regiment of the Spinii one Captain Spurio, with his cicatrice, an emblem of war, here on his sinister cheek; it was this very sword entrenched it. Say to him I live, and observe his reports for me.

FIRST LORD We shall, noble captain.   *Exeunt the Lords*

PAROLLES Mars dote on you for his novices! (*To Bertram*) What will ye do?

BERTRAM Stay: the King.

PAROLLES Use a more spacious ceremony to the noble 50 lords; you have restrained yourself within the list of too cold an adieu. Be more expressive to them, for they wear themselves in the cap of the time; there do muster true gait, eat, speak, and move, under the influence of the most received star; and though the devil lead the measure, such are to be followed. After them, and take a more dilated farewell.

BERTRAM And I will do so.

PAROLLES Worthy fellows, and like to prove most sinewy sword-men.   *Exeunt Bertram and Parolles* 60

II.1

Enter Lafew. The King comes forward

LAFEW (*kneeling*)

    Pardon, my lord, for me and for my tidings.

KING

    I'll sue thee to stand up.

LAFEW

    Then here's a man stands that has brought his pardon.
    I would you had kneeled, my lord, to ask me mercy,
    And that at my bidding you could so stand up.

KING

    I would I had, so I had broke thy pate
    And asked thee mercy for't.

LAFEW   Good faith, across!
    But, my good lord, 'tis thus: will you be cured
    Of your infirmity?

KING   No.

LAFEW   O, will you eat

70   No grapes, my royal fox? Yes, but you will
    My noble grapes, and if my royal fox
    Could reach them. I have seen a medicine
    That's able to breathe life into a stone,
    Quicken a rock, and make you dance canary
    With sprightly fire and motion; whose simple touch
    Is powerful to araise King Pippen, nay,
    To give great Charlemain a pen in's hand
    And write to her a love-line.

KING   What 'her' is this?

LAFEW

    Why, Doctor She! My lord, there's one arrived,
80   If you will see her. Now by my faith and honour,
    If seriously I may convey my thoughts
    In this my light deliverance, I have spoke
    With one that in her sex, her years, profession,
    Wisdom, and constancy hath amazed me more

Than I dare blame my weakness. Will you see her,
For that is her demand, and know her business?
That done, laugh well at me.

KING   Now, good Lafew,
Bring in the admiration, that we with thee
May spend our wonder too, or take off thine
By wondering how thou tookest it.

LAFEW   Nay, I'll fit you, 90
And not be all day neither.
          He goes to the door

KING
Thus he his special nothing ever prologues.

LAFEW
Nay, come your ways.
          Enter Helena

KING   This haste hath wings indeed.

LAFEW
Nay, come your ways.
This is his majesty: say your mind to him.
A traitor you do look like, but such traitors
His majesty seldom fears. I am Cressid's uncle
That dare leave two together. Fare you well.   *Exit*

KING
Now, fair one, does your business follow us?

HELENA
Ay, my good lord.   100
Gerard de Narbon was my father,
In what he did profess, well found.

KING   I knew him.

HELENA
The rather will I spare my praises towards him;
Knowing him is enough. On's bed of death
Many receipts he gave me; chiefly one,
Which, as the dearest issue of his practice,

And of his old experience th'only darling,
He bade me store up as a triple eye,
Safer than mine own two, more dear; I have so,
110 And hearing your high majesty is touched
With that malignant cause wherein the honour
Of my dear father's gift stands chief in power,
I come to tender it and my appliance,
With all bound humbleness.

KING   We thank you, maiden,
But may not be so credulous of cure,
When our most learnèd doctors leave us, and
The congregated college have concluded
That labouring art can never ransom nature
From her inaidible estate. I say we must not
120 So stain our judgement or corrupt our hope,
To prostitute our past-cure malady
To empirics, or to dissever so
Our great self and our credit, to esteem
A senseless help, when help past sense we deem.

HELENA
My duty then shall pay me for my pains.
I will no more enforce mine office on you,
Humbly entreating from your royal thoughts
A modest one to bear me back again.

KING
I cannot give thee less, to be called grateful.
130 Thou thoughtest to help me, and such thanks I give
As one near death to those that wish him live.
But what at full I know, thou knowest no part;
I knowing all my peril, thou no art.

HELENA
What I can do can do no hurt to try,
Since you set up your rest 'gainst remedy.
He that of greatest works is finisher

Oft does them by the weakest minister.
So holy writ in babes hath judgement shown,
When judges have been babes; great floods have flown
From simple sources; and great seas have dried 140
When miracles have by the greatest been denied.
Oft expectation fails, and most oft there
Where most it promises, and oft it hits
Where hope is coldest and despair most fits.

KING

I must not hear thee. Fare thee well, kind maid.
Thy pains, not used, must by thyself be paid;
Proffers not took reap thanks for their reward.

HELENA

Inspirèd merit so by breath is barred.
It is not so with Him that all things knows
As 'tis with us that square our guess by shows; 150
But most it is presumption in us when
The help of heaven we count the act of men.
Dear sir, to my endeavours give consent.
Of heaven, not me, make an experiment.
I am not an impostor, that proclaim
Myself against the level of mine aim,
But know I think, and think I know most sure,
My art is not past power, nor you past cure.

KING

Art thou so confident? Within what space
Hopest thou my cure?

HELENA   The greatest grace lending grace, 160
Ere twice the horses of the sun shall bring
Their fiery torcher his diurnal ring,
Ere twice in murk and occidental damp
Moist Hesperus hath quenched her sleepy lamp,
Or four and twenty times the pilot's glass
Hath told the thievish minutes how they pass,

What is infirm from your sound parts shall fly,
Health shall live free and sickness freely die.

KING

Upon thy certainty and confidence
170 What darest thou venture?

HELENA   Tax of impudence,
A strumpet's boldness, a divulgèd shame;
Traduced by odious ballads my maiden's name;
Seared otherwise, ne worse of worst, extended
With vildest torture let my life be ended.

KING

Methinks in thee some blessèd spirit doth speak
His powerful sound within an organ weak;
And what impossibility would slay
In common sense, sense saves another way.
Thy life is dear, for all that life can rate
180 Worth name of life in thee hath estimate:
Youth, beauty, wisdom, courage – all
That happiness and prime can' happy call.
Thou this to hazard needs must intimate
Skill infinite, or monstrous desperate.
Sweet practiser, thy physic I will try,
That ministers thine own death if I die.

HELENA

If I break time, or flinch in property
Of what I spoke, unpitied let me die,
And well deserved. Not helping, death's my fee;
190 But if I help, what do you promise me?

KING

Make thy demand.

HELENA   But will you make it even?

KING

Ay, by my sceptre and my hopes of heaven.

HELENA

Then shalt thou give me with thy kingly hand
What husband in thy power I will command:
Exempted be from me the arrogance
To choose from forth the royal blood of France
My low and humble name to propagate
With any branch or image of thy state;
But such a one, thy vassal, whom I know
Is free for me to ask, thee to bestow.   200

KING

Here is my hand; the premises observed,
Thy will by my performance shall be served.
So make the choice of thy own time, for I,
Thy resolved patient, on thee still rely.
More should I question thee, and more I must,
Though more to know could not be more to trust:
From whence thou camest, how tended on – but rest
Unquestioned welcome, and undoubted blessed.
Give me some help here, ho! If thou proceed
As high as word, my deed shall match thy deed.   210

Flourish. Exeunt

Enter the Countess and the Clown   II.2

COUNTESS Come on, sir. I shall now put you to the
height of your breeding.

CLOWN I will show myself highly fed and lowly taught. I
know my business is but to the court.

COUNTESS To the court! Why, what place make you
special, when you put off that with such contempt? But
to the court!

CLOWN Truly, madam, if God have lent a man any
manners he may easily put it off at court. He that cannot

77

10   make a leg, put off's cap, kiss his hand, and say nothing, has neither leg, hands, lip, nor cap; and indeed such a fellow, to say precisely, were not for the court. But for me, I have an answer will serve all men.

COUNTESS Marry, that's a bountiful answer that fits all questions.

CLOWN It is like a barber's chair that fits all buttocks: the pin-buttock, the quatch-buttock, the brawn-buttock, or any buttock.

COUNTESS Will your answer serve fit to all questions?

20 CLOWN As fit as ten groats is for the hand of an attorney, as your French crown for your taffety punk, as Tib's rush for Tom's forefinger, as a pancake for Shrove Tuesday, a morris for May-day, as the nail to his hole, the cuckold to his horn, as a scolding quean to a wrangling knave, as the nun's lip to the friar's mouth; nay, as the pudding to his skin.

COUNTESS Have you, I say, an answer of such fitness for all questions?

CLOWN From below your duke to beneath your constable,
30   it will fit any question.

COUNTESS It must be an answer of most monstrous size that must fit all demands.

CLOWN But a trifle neither, in good faith, if the learned should speak truth of it. Here it is, and all that belongs to't. Ask me if I am a courtier; it shall do you no harm to learn.

COUNTESS To be young again, if we could! I will be a fool in question, hoping to be the wiser by your answer. I pray you, sir, are you a courtier?

40 CLOWN O Lord, sir! – There's a simple putting off. More, more, a hundred of them.

COUNTESS Sir, I am a poor friend of yours that loves you.

CLOWN O Lord, sir! – Thick, thick; spare not me.

COUNTESS I think, sir, you can eat none of this homely meat.

CLOWN O Lord, sir! – Nay, put me to't, I warrant you.

COUNTESS You were lately whipped, sir, as I think.

CLOWN O Lord, sir! – Spare not me.

COUNTESS Do you cry 'O Lord, sir!' at your whipping, and 'spare not me'? Indeed your 'O Lord, sir!' is very 50 sequent to your whipping: you would answer very well to a whipping, if you were but bound to't.

CLOWN I ne'er had worse luck in my life in my 'O Lord, sir!' I see things may serve long, but not serve ever.

COUNTESS
I play the noble housewife with the time,
To entertain it so merrily with a fool.

CLOWN
O Lord, sir! – Why, there't serves well again.

COUNTESS
An end, sir! To your business: give Helen this,
And urge her to a present answer back.
Commend me to my kinsmen and my son.   60
This is not much.

CLOWN Not much commendation to them?

COUNTESS Not much employment for you. You understand me?

CLOWN Most fruitfully. I am there before my legs.

COUNTESS Haste you again.

Exeunt

Enter Bertram, Lafew, and Parolles   II.3

LAFEW They say miracles are past, and we have our philosophical persons to make modern and familiar, things supernatural and causeless. Hence is it that we make trifles of terrors, ensconcing ourselves into

79

seeming knowledge when we should submit ourselves
to an unknown fear.

PAROLLES Why, 'tis the rarest argument of wonder that
hath shot out in our latter times.

BERTRAM And so 'tis.

10 LAFEW To be relinquished of the artists –

PAROLLES So I say – both of Galen and Paracelsus.

LAFEW Of all the learnèd and authentic fellows –

PAROLLES Right, so I say.

LAFEW That gave him out incurable –

PAROLLES Why, there 'tis, so say I too.

LAFEW Not to be helped.

PAROLLES Right, as 'twere a man assured of a –

LAFEW Uncertain life and sure death.

PAROLLES Just, you say well. So would I have said.

20 LAFEW I may truly say it is a novelty to the world.

PAROLLES It is indeed. If you will have it in showing, you
shall read it in what-do-ye-call there.

LAFEW A showing of a heavenly effect in an earthly actor.

PAROLLES That's it, I would have said the very same.

LAFEW Why, your dolphin is not lustier. Fore me, I speak
in respect –

PAROLLES Nay, 'tis strange, 'tis very strange, that is the
brief and the tedious of it; and he's of a most facinerious
spirit that will not acknowledge it to be the –

30 LAFEW Very hand of heaven.

PAROLLES Ay, so I say.

LAFEW In a most weak –

PAROLLES And debile minister, great power, great
transcendence, which should indeed give us a further
use to be made than alone the recovery of the King, as
to be –

LAFEW Generally thankful.

Enter the King, Helena, and attendants

PAROLLES I would have said it, you say well. Here comes
the King.

LAFEW Lustique, as the Dutchman says. I'll like a maid 40
the better whilst I have a tooth in my head. Why, he's
able to lead her a coranto.

PAROLLES *Mor du vinager*! Is not this Helen?

LAFEW Fore God, I think so.

KING

Go, call before me all the lords in court.

Exit an attendant

Sit, my preserver, by thy patient's side,
And with this healthful hand, whose banished sense
Thou hast repealed, a second time receive
The confirmation of my promised gift,
Which but attends thy naming. 50

Enter four Lords

Fair maid, send forth thine eye. This youthful parcel
Of noble bachelors stand at my bestowing,
O'er whom both sovereign power and father's voice
I have to use. Thy frank election make;
Thou hast power to choose, and they none to forsake.

HELENA

To each of you one fair and virtuous mistress
Fall, when love please! Marry, to each but one!

LAFEW

I'd give bay curtal and his furniture
My mouth no more were broken than these boys',
And writ as little beard.

KING Peruse them well. 60

Not one of those but had a noble father.

Helena addresses the Lords

HELENA

Gentlemen,
Heaven hath through me restored the King to health.

81

ALL THE LORDS

We understand it, and thank heaven for you.

HELENA

I am a simple maid, and therein wealthiest
That I protest I simply am a maid.
Please it your majesty, I have done already.
The blushes in my cheeks thus whisper me:
'We blush that thou shouldst choose, but, be refused,
70   Let the white death sit on thy cheek for ever,
We'll ne'er come there again.'

KING   Make choice and see,
Who shuns thy love shuns all his love in me.

HELENA

Now, Dian, from thy altar do I fly,
And to imperial Love, that god most high,
Do my sighs stream. (*To First Lord*) Sir, will you hear
        my suit?

FIRST LORD

And grant it.

HELENA   Thanks, sir. All the rest is mute.

LAFEW I had rather be in this choice than throw ames-ace
for my life.

HELENA (*to Second Lord*)

The honour, sir, that flames in your fair eyes
80   Before I speak, too threateningly replies.
Love make your fortunes twenty times above
Her that so wishes, and her humble love!

SECOND LORD

No better, if you please.

HELENA   My wish receive,
Which great Love grant. And so I take my leave.

LAFEW Do all they deny her? An they were sons of mine
I'd have them whipped, or I would send them to
th'Turk to make eunuchs of.

HELENA (*to Third Lord*)
  Be not afraid that I your hand should take;
  I'll never do you wrong, for your own sake.
  Blessing upon your vows, and in your bed   90
  Find fairer fortune if you ever wed!

LAFEW These boys are boys of ice; they'll none have her.
  Sure, they are bastards to the English; the French ne'er
  got 'em.

HELENA (*to Fourth Lord*)
  You are too young, too happy, and too good
  To make yourself a son out of my blood.

FOURTH LORD Fair one, I think not so.

LAFEW There's one grape yet. I am sure thy father drunk
  wine; but if thou beest not an ass, I am a youth of four-
  teen; I have known thee already.   100

HELENA (*to Bertram*)
  I dare not say I take you, but I give
  Me and my service, ever whilst I live,
  Into your guiding power. This is the man.

KING
  Why, then, young Bertram, take her, she's thy wife.

BERTRAM
  My wife, my liege! I shall beseech your highness,
  In such a business give me leave to use
  The help of mine own eyes.

KING   Knowest thou not, Bertram,
  What she has done for me?

BERTRAM   Yes, my good lord,
  But never hope to know why I should marry her.

KING
  Thou knowest she has raised me from my sickly bed. 110

BERTRAM
  But follows it, my lord, to bring me down
  Must answer for your raising? I know her well:

She had her breeding at my father's charge.
A poor physician's daughter my wife! Disdain
Rather corrupt me ever!

KING

'Tis only title thou disdainest in her, the which
I can build up. Strange is it that our bloods,
Of colour, weight, and heat, poured all together,
Would quite confound distinction, yet stands off
120 In differences so mighty. If she be
All that is virtuous, save what thou dislikest –
A poor physician's daughter – thou dislikest
Of virtue for the name. But do not so.
From lowest place when virtuous things proceed,
The place is dignified by th'doer's deed.
Where great additions swell's and virtue none,
It is a dropsied honour. Good alone
Is good, without a name: vileness is so;
The property by what it is should go,
130 Not by the title. She is young, wise, fair;
In these to nature she's immediate heir,
And these breed honour; that is honour's scorn
Which challenges itself as honour's born
And is not like the sire. Honours thrive
When rather from our acts we them derive
Than our foregoers. The mere word's a slave,
Debauched on every tomb, on every grave
A lying trophy, and as oft is dumb
Where dust and damned oblivion is the tomb
140 Of honoured bones indeed. What should be said?
If thou canst like this creature as a maid,
I can create the rest. Virtue and she
Is her own dower; honour and wealth from me.

BERTRAM

I cannot love her nor will strive to do't.

KING

    Thou wrongest thyself if thou shouldst strive to choose.

HELENA

    That you are well restored, my lord, I'm glad.
    Let the rest go.

KING

    My honour's at the stake, which to defeat,
    I must produce my power. Here, take her hand,
    Proud, scornful boy, unworthy this good gift,   150
    That dost in vile misprision shackle up
    My love and her desert; that canst not dream
    We, poising us in her defective scale,
    Shall weigh thee to the beam; that wilt not know
    It is in us to plant thine honour where
    We please to have it grow. Check thy contempt.
    Obey our will which travails in thy good.
    Believe not thy disdain, but presently
    Do thine own fortunes that obedient right
    Which both thy duty owes and our power claims;   160
    Or I will throw thee from my care for ever
    Into the staggers and the careless lapse
    Of youth and ignorance, both my revenge and hate
    Loosing upon thee in the name of justice,
    Without all terms of pity. Speak. Thine answer.

BERTRAM

    Pardon, my gracious lord; for I submit
    My fancy to your eyes. When I consider
    What great creation and what dole of honour
    Flies where you bid it, I find that she, which late
    Was in my nobler thoughts most base, is now   170
    The praisèd of the King; who, so ennobled,
    Is as 'twere born so.

KING   Take her by the hand
    And tell her she is thine; to whom I promise

A counterpoise, if not to thy estate,
A balance more replete.

BERTRAM   I take her hand.

KING

Good fortune and the favour of the King
Smile upon this contract, whose ceremony
Shall seem expedient on the now-born brief,
And be performed tonight. The solemn feast

180 Shall more attend upon the coming space,
Expecting absent friends. As thou lovest her
Thy love's to me religious; else, does err.

Exeunt all but Parolles and Lafew,
who stay behind, commenting on this wedding

LAFEW Do you hear, monsieur? A word with you.

PAROLLES Your pleasure, sir.

LAFEW Your lord and master did well to make his recantation.

PAROLLES Recantation! My lord! My master!

LAFEW Ay. Is it not a language I speak?

PAROLLES A most harsh one, and not to be understood

190 without bloody succeeding. My master!

LAFEW Are you companion to the Count Rossillion?

PAROLLES To any Count, to all Counts, to what is man.

LAFEW To what is Count's man; Count's master is of another style.

PAROLLES You are too old, sir; let it satisfy you, you are too old.

LAFEW I must tell thee, sirrah, I write man, to which title age cannot bring thee.

PAROLLES What I dare too well do, I dare not do.

200 LAFEW I did think thee for two ordinaries to be a pretty wise fellow. Thou didst make tolerable vent of thy travel; it might pass. Yet the scarfs and the bannerets about thee did manifoldly dissuade me from believing

thee a vessel of too great a burden. I have now found thee; when I lose thee again I care not. Yet art thou good for nothing but taking up, and that thou'rt scarce worth.

PAROLLES Hadst thou not the privilege of antiquity upon thee –

LAFEW Do not plunge thyself too far in anger, lest thou 210 hasten thy trial; which if – Lord have mercy on thee for a hen! So, my good window of lattice, fare thee well; thy casement I need not open, for I look through thee. Give me thy hand.

PAROLLES My lord, you give me most egregious indignity.

LAFEW Ay, with all my heart; and thou art worthy of it.

PAROLLES I have not, my lord, deserved it.

LAFEW Yes, good faith, every dram of it, and I will not bate thee a scruple. 220

PAROLLES Well, I shall be wiser.

LAFEW Even as soon as thou canst, for thou hast to pull at a smack o'th'contrary. If ever thou beest bound in thy scarf and beaten, thou shall find what it is to be proud of thy bondage. I have a desire to hold my acquaintance with thee, or rather my knowledge, that I may say, in the default, 'He is a man I know'.

PAROLLES My lord, you do me most insupportable vexation.

LAFEW I would it were hell-pains for thy sake, and my 230 poor doing eternal; for doing I am past, as I will by thee, in what motion age will give me leave. *Exit*

PAROLLES Well, thou hast a son shall take this disgrace off me, scurvy, old, filthy, scurvy lord! Well, I must be patient, there is no fettering of authority. I'll beat him, by my life, if I can meet him with any convenience, an he were double and double a lord. I'll have no more

pity of his age than I would have of – I'll beat him an if
I could but meet him again.

Enter Lafew

240 LAFEW Sirrah, your lord and master's married, there's
news for you; you have a new mistress.

PAROLLES I most unfeignedly beseech your lordship to
make some reservation of your wrongs. He is my good
lord: whom I serve above is my master.

LAFEW Who? God?

PAROLLES Ay, sir.

LAFEW The devil it is that's thy master. Why dost thou
garter up thy arms o'this fashion? Dost make hose of
thy sleeves? Do other servants so? Thou wert best set
250 thy lower part where thy nose stands. By mine honour,
if I were but two hours younger I'd beat thee. Me-
thinkst thou art a general offence and every man should
beat thee. I think thou wast created for men to breathe
themselves upon thee.

PAROLLES This is hard and undeserved measure, my
lord.

LAFEW Go to, sir. You were beaten in Italy for picking a
kernel out of a pomegranate. You are a vagabond and no
true traveller. You are more saucy with lords and
260 honourable personages than the commission of your
birth and virtue gives you heraldry. You are not worth
another word, else I'd call you knave. I leave you. *Exit*

Enter Bertram

PAROLLES Good, very good, it is so then. Good, very
good; let it be concealed awhile.

BERTRAM
Undone and forfeited to cares for ever!

PAROLLES What's the matter, sweetheart?

BERTRAM
Although before the solemn priest I have sworn,

I will not bed her.

PAROLLES

What, what, sweetheart?

BERTRAM

O my Parolles, they have married me!   270
I'll to the Tuscan wars and never bed her.

PAROLLES

France is a dog-hole and it no more merits
The tread of a man's foot. To th'wars!

BERTRAM

There's letters from my mother: what th'import is
I know not yet.

PAROLLES

Ay, that would be known. To th'wars, my boy, to
        th'wars!
He wears his honour in a box unseen
That hugs his kicky-wicky here at home,
Spending his manly marrow in her arms,
Which should sustain the bound and high curvet   280
Of Mars's fiery steed. To other regions!
France is a stable, we that dwell in't jades.
Therefore to th'war!

BERTRAM

It shall be so. I'll send her to my house,
Acquaint my mother with my hate to her
And wherefore I am fled; write to the King
That which I durst not speak. His present gift
Shall furnish me to those Italian fields
Where noble fellows strike. Wars is no strife
To the dark house and the detested wife.   290

PAROLLES

Will this capriccio hold in thee, art sure?

BERTRAM

Go with me to my chamber and advise me.

I'll send her straight away. Tomorrow
I'll to the wars, she to her single sorrow.

PAROLLES

Why, these balls bound, there's noise in it. 'Tis hard:
A young man married is a man that's marred.
Therefore away, and leave her bravely; go.
The King has done you wrong, but hush, 'tis so.

Exeunt

II.4   *Enter Helena and the Clown*

HELENA My mother greets me kindly. Is she well?

CLOWN She is not well, but yet she has her health; she's
very merry, but yet she is not well. But thanks be given
she's very well and wants nothing i'th'world; but yet she
is not well.

HELENA If she be very well, what does she ail that she's
not very well?

CLOWN Truly, she's very well indeed, but for two things.

HELENA What two things?

10 CLOWN One, that she's not in heaven, whither God send
her quickly! The other, that she's in earth, from whence
God send her quickly!

Enter Parolles

PAROLLES Bless you, my fortunate lady.

HELENA I hope, sir, I have your good will to have mine
own good fortune.

PAROLLES You had my prayers to lead them on, and to
keep them on have them still. O, my knave! How does
my old lady?

CLOWN So that you had her wrinkles and I her money, I
20 would she did as you say.

PAROLLES Why, I say nothing.

CLOWN Marry, you are the wiser man, for many a man's

tongue shakes out his master's undoing. To say nothing, to do nothing, to know nothing, and to have nothing, is to be a great part of your title, which is within a very little of nothing.

PAROLLES Away! Th' art a knave.

CLOWN You should have said, sir, 'Before a knave th' art a knave'; that's 'Before me, th' art a knave'. This had been truth, sir.   30

PAROLLES Go to, thou art a witty fool: I have found thee.

CLOWN Did you find me in your self, sir, or were you taught to find me? The search, sir, was profitable; and much fool may you find in you, even to the world's pleasure and the increase of laughter.

PAROLLES
A good knave i'faith, and well fed.
Madam, my lord will go away tonight:
A very serious business calls on him.
The great prerogative and rite of love,
Which as your due time claims, he does acknowledge,   40
But puts it off to a compelled restraint;
Whose want and whose delay is strewed with sweets,
Which they distil now in the curbèd time,
To make the coming hour o'erflow with joy
And pleasure drown the brim.

HELENA   What's his will else?

PAROLLES
That you will take your instant leave o'th'King,
And make this haste as your own good proceeding,
Strengthened with what apology you think
May make it probable need.

HELENA   What more commands he?

PAROLLES
That, having this obtained, you presently   50
Attend his further pleasure.

HELENA
In everything I wait upon his will.

PAROLLES
I shall report it so. *Exit*

HELENA
I pray you. Come, sirrah. *Exeunt*

II.5 *Enter Lafew and Bertram*

LAFEW But I hope your lordship thinks not him a soldier.

BERTRAM Yes, my lord, and of very valiant approof.

LAFEW You have it from his own deliverance.

BERTRAM And by other warranted testimony.

LAFEW Then my dial goes not true: I took this lark for a bunting.

BERTRAM I do assure you, my lord, he is very great in knowledge, and accordingly valiant.

LAFEW I have then sinned against his experience and
10 transgressed against his valour, and my state that way is dangerous, since I cannot yet find in my heart to repent. Here he comes. I pray you make us friends; I will pursue the amity.

Enter Parolles

PAROLLES (*to Bertram*) These things shall be done, sir.

LAFEW Pray you, sir, who's his tailor?

PAROLLES Sir!

LAFEW O, I know him well. Ay, sir, he, sir, 's a good workman, a very good tailor.

BERTRAM (*aside to Parolles*) Is she gone to the King?
20 PAROLLES She is.

BERTRAM Will she away tonight?

PAROLLES As you'll have her.

BERTRAM
I have writ my letters, casketed my treasure,

Given order for our horses; and tonight,
When I should take possession of the bride,
End ere I do begin.

LAFEW (*aside*) A good traveller is something at the latter
end of a dinner; but one that lies three thirds and uses a
known truth to pass a thousand nothings with, should
be once heard and thrice beaten. (*Aloud*) God save you, 30
captain!

BERTRAM Is there any unkindness between my lord and
you, monsieur?

PAROLLES I know not how I have deserved to run into
my lord's displeasure.

LAFEW You have made shift to run into't, boots and spurs
and all, like him that leaped into the custard; and out of
it you'll run again rather than suffer question for your
residence.

BERTRAM It may be you have mistaken him, my lord. 40

LAFEW And shall do so ever, though I took him at's
prayers. Fare you well, my lord, and believe this of me:
there can be no kernel in this light nut. The soul of this
man is his clothes. Trust him not in matter of heavy
consequence. I have kept of them tame, and know their
natures. Farewell, monsieur; I have spoken better of
you than you have or will to deserve at my hand, but we
must do good against evil.   *Exit*

PAROLLES An idle lord, I swear.

BERTRAM I think not so.   50

PAROLLES Why, do you not know him?

BERTRAM
Yes, I do know him well, and common speech
Gives him a worthy pass. Here comes my clog.
        Enter Helena

HELENA
I have, sir, as I was commanded from you,

Spoke with the King, and have procured his leave
For present parting; only he desires
Some private speech with you.

BERTRAM   I shall obey his will.
You must not marvel, Helen, at my course,
Which holds not colour with the time, nor does
60 The ministration and requirèd office
On my particular. Prepared I was not
For such a business, therefore am I found
So much unsettled. This drives me to entreat you
That presently you take your way for home,
And rather muse than ask why I entreat you;
For my respects are better than they seem,
And my appointments have in them a need
Greater than shows itself at the first view
To you that know them not. This to my mother.

  He gives Helena a letter
70 'Twill be two days ere I shall see you, so
I leave you to your wisdom.

HELENA   Sir, I can nothing say
But that I am your most obedient servant.

BERTRAM
Come, come, no more of that.

HELENA   And ever shall
With true observance seek to eke out that
Wherein toward me my homely stars have failed
To equal my great fortune.

BERTRAM   Let that go.
My haste is very great. Farewell. Hie home.

HELENA
Pray, sir, your pardon.

BERTRAM   Well, what would you say?

HELENA
I am not worthy of the wealth I owe,

94

Nor dare I say 'tis mine – and yet it is;   80
But, like a timorous thief, most fain would steal
What law does vouch mine own.

BERTRAM   What would you have?

HELENA
Something, and scarce so much; nothing indeed.
I would not tell you what I would, my lord.
Faith, yes:
Strangers and foes do sunder and not kiss.

BERTRAM
I pray you, stay not, but in haste to horse.

HELENA
I shall not break your bidding, good my lord.
Where are my other men? Monsieur, farewell.   *Exit*

BERTRAM
Go thou toward home, where I will never come   90
Whilst I can shake my sword or hear the drum.
Away, and for our flight.

PAROLLES   Bravely. Coragio!   *Exeunt*

＊

   Flourish. Enter the Duke of Florence, and the two III.1
   French Lords, with a troop of soldiers

DUKE
So that from point to point now have you heard
The fundamental reasons of this war,
Whose great decision hath much blood let forth,
And more thirsts after.

FIRST LORD   Holy seems the quarrel
Upon your grace's part, black and fearful
On the opposer.

95

DUKE
    Therefore we marvel much our cousin France
    Would in so just a business shut his bosom
    Against our borrowing prayers.

SECOND LORD   Good my lord,
10   The reasons of our state I cannot yield,
    But like a common and an outward man
    That the great figure of a council frames
    By self-unable motion; therefore dare not
    Say what I think of it, since I have found
    Myself in my incertain grounds to fail
    As often as I guessed.

DUKE   Be it his pleasure.

FIRST LORD
    But I am sure the younger of our nature
    That surfeit on their ease will day by day
    Come here for physic.

DUKE   Welcome shall they be,
20   And all the honours that can fly from us
    Shall on them settle. You know your places well;
    When better fall, for your avails they fell.
    Tomorrow to the field.   *Flourish. Exeunt*

III.2   *Enter the Countess and the Clown*

COUNTESS It hath happened all as I would have had it,
    save that he comes not along with her.

CLOWN By my troth, I take my young lord to be a very
    melancholy man.

COUNTESS By what observance, I pray you?

CLOWN Why, he will look upon his boot and sing, mend
    the ruff and sing, ask questions and sing, pick his teeth
    and sing. I knew a man that had this trick of melancholy
    hold a goodly manor for a song.

COUNTESS Let me see what he writes, and when he 10
means to come.

    She opens the letter

CLOWN I have no mind to Isbel since I was at court. Our
old lings and our Isbels o'th'country are nothing like
your old ling and your Isbels o'th'court. The brains of
my Cupid's knocked out, and I begin to love as an old
man loves money, with no stomach.

COUNTESS What have we here?

CLOWN E'en that you have there.   *Exit*

COUNTESS (*reading the letter aloud*) *I have sent you a
daughter-in-law; she hath recovered the King and undone* 20
*me. I have wedded her, not bedded her, and sworn to make
the 'not' eternal. You shall hear I am run away; know it
before the report come. If there be breadth enough in the
world I will hold a long distance. My duty to you.*

                Your unfortunate son,
                      Bertram.

This is not well, rash and unbridled boy,
To fly the favours of so good a King,
To pluck his indignation on thy head
By the misprizing of a maid too virtuous   30
For the contempt of empire.

    Enter Clown

CLOWN O madam, yonder is heavy news within, between
two soldiers and my young lady.

COUNTESS What is the matter?

CLOWN Nay, there is some comfort in the news, some
comfort: your son will not be killed so soon as I thought
he would.

COUNTESS Why should he be killed?

CLOWN So say I, madam, if he run away, as I hear he
does. The danger is in standing to't; that's the loss of 40
men, though it be the getting of children. Here they

come will tell you more. For my part, I only hear your
son was run away. *Exit*

Enter Helena and the two French Lords

FIRST LORD
Save you, good madam.

HELENA
Madam, my lord is gone, for ever gone.

SECOND LORD
Do not say so.

COUNTESS
Think upon patience. Pray you, gentlemen –
I have felt so many quirks of joy and grief
That the first face of neither on the start
50 Can woman me unto't. Where is my son, I pray you?

SECOND LORD
Madam, he's gone to serve the Duke of Florence.
We met him thitherward, for thence we came,
And, after some dispatch in hand at court,
Thither we bend again.

HELENA
Look on his letter, madam: here's my passport.
(*She reads the letter aloud*)
*When thou canst get the ring upon my finger, which never
shall come off, and show me a child begotten of thy body
that I am father to, then call me husband; but in such a
'then' I write a 'never'.*
60 This is a dreadful sentence.

COUNTESS Brought you this letter, gentlemen?

FIRST LORD Ay, madam, and for the contents' sake are
sorry for our pains.

COUNTESS
I prithee, lady, have a better cheer.
If thou engrossest all the griefs are thine
Thou robbest me of a moiety. He was my son,

98

But I do wash his name out of my blood
And thou art all my child. Towards Florence is he?

SECOND LORD
Ay, madam.

COUNTESS   And to be a soldier?

SECOND LORD
Such is his noble purpose; and, believe't,   70
The Duke will lay upon him all the honour
That good convenience claims.

COUNTESS   Return you thither?

FIRST LORD
Ay, madam, with the swiftest wing of speed.

HELENA (*reading*)
Till I have no wife I have nothing in France.
'Tis bitter.

COUNTESS   Find you that there?

HELENA   Ay, madam.

FIRST LORD 'Tis but the boldness of his hand, haply,
which his heart was not consenting to.

COUNTESS
Nothing in France until he have no wife!
There's nothing here that is too good for him
But only she, and she deserves a lord   80
That twenty such rude boys might tend upon
And call her, hourly, mistress. Who was with him?

FIRST LORD A servant only, and a gentleman which I
have sometime known.

COUNTESS Parolles, was it not?

FIRST LORD Ay, my good lady, he.

COUNTESS
A very tainted fellow, and full of wickedness.
My son corrupts a well-derivèd nature
With his inducement.

FIRST LORD   Indeed, good lady,

90   The fellow has a deal of that too much
     Which holds him much to have.

COUNTESS   Y'are welcome, gentlemen.
     I will entreat you, when you see my son,
     To tell him that his sword can never win
     The honour that he loses. More I'll entreat you
     Written to bear along.

SECOND LORD   We serve you, madam,
     In that and all your worthiest affairs.

COUNTESS
     Not so, but as we change our courtesies.
     Will you draw near?   *Exeunt the Countess and the Lords*

HELENA
     'Till I have no wife I have nothing in France.'
100 Nothing in France until he has no wife!
     Thou shalt have none, Rossillion, none in France,
     Then hast thou all again. Poor lord, is't I
     That chase thee from thy country, and expose
     Those tender limbs of thine to the event
     Of the none-sparing war? And is it I
     That drive thee from the sportive court, where thou
     Wast shot at with fair eyes, to be the mark
     Of smoky muskets? O you leaden messengers,
     That ride upon the violent speed of fire,
110 Fly with false aim, move the still-piecing air
     That sings with piercing, do not touch my lord.
     Whoever shoots at him, I set him there.
     Whoever charges on his forward breast,
     I am the caitiff that do hold him to't;
     And though I kill him not, I am the cause
     His death was so effected. Better 'twere
     I met the ravin lion when he roared
     With sharp constraint of hunger; better 'twere
     That all the miseries which nature owes

Were mine at once. No, come thou home, Rossillion,   120
Whence honour but of danger wins a scar,
As oft it loses all. I will be gone;
My being here it is that holds thee hence.
Shall I stay here to do't? No, no, although
The air of paradise did fan the house
And angels officed all. I will be gone,
That pitiful rumour may report my flight
To consolate thine ear. Come, night; end, day!
For with the dark, poor thief, I'll steal away.   *Exit*

 Flourish. Enter the Duke of Florence, Bertram, drum III.3
  and trumpets, soldiers, Parolles

DUKE
 The general of our horse thou art, and we,
 Great in our hope, lay our best love and credence
 Upon thy promising fortune.

BERTRAM   Sir, it is
 A charge too heavy for my strength; but yet
 We'll strive to bear it for your worthy sake
 To th'extreme edge of hazard.

DUKE   Then go thou forth,
 And fortune play upon thy prosperous helm
 As thy auspicious mistress!

BERTRAM   This very day,
 Great Mars, I put myself into thy file;
 Make me but like my thoughts and I shall prove   10
 A lover of thy drum, hater of love.   *Exeunt*

 Enter the Countess and the Steward   III.4

COUNTESS
 Alas! and would you take the letter of her?

Might you not know she would do as she has done
By sending me a letter? Read it again.

STEWARD (*reading*)

I am Saint Jaques' pilgrim, thither gone.
  Ambitious love hath so in me offended
That barefoot plod I the cold ground upon,
  With sainted vow my faults to have amended.
Write, write, that from the bloody course of war
  My dearest master, your dear son, may hie.
Bless him at home in peace, whilst I from far
  His name with zealous fervour sanctify.
His taken labours bid him me forgive;
  I, his despiteful Juno, sent him forth
From courtly friends, with camping foes to live
  Where death and danger dogs the heels of worth.
He is too good and fair for death and me;
  Whom I myself embrace to set him free.

COUNTESS

Ah, what sharp stings are in her mildest words!
Rynaldo, you did never lack advice so much
As letting her pass so. Had I spoke with her,
I could have well diverted her intents,
Which thus she hath prevented.

STEWARD   Pardon me, madam.
If I had given you this at overnight
She might have been o'erta'en; and yet she writes
Pursuit would be but vain.

COUNTESS   What angel shall
Bless this unworthy husband? He cannot thrive,
Unless her prayers, whom heaven delights to hear
And loves to grant, reprieve him from the wrath
Of greatest justice. Write, write, Rynaldo,
To this unworthy husband of his wife.
Let every word weigh heavy of her worth

That he does weigh too light. My greatest grief,
Though little he do feel it, set down sharply.
Dispatch the most convenient messenger.
When haply he shall hear that she is gone,
He will return; and hope I may that she,
Hearing so much, will speed her foot again,
Led hither by pure love. Which of them both
Is dearest to me I have no skill in sense
To make distinction. Provide this messenger.   40
My heart is heavy and mine age is weak;
Grief would have tears, and sorrow bids me speak.

Exeunt

A tucket afar off. Enter the old Widow of Florence, III.5
*her daughter Diana, and Mariana, with other
citizens*

WIDOW Nay, come, for if they do approach the city, we
shall lose all the sight.

DIANA They say the French Count has done most
honourable service.

WIDOW It is reported that he has taken their greatest
commander, and that with his own hand he slew the
Duke's brother.

Tucket

We have lost our labour; they are gone a contrary way.
Hark! You may know by their trumpets.

MARIANA Come, let's return again and suffice ourselves   10
with the report of it. Well, Diana, take heed of this
French Earl. The honour of a maid is her name, and no
legacy is so rich as honesty.

WIDOW I have told my neighbour how you have been
solicited by a gentleman his companion.

MARIANA I know that knave, hang him! one Parolles; a

filthy officer he is in those suggestions for the young
Earl. Beware of them, Diana: their promises, entice-
ments, oaths, tokens, and all these engines of lust, are
20 not the things they go under. Many a maid hath been
seduced by them, and the misery is, example, that so
terrible shows in the wrack of maidenhood, cannot for
all that dissuade succession, but that they are limed with
the twigs that threatens them. I hope I need not to
advise you further; but I hope your own grace will keep
you where you are, though there were no further danger
known but the modesty which is so lost.

DIANA You shall not need to fear me.

Enter Helena

WIDOW I hope so. Look, here comes a pilgrim. I know
30 she will lie at my house; thither they send one another.
I'll question her. God save you, pilgrim! Whither are
bound?

HELENA
To Saint Jaques le Grand.
Where do the palmers lodge, I do beseech you?

WIDOW
At the Saint Francis here beside the port.

HELENA
Is this the way?

A march afar

WIDOW
Ay, marry, is't. Hark you, they come this way.
If you will tarry, holy pilgrim,
But till the troops come by,
40 I will conduct you where you shall be lodged;
The rather for I think I know your hostess
As ample as myself.

HELENA   Is it yourself?

WIDOW

If you shall please so, pilgrim.

HELENA

I thank you and will stay upon your leisure.

WIDOW

You came, I think, from France?

HELENA   I did so.

WIDOW

Here you shall see a countryman of yours
That has done worthy service.

HELENA   His name, I pray you?

DIANA

The Count Rossillion. Know you such a one?

HELENA

But by the ear, that hears most nobly of him;
His face I know not.

DIANA   Whatsome'er he is,   50
He's bravely taken here. He stole from France,
As 'tis reported, for the King had married him
Against his liking. Think you it is so?

HELENA

Ay, surely, mere the truth. I know his lady.

DIANA

There is a gentleman that serves the Count
Reports but coarsely of her.

HELENA   What's his name?

DIANA

Monsieur Parolles.

HELENA   O, I believe with him,
In argument of praise or to the worth
Of the great Count himself, she is too mean
To have her name repeated; all her deserving   60
Is a reservèd honesty, and that

I have not heard examined.

DIANA   Alas, poor lady!
'Tis a hard bondage to become the wife
Of a detesting lord.

WIDOW

I warrant, good creature, wheresoe'er she is,
Her heart weighs sadly. This young maid might do her
A shrewd turn if she pleased.

HELENA   How do you mean?
Maybe the amorous Count solicits her
In the unlawful purpose?

WIDOW   He does indeed,
70 And brokes with all that can in such a suit
Corrupt the tender honour of a maid;
But she is armed for him and keeps her guard
In honestest defence.

> Drum and colours. Enter Bertram, Parolles, and the
> whole army

MARIANA   The gods forbid else!

WIDOW

So, now they come.
That is Antonio, the Duke's eldest son;
That Escalus.

HELENA   Which is the Frenchman?

DIANA   He –
That with the plume. 'Tis a most gallant fellow.
I would he loved his wife; if he were honester
He were much goodlier. Is't not a handsome gentleman?

HELENA

80 I like him well.

DIANA

'Tis pity he is not honest. Yond's that same knave
That leads him to these places. Were I his lady
I would poison that vile rascal.

HELENA   Which is he?

DIANA That jackanapes with scarfs. Why is he melan-
     choly?

HELENA Perchance he's hurt i'th'battle.

PAROLLES Lose our drum! Well!

MARIANA He's shrewdly vexed at something. Look, he
     has spied us.

WIDOW Marry, hang you!   90

MARIANA And your courtesy, for a ring-carrier!
                    Exeunt Bertram, Parolles, and the army

WIDOW
     The troop is past. Come, pilgrim, I will bring you
     Where you shall host. Of enjoined penitents
     There's four or five, to great Saint Jaques bound,
     Already at my house.

HELENA   I humbly thank you.
     Please it this matron and this gentle maid
     To eat with us tonight; the charge and thanking
     Shall be for me, and, to requite you further,
     I will bestow some precepts of this virgin,
     Worthy the note.

WIDOW *and* MARIANA
                    We'll take your offer kindly.   *Exeunt* 100

              Enter Bertram and the two French Lords   III.6

FIRST LORD Nay, good my lord, put him to't, let him
     have his way.

SECOND LORD If your lordship find him not a hilding,
     hold me no more in your respect.

FIRST LORD On my life, my lord, a bubble.

BERTRAM Do you think I am so far deceived in him?

FIRST LORD Believe it, my lord, in mine own direct
     knowledge, without any malice, but to speak of him as

my kinsman, he's a most notable coward, an infinite and
10   endless liar, an hourly promise-breaker, the owner of no
one good quality worthy your lordship's entertainment.

SECOND LORD It were fit you knew him; lest, reposing
too far in his virtue which he hath not, he might at some
great and trusty business in a main danger fail you.

BERTRAM I would I knew in what particular action to try
him.

SECOND LORD None better than to let him fetch off his
drum, which you hear him so confidently undertake to
do.

20 FIRST LORD I, with a troop of Florentines, will suddenly
surprise him; such I will have whom I am sure he
knows not from the enemy. We will bind and hoodwink
him so, that he shall suppose no other but that he is
carried into the leaguer of the adversaries when we
bring him to our own tents. Be but your lordship present
at his examination. If he do not for the promise of his
life, and in the highest compulsion of base fear, offer to
betray you and deliver all the intelligence in his power
against you, and that with the divine forfeit of his soul
30   upon oath, never trust my judgement in anything.

SECOND LORD O, for the love of laughter, let him fetch
his drum; he says he has a stratagem for't. When your
lordship sees the bottom of his success in't, and to what
metal this counterfeit lump of ore will be melted, if you
give him not John Drum's entertainment your inclining
cannot be removed. Here he comes.

Enter Parolles

FIRST LORD O, for the love of laughter, hinder not the
honour of his design; let him fetch off his drum in any
hand.

40 BERTRAM How now, monsieur! This drum sticks sorely
in your disposition.

SECOND LORD A pox on't! Let it go, 'tis but a drum.

PAROLLES But a drum! Is't but a drum? A drum so lost! There was excellent command: to charge in with our horse upon our own wings and to rend our own soldiers!

SECOND LORD That was not to be blamed in the command of the service; it was a disaster of war that Caesar himself could not have prevented if he had been there to command.

BERTRAM Well, we cannot greatly condemn our success; 50 some dishonour we had in the loss of that drum, but it is not to be recovered.

PAROLLES It might have been recovered.

BERTRAM It might, but it is not now.

PAROLLES It is to be recovered. But that the merit of service is seldom attributed to the true and exact performer, I would have that drum or another, or *hic jacet*.

BERTRAM Why, if you have a stomach, to't, monsieur! If you think your mystery in stratagem can bring this instrument of honour again into his native quarter, be 60 magnanimious in the enterprise and go on. I will grace the attempt for a worthy exploit. If you speed well in it the Duke shall both speak of it and extend to you what further becomes his greatness, even to the utmost syllable of your worthiness.

PAROLLES By the hand of a soldier, I will undertake it.

BERTRAM But you must not now slumber in it.

PAROLLES I'll about it this evening, and I will presently pen down my dilemmas, encourage myself in my certainty, put myself into my mortal preparation; and by 70 midnight look to hear further from me.

BERTRAM May I be bold to acquaint his grace you are gone about it?

PAROLLES I know not what the success will be, my lord, but the attempt I vow.

BERTRAM I know th' art valiant, and to the possibility of thy soldiership will subscribe for thee. Farewell.

PAROLLES I love not many words. *Exit*

FIRST LORD No more than a fish loves water. Is not this a
80 strange fellow, my lord, that so confidently seems to undertake this business, which he knows is not to be done, damns himself to do, and dares better be damned than to do't.

SECOND LORD You do not know him, my lord, as we do. Certain it is that he will steal himself into a man's favour and for a week escape a great deal of discoveries, but when you find him out you have him ever after.

BERTRAM Why, do you think he will make no deed at all of this that so seriously he does address himself unto?

90 FIRST LORD None in the world, but return with an invention, and clap upon you two or three probable lies. But we have almost embossed him. You shall see his fall tonight; for indeed he is not for your lordship's respect.

SECOND LORD We'll make you some sport with the fox ere we case him. He was first smoked by the old Lord Lafew. When his disguise and he is parted tell me what a sprat you shall find him; which you shall see this very night.

100 FIRST LORD I must go look my twigs. He shall be caught.

BERTRAM Your brother, he shall go along with me.

FIRST LORD As't please your lordship. I'll leave you.

Exit

BERTRAM
Now will I lead you to the house and show you
The lass I spoke of.

SECOND LORD   But you say she's honest.

BERTRAM
That's all the fault. I spoke with her but once

And found her wondrous cold, but I sent to her
By this same coxcomb that we have i'th'wind
Tokens and letters which she did re-send,
And this is all I have done. She's a fair creature;
Will you go see her?

SECOND LORD   With all my heart, my lord. *Exeunt* 110

Enter Helena and the Widow   III.7

HELENA
If you misdoubt me that I am not she,
I know not how I shall assure you further
But I shall lose the grounds I work upon.

WIDOW
Though my estate be fallen, I was well born,
Nothing acquainted with these businesses,
And would not put my reputation now
In any staining act.

HELENA   Nor would I wish you.
First give me trust the Count he is my husband,
And what to your sworn counsel I have spoken
Is so from word to word, and then you cannot,   10
By the good aid that I of you shall borrow,
Err in bestowing it.

WIDOW   I should believe you,
For you have showed me that which well approves
Y'are great in fortune.

HELENA   Take this purse of gold,
And let me buy your friendly help thus far,
Which I will over-pay, and pay again
When I have found it. The Count he woos your
          daughter,
Lays down his wanton siege before her beauty,
Resolved to carry her; let her in fine consent

20 As we'll direct her how 'tis best to bear it.
Now his important blood will naught deny
That she'll demand. A ring the County wears
That downward hath succeeded in his house
From son to son some four or five descents
Since the first father wore it. This ring he holds
In most rich choice, yet, in his idle fire,
To buy his will it would not seem too dear,
Howe'er repented after.

WIDOW   Now I see
The bottom of your purpose.

HELENA
30 You see it lawful then. It is no more
But that your daughter, ere she seems as won,
Desires this ring; appoints him an encounter;
In fine, delivers me to fill the time,
Herself most chastely absent. After,
To marry her I'll add three thousand crowns
To what is passed already.

WIDOW   I have yielded.
Instruct my daughter how she shall persever
That time and place with this deceit so lawful
May prove coherent. Every night he comes
40 With musics of all sorts, and songs composed
To her unworthiness. It nothing steads us
To chide him from our eaves, for he persists
As if his life lay on't.

HELENA   Why then tonight
Let us assay our plot, which, if it speed,
Is wicked meaning in a lawful deed,
And lawful meaning in a lawful act,
Where both not sin, and yet a sinful fact.
But let's about it.   *Exeunt*

✳

Enter the First French Lord, with five or six other Soldiers in ambush

FIRST LORD He can come no other way but by this hedge-corner. When you sally upon him speak what terrible language you will; though you understand it not yourselves, no matter; for we must not seem to understand him, unless some one among us, whom we must produce for an interpreter.

FIRST SOLDIER Good captain, let me be th'interpreter.

FIRST LORD Art not acquainted with him? Knows he not thy voice?

FIRST SOLDIER No, sir, I warrant you. 10

FIRST LORD But what linsey-woolsey hast thou to speak to us again?

FIRST SOLDIER E'en such as you speak to me.

FIRST LORD He must think us some band of strangers i'th'adversary's entertainment. Now he hath a smack of all neighbouring languages, therefore we must every one be a man of his own fancy, not to know what we speak one to another; so we seem to know is to know straight our purpose – choughs' language, gabble enough and good enough. As for you, interpreter, you must seem 20 very politic. But couch, ho! Here he comes to beguile two hours in a sleep, and then to return and swear the lies he forges.

Enter Parolles

PAROLLES Ten o'clock. Within these three hours 'twill be time enough to go home. What shall I say I have done? It must be a very plausive invention that carriés it. They begin to smoke me, and disgraces have of late knocked too often at my door. I find my tongue is too foolhardy, but my heart hath the fear of Mars before it and of his creatures, not daring the reports of my tongue. 30

FIRST LORD This is the first truth that e'er thine own
tongue was guilty of.

PAROLLES What the devil should move me to undertake
the recovery of this drum, being not ignorant of the
impossibility, and knowing I had no such purpose? I
must give myself some hurts, and say I got them in
exploit. Yet slight ones will not carry it: they will say
'Came you off with so little?' And great ones I dare not
give. Wherefore, what's the instance? Tongue, I must
40   put you into a butter-woman's mouth, and buy myself
another of Bajazeth's mule, if you prattle me into these
perils.

FIRST LORD Is it possible he should know what he is, and
be that he is?

PAROLLES I would the cutting of my garments would
serve the turn, or the breaking of my Spanish sword.

FIRST LORD We cannot afford you so.

PAROLLES Or the baring of my beard, and to say it was in
stratagem.

50 FIRST LORD 'Twould not do.

PAROLLES Or to drown my clothes and say I was stripped.

FIRST LORD Hardly serve.

PAROLLES Though I swore I leaped from the window of
the citadel –

FIRST LORD How deep?

PAROLLES Thirty fathom.

FIRST LORD Three great oaths would scarce make that be
believed.

PAROLLES I would I had any drum of the enemy's; I
60   would swear I recovered it.

FIRST LORD You shall hear one anon.

PAROLLES A drum now of the enemy's –
        Alarum within

FIRST LORD *Throca movousus, cargo, cargo, cargo.*

ALL *Cargo, cargo, cargo, villianda par corbo, cargo.*
> *They seize him*

PAROLLES

O, ransom, ransom!
> *They blindfold him*

                          Do not hide mine eyes.

FIRST SOLDIER *Boskos thromuldo boskos.*

PAROLLES

I know you are the Muskos' regiment,
And I shall lose my life for want of language.
If there be here German, or Dane, Low Dutch,
Italian, or French, let him speak to me,   70
I'll discover that which shall undo the Florentine.

FIRST SOLDIER *Boskos vauvado.* I understand thee, and
can speak thy tongue. *Kerelybonto.* Sir, betake thee to
thy faith, for seventeen poniards are at thy bosom.

PAROLLES O!

FIRST SOLDIER O, pray, pray, pray! *Manka revania
dulche.*

FIRST LORD *Oscorbidulchos volivorco.*

FIRST SOLDIER

The General is content to spare thee yet,
And, hoodwinked as thou art, will lead thee on   80
To gather from thee. Haply thou mayst inform
Something to save thy life.

PAROLLES   O, let me live,
And all the secrets of our camp I'll show,
Their force, their purposes; nay, I'll speak that
Which you will wonder at.

FIRST SOLDIER   But wilt thou faithfully?

PAROLLES

If I do not, damn me.

FIRST SOLDIER   *Acordo linta.*
    Come on, thou art granted space.
                                        Exit with Parolles guarded
                A short alarum within
FIRST LORD
    Go tell the Count Rossillion and my brother
    We have caught the woodcock and will keep him muffled
90 Till we do hear from them.
SECOND SOLDIER   Captain, I will.
FIRST LORD
    'A will betray us all unto ourselves:
    Inform on that.
SECOND SOLDIER
    So I will, sir.
FIRST LORD
    Till then I'll keep him dark and safely locked.   *Exeunt*

IV.2   *Enter Bertram and Diana*
BERTRAM
    They told me that your name was Fontybell.
DIANA
    No, my good lord, Diana.
BERTRAM   Titled goddess,
    And worth it, with addition! But, fair soul,.
    In your fine frame hath love no quality?
    If the quick fire of youth light not your mind
    You are no maiden but a monument.
    When you are dead you should be such a one
    As you are now; for you are cold and stern,
    And now you should be as your mother was
10 When your sweet self was got.
DIANA
    She then was honest.

BERTRAM   So should you be.
DIANA   No.
  My mother did but duty, such, my lord,
  As you owe to your wife.
BERTRAM   No more o'that!
  I prithee do not strive against my vows.
  I was compelled to her, but I love thee
  By love's own sweet constraint, and will for ever
  Do thee all rights of service.
DIANA   Ay, so you serve us
  Till we serve you; but when you have our roses,
  You barely leave our thorns to prick ourselves,
  And mock us with our bareness.
BERTRAM   How have I sworn!   20
DIANA
  'Tis not the many oaths that makes the truth,
  But the plain single vow that is vowed true.
  What is not holy, that we swear not by,
  But take the highest to witness. Then, pray you, tell
     me:
  If I should swear by Love's great attributes
  I loved you dearly, would you believe my oaths
  When I did love you ill? This has no holding,
  To swear by him whom I protest to love
  That I will work against him. Therefore your oaths
  Are words, and poor conditions but unsealed –   30
  At least in my opinion.
BERTRAM   Change it, change it.
  Be not so holy-cruel. Love is holy,
  And my integrity ne'er knew the crafts
  That you do charge men with. Stand no more off,
  But give thyself unto my sick desires,
  Who then recovers. Say thou art mine, and ever
  My love as it begins shall so persever.

DIANA

I see that men make vows in such a flame
That we'll forsake ourselves. Give me that ring.

BERTRAM

40 I'll lend it thee, my dear, but have no power
To give it from me.

DIANA   Will you not, my lord?

BERTRAM

It is an honour 'longing to our house,
Bequeathèd down from many ancestors,
Which were the greatest obloquy i'th'world
In me to lose.

DIANA   Mine honour's such a ring;
My chastity's the jewel of our house,
Bequeathèd down from many ancestors,
Which were the greatest obloquy i'th'world
In me to lose. Thus your own proper wisdom

50 Brings in the champion Honour on my part
Against your vain assault.

BERTRAM   Here, take my ring.
My house, mine honour, yea, my life be thine,
And I'll be bid by thee.

DIANA

When midnight comes, knock at my chamber window;
I'll order take my mother shall not hear.
Now will I charge you in the band of truth,
When you have conquered my yet maiden bed,
Remain there but an hour, nor speak to me.
My reasons are most strong and you shall know them

60 When back again this ring shall be delivered.
And on your finger in the night I'll put
Another ring, that what in time proceeds
May token to the future our past deeds.
Adieu till then; then, fail not. You have won

A wife of me, though there my hope be done.

BERTRAM

A heaven on earth I have won by wooing thee. *Exit*

DIANA

For which live long to thank both heaven and me!
You may so in the end.
My mother told me just how he would woo
As if she sat in's heart. She says all men   70
Have the like oaths. He had sworn to marry me
When his wife's dead; therefore I'll lie with him
When I am buried. Since Frenchmen are so braid,
Marry that will, I live and die a maid.
Only, in this disguise, I think't no sin
To cozen him that would unjustly win.   *Exit*

Enter the two French Lords, and two or three soldiers **IV.3**

FIRST LORD You have not given him his mother's letter?

SECOND LORD I have delivered it an hour since. There is something in't that stings his nature, for on the reading it he changed almost into another man.

FIRST LORD He has much worthy blame laid upon him for shaking off so good a wife and so sweet a lady.

SECOND LORD Especially he hath incurred the ever-lasting displeasure of the King, who had even tuned his bounty to sing happiness to him. I will tell you a thing, but you shall let it dwell darkly with you.   10

FIRST LORD When you have spoken it 'tis dead, and I am the grave of it.

SECOND LORD He hath perverted a young gentlewoman here in Florence, of a most chaste renown, and this night he fleshes his will in the spoil of her honour. He hath given her his monumental ring, and thinks himself made in the unchaste composition.

FIRST LORD Now, God delay our rebellion! As we are ourselves, what things are we!

20 SECOND LORD Merely our own traitors. And as in the common course of all treasons we still see them reveal themselves till they attain to their abhorred ends, so he that in this action contrives against his own nobility, in his proper stream o'erflows himself.

FIRST LORD Is it not meant damnable in us to be trumpeters of our unlawful intents? We shall not then have his company tonight?

SECOND LORD Not till after midnight, for he is dieted to his hour.

30 FIRST LORD That approaches apace. I would gladly have him see his company anatomized, that he might take a measure of his own judgements wherein so curiously he had set this counterfeit.

SECOND LORD We will not meddle with him till he come, for his presence must be the whip of the other.

FIRST LORD In the meantime, what hear you of these wars?

SECOND LORD I hear there is an overture of peace.

FIRST LORD Nay, I assure you, a peace concluded.

40 SECOND LORD What will Count Rossillion do then? Will he travel higher, or return again into France?

FIRST LORD I perceive by this demand you are not altogether of his counsel.

SECOND LORD Let it be forbid, sir; so should I be a great deal of his act.

FIRST LORD Sir, his wife some two months since fled from his house. Her pretence is a pilgrimage to Saint Jaques le Grand; which holy undertaking with most austere sanctimony she accomplished; and there resid-

50 ing, the tenderness of her nature became as a prey to her

grief; in fine, made a groan of her last breath, and now she sings in heaven.

SECOND LORD How is this justified?

FIRST LORD The stronger part of it by her own letters, which makes her story true even to the point of her death. Her death itself, which could not be her office to say is come, was faithfully confirmed by the rector of the place.

SECOND LORD Hath the Count all this intelligence?

FIRST LORD Ay, and the particular confirmations, point from point, to the full arming of the verity. 60

SECOND LORD I am heartily sorry that he'll be glad of this.

FIRST LORD How mightily sometimes we make us comforts of our losses!

SECOND LORD And how mightily some other times we drown our gain in tears! The great dignity that his valour hath here acquired for him shall at home be encountered with a shame as ample.

FIRST LORD The web of our life is of a mingled yarn, good 70 and ill together. Our virtues would be proud if our faults whipped them not, and our crimes would despair if they were not cherished by our virtues.

Enter a Messenger

How now? Where's your master?

MESSENGER He met the Duke in the street, sir, of whom he hath taken a solemn leave: his lordship will next morning for France. The Duke hath offered him letters of commendations to the King.

SECOND LORD They shall be no more than needful there, if they were more than they can commend. 80

Enter Bertram

FIRST LORD They cannot be too sweet for the King's

tartness. Here's his lordship now. How now, my lord? Is't not after midnight?

BERTRAM I have tonight dispatched sixteen businesses a month's length apiece. By an abstract of success: I have congied with the Duke, done my adieu with his nearest, buried a wife, mourned for her, writ to my lady mother I am returning, entertained my convoy, and between these main parcels of dispatch effected many nicer
90 needs; the last was the greatest, but that I have not ended yet.

SECOND LORD If the business be of any difficulty, and this morning your departure hence, it requires haste of your lordship.

BERTRAM I mean, the business is not ended, as fearing to hear of it hereafter. But shall we have this dialogue between the Fool and the Soldier? Come, bring forth this counterfeit module has deceived me like a double-meaning prophesier.

100 SECOND LORD Bring him forth.

Exeunt the Soldiers

Has sat i'th'stocks all night, poor gallant knave.

BERTRAM No matter. His heels have deserved it in usurping his spurs so long. How does he carry himself?

SECOND LORD I have told your lordship already: the stocks carry him. But to answer you as you would be understood, he weeps like a wench that had shed her milk. He hath confessed himself to Morgan, whom he supposes to be a friar, from the time of his remembrance to this very instant disaster of his setting i'th'stocks.
110 And what think you he hath confessed?

BERTRAM Nothing of me, has 'a?

SECOND LORD His confession is taken, and it shall be read to his face; if your lordship be in't, as I believe you are, you must have the patience to hear it.

Enter Parolles guarded, with the First Soldier as his interpreter

BERTRAM A plague upon him! Muffled! He can say nothing of me.

FIRST LORD (*aside to Bertram*) Hush, hush! Hoodman comes. (*Aloud*) *Portotartarossa*.

FIRST SOLDIER He calls for the tortures. What will you say without 'em? 120

PAROLLES I will confess what I know without constraint. If ye pinch me like a pasty I can say no more.

FIRST SOLDIER *Bosko chimurcho.*

FIRST LORD *Boblibindo chicurmurco.*

FIRST SOLDIER You are a merciful general. Our General bids you answer to what I shall ask you out of a note.

PAROLLES And truly, as I hope to live.

FIRST SOLDIER (*reading*) *First demand of him how many horse the Duke is strong.* What say you to that?

PAROLLES Five or six thousand, but very weak and un- 130 serviceable. The troops are all scattered and the commanders very poor rogues, upon my reputation and credit, and as I hope to live.

FIRST SOLDIER Shall I set down your answer so?

PAROLLES Do. I'll take the sacrament on't, how and which way you will.

BERTRAM All's one to him. What a past-saving slave is this!

FIRST LORD Y'are deceived, my lord; this is Monsieur Parolles, the gallant militarist – that was his own phrase 140 – that had the whole theoric of war in the knot of his scarf, and the practice in the chape of his dagger.

SECOND LORD I will never trust a man again for keeping his sword clean, nor believe he can have everything in him by wearing his apparel neatly.

FIRST SOLDIER Well, that's set down.

PAROLLES 'Five or six thousand horse' I said – I will say true – 'or thereabouts' set down, for I'll speak truth.

FIRST LORD He's very near the truth in this.

150 BERTRAM But I con him no thanks for't, in the nature he delivers it.

PAROLLES 'Poor rogues' I pray you say.

FIRST SOLDIER Well, that's set down.

PAROLLES I humbly thank you, sir. A truth's a truth, the rogues are marvellous poor.

FIRST SOLDIER (reading) Demand of him of what strength they are a-foot. What say you to that?

PAROLLES By my troth, sir, if I were to live this present hour, I will tell true. Let me see: Spurio, a hundred and 160 fifty; Sebastian, so many; Corambus, so many; Jaques, so many; Guiltian, Cosmo, Lodowick, and Gratii, two hundred fifty each; mine own company, Chitopher, Vaumond, Bentii, two hundred fifty each; so that the muster-file, rotten and sound, upon my life, amounts not to fifteen thousand poll; half of the which dare not shake the snow from off their cassocks lest they shake themselves to pieces.

BERTRAM What shall be done to him?

FIRST LORD Nothing but let him have thanks. Demand 170 of him my condition, and what credit I have with the Duke.

FIRST SOLDIER Well, that's set down. (Reading) You shall demand of him whether one Captain Dumaine be i'th'camp, a Frenchman; what his reputation is with the Duke, what his valour, honesty, and expertness in wars; or whether he thinks it were not possible with well-weighing sums of gold to corrupt him to a revolt. What say you to this? What do you know of it?

PAROLLES I beseech you, let me answer to the particular 180 of the inter'gatories. Demand them singly.

FIRST SOLDIER Do you know this Captain Dumaine?

PAROLLES I know him: 'a was a botcher's prentice in Paris, from whence he was whipped for getting the shrieve's fool with child, a dumb innocent that could not say him nay.

BERTRAM Nay, by your leave, hold your hands – though I know his brains are forfeit to the next tile that falls.

FIRST SOLDIER Well, is this captain in the Duke of Florence's camp?

PAROLLES Upon my knowledge he is, and lousy.   190

FIRST LORD Nay, look not so upon me; we shall hear of your lordship anon.

FIRST SOLDIER What is his reputation with the Duke?

PAROLLES The Duke knows him for no other but a poor officer of mine, and writ to me this other day to turn him out o'th'band. I think I have his letter in my pocket.

FIRST SOLDIER Marry, we'll search.

PAROLLES In good sadness, I do not know; either it is there or it is upon a file with the Duke's other letters in my tent.   200

FIRST SOLDIER Here 'tis; here's a paper. Shall I read it to you?

PAROLLES I do not know if it be it or no.

BERTRAM Our interpreter does it well.

FIRST LORD Excellently.

FIRST SOLDIER (reading)
Dian, the Count's a fool, and full of gold.

PAROLLES That is not the Duke's letter, sir; that is an advertisement to a proper maid in Florence, one Diana, to take heed of the allurement of one Count Rossillion, a foolish idle boy, but for all that very ruttish. I pray you,   210
sir, put it up again.

FIRST SOLDIER Nay, I'll read it first by your favour.

PAROLLES My meaning in't, I protest, was very honest in

the behalf of the maid; for I knew the young Count to be a dangerous and lascivious boy, who is a whale to virginity, and devours up all the fry it finds.

BERTRAM Damnable both-sides rogue!

FIRST SOLDIER (*reading*)
When he swears oaths, bid him drop gold, and take it;
After he scores he never pays the score.
220 *Half-won is match well made; match, and well make it.*
He ne'er pays after-debts, take it before.
And say a soldier, Dian, told thee this:
Men are to mell with, boys are not to kiss;
For count of this, the Count's a fool, I know it,
Who pays before, but not when he does owe it.
> *Thine, as he vowed to thee in thine ear,*
> *Parolles.*

BERTRAM He shall be whipped through the army, with this rhyme in's forehead.

230 SECOND LORD This is your devoted friend, sir, the manifold linguist, and the armipotent soldier.

BERTRAM I could endure anything before but a cat, and now he's a cat to me.

FIRST SOLDIER I perceive, sir, by the General's looks, we shall be fain to hang you.

PAROLLES My life, sir, in any case! Not that I am afraid to die, but that, my offences being many, I would repent out the remainder of nature. Let me live, sir, in a dungeon, i'th'stocks, or anywhere, so I may live.

240 FIRST SOLDIER We'll see what may be done, so you confess freely. Therefore once more to this Captain Dumaine: you have answered to his reputation with the Duke and to his valour; what is his honesty?

PAROLLES He will steal, sir, an egg out of a cloister. For rapes and ravishments he parallels Nessus. He professes not keeping of oaths; in breaking 'em he is stronger than

Hercules. He will lie, sir, with such volubility that you
would think truth were a fool. Drunkenness is his best
virtue, for he will be swine-drunk, and in his sleep he
does little harm, save to his bedclothes about him; but 250
they know his conditions and lay him in straw. I have
but little more to say, sir, of his honesty: he has everything that an honest man should not have; what an
honest man should have, he has nothing.

FIRST LORD I begin to love him for this.

BERTRAM For this description of thine honesty? A pox
upon him! For me, he's more and more a cat.

FIRST SOLDIER What say you to his expertness in war?

PAROLLES Faith, sir, has led the drum before the English
tragedians – to belie him I will not – and more of his 260
soldiership I know not, except in that country he had
the honour to be the officer at a place there called Mile-
end, to instruct for the doubling of files. I would do the
man what honour I can, but of this I am not certain.

FIRST LORD He hath out-villained villainy so far that the
rarity redeems him.

BERTRAM A pox on him! He's a cat still.

FIRST SOLDIER His qualities being at this poor price, I
need not to ask you if gold will corrupt him to revolt.

PAROLLES Sir, for a cardecue he will sell the fee-simple 270
of his salvation, the inheritance of it, and cut th'entail
from all remainders, and a perpetual succession for it
perpetually.

FIRST SOLDIER What's his brother, the other Captain
Dumaine?

SECOND LORD Why does he ask him of me?

FIRST SOLDIER What's he?

PAROLLES E'en a crow o'th'same nest; not altogether so
great as the first in goodness, but greater a great deal in
evil. He excels his brother for a coward, yet his brother 280

is reputed one of the best that is. In a retreat he outruns any lackey; marry, in coming on he has the cramp.

FIRST SOLDIER If your life be saved will you undertake to betray the Florentine?

PAROLLES Ay, and the captain of his horse, Count Rossillion.

FIRST SOLDIER I'll whisper with the General and know his pleasure.

PAROLLES I'll no more drumming. A plague of all
290 drums! Only to seem to deserve well, and to beguile the supposition of that lascivious young boy, the Count, have I run into this danger. Yet who would have suspected an ambush where I was taken?

FIRST SOLDIER There is no remedy, sir, but you must die. The General says you that have so traitorously discovered the secrets of your army, and made such pestiferous reports of men very nobly held, can serve the world for no honest use; therefore you must die. Come, headsman, off with his head.

300 PAROLLES O Lord, sir, let me live, or let me see my death!

FIRST SOLDIER That shall you, and take your leave of all your friends.

He removes the blindfold

So: look about you. Know you any here?

BERTRAM Good morrow, noble captain.

SECOND LORD God bless you, Captain Parolles.

FIRST LORD God save you, noble captain.

SECOND LORD Captain, what greeting will you to my Lord Lafew? I am for France.

FIRST LORD Good captain, will you give me a copy of the
310 sonnet you writ to Diana in behalf of the Count Rossillion? An I were not a very coward I'd compel it of you; but fare you well.

Exeunt Bertram and the Lords

FIRST SOLDIER You are undone, captain – all but your
scarf; that has a knot on't yet.

PAROLLES Who cannot be crushed with a plot?

FIRST SOLDIER If you could find out a country where
but women were that had received so much shame you
might begin an impudent nation. Fare ye well, sir. I am
for France too; we shall speak of you there.

Exeunt the Soldiers

PAROLLES

Yet am I thankful. If my heart were great   320
'Twould burst at this. Captain I'll be no more,
But I will eat and drink and sleep as soft
As captain shall. Simply the thing I am
Shall make me live. Who knows himself a braggart,
Let him fear this; for it will come to pass
That every braggart shall be found an ass.
Rust, sword; cool, blushes; and Parolles live
Safest in shame; being fooled, by foolery thrive.
There's place and means for every man alive.
I'll after them.   *Exit* 330

Enter Helena, the Widow, and Diana   IV.4

HELENA

That you may well perceive I have not wronged you
One of the greatest in the Christian world
Shall be my surety; fore whose throne 'tis needful,
Ere I can perfect mine intents, to kneel.
Time was, I did him a desirèd office,
Dear almost as his life, which gratitude
Through flinty Tartar's bosom would peep forth
And answer thanks. I duly am informed
His grace is at Marcellus, to which place
We have convenient convoy. You must know   10

129

I am supposèd dead. The army breaking,
My husband hies him home, where, heaven aiding,
And by the leave of my good lord the King,
We'll be before our welcome.

WIDOW   Gentle madam,
You never had a servant to whose trust
Your business was more welcome.

HELENA   Nor you, mistress,
Ever a friend whose thoughts more truly labour
To recompense your love. Doubt not but heaven
Hath brought me up to be your daughter's dower,
20 As it hath fated her to be my motive
And helper to a husband. But, O strange men!
That can such sweet use make of what they hate,
When saucy trusting of the cozened thoughts
Defiles the pitchy night; so lust doth play
With what it loathes for that which is away.
But more of this hereafter. You, Diana,
Under my poor instructions yet must suffer
Something in my behalf.

DIANA   Let death and honesty
Go with your impositions, I am yours,
30 Upon your will to suffer.

HELENA   Yet, I pray you.
But with the word the time will bring on summer,
When briars shall have leaves as well as thorns
And be as sweet as sharp. We must away;
Our wagon is prepared, and time revives us.
All's well that ends well; still the fine's the crown.
Whate'er the course, the end is the renown.   *Exeunt*

IV.5   *Enter the Countess, Lafew, and the Clown*
LAFEW No, no, no, your son was misled with a snipped-

taffeta fellow there, whose villainous saffron would have made all the unbaked and doughy youth of a nation in his colour. Your daughter-in-law had been alive at this hour, and your son here at home, more advanced by the King than by that red-tailed humble-bee I speak of.

COUNTESS I would I had not known him; it was the death of the most virtuous gentlewoman that ever nature had praise for creating. If she had partaken of my flesh and cost me the dearest groans of a mother I 10 could not have owed her a more rooted love.

LAFEW 'Twas a good lady, 'twas a good lady. We may pick a thousand sallets ere we light on such another herb.

CLOWN Indeed, sir, she was the sweet-marjoram of the sallet, or, rather, the herb of grace.

LAFEW They are not herbs, you knave, they are nose-herbs.

CLOWN I am no great Nabuchadnezzar, sir, I have not much skill in grass.

LAFEW Whether dost thou profess thyself, a knave or a 20 fool?

CLOWN A fool, sir, at a woman's service, and a knave at a man's.

LAFEW Your distinction?

CLOWN I would cozen the man of his wife and do his service.

LAFEW So you were a knave at his service indeed.

CLOWN And I would give his wife my bauble, sir, to do her service.

LAFEW I will subscribe for thee, thou art both knave and 30 fool.

CLOWN At your service.

LAFEW No, no, no.

CLOWN Why, sir, if I cannot serve you I can serve as great a prince as you are.

LAFEW Who's that? A Frenchman?

CLOWN Faith, sir, 'a has an English name; but his fisnomy is more hotter in France than there.

LAFEW What prince is that?

40 CLOWN The Black Prince, sir, alias the prince of darkness, alias the devil.

LAFEW Hold thee, there's my purse. I give thee not this to suggest thee from thy master thou talkest of; serve him still.

CLOWN I am a woodland fellow, sir, that always loved a great fire, and the master I speak of ever keeps a good fire. But sure he is the prince of the world; let his nobility remain in's court. I am for the house with the narrow gate, which I take to be too little for pomp to 50 enter; some that humble themselves may, but the many will be too chill and tender, and they'll be for the flowery way that leads to the broad gate and the great fire.

LAFEW Go thy ways. I begin to be aweary of thee, and I tell thee so before, because I would not fall out with thee. Go thy ways. Let my horses be well looked to, without any tricks.

CLOWN If I put any tricks upon 'em, sir, they shall be jades' tricks, which are their own right by the law of 60 nature.   *Exit*

LAFEW A shrewd knave and an unhappy.

COUNTESS So 'a is. My lord that's gone made himself much sport out of him; by his authority he remains here, which he thinks is a patent for his sauciness; and indeed he has no pace, but runs where he will.

LAFEW I like him well, 'tis not amiss. And I was about to tell you, since I heard of the good lady's death and that my lord your son was upon his return home, I moved

the King my master to speak in the behalf of my
daughter; which, in the minority of them both, his 70
majesty out of a self-gracious remembrance did first
propose. His highness hath promised me to do it; and to
stop up the displeasure he hath conceived against your
son there is no fitter matter. How does your ladyship
like it?

COUNTESS With very much content, my lord, and I wish
it happily effected.

LAFEW His highness comes post from Marcellus, of as
able body as when he numbered thirty. 'A will be here
tomorrow, or I am deceived by him that in such 80
intelligence hath seldom failed.

COUNTESS It rejoices me that I hope I shall see him ere I
die. I have letters that my son will be here tonight. I
shall beseech your lordship to remain with me till they
meet together.

LAFEW Madam, I was thinking with what manners I
might safely be admitted.

COUNTESS You need but plead your honourable privilege.

LAFEW Lady, of that I have made a bold charter, but, I
thank my God, it holds yet.   90

Enter Clown

CLOWN O madam, yonder's my lord your son with a patch
of velvet on's face; whether there be a scar under't or no,
the velvet knows, but 'tis a goodly patch of velvet. His
left cheek is a cheek of two pile and a half, but his right
cheek is worn bare.

LAFEW A scar nobly got, or a noble scar, is a good livery
of honour; so belike is that.

CLOWN But it is your carbonadoed face.

LAFEW Let us go see your son, I pray you. I long to talk
with the young noble soldier.   100

CLOWN Faith, there's a dozen of 'em with delicate fine hats, and most courteous feathers which bow the head and nod at every man. *Exeunt*

*

V.1 *Enter Helena, the Widow, and Diana, with two attendants*

HELENA
But this exceeding posting day and night
Must wear your spirits low. We cannot help it;
But since you have made the days and nights as one
To wear your gentle limbs in my affairs,
Be bold you do so grow in my requital
As nothing can unroot you.
  Enter a Gentleman, Astringer to the King
                              In happy time!
This man may help me to his majesty's ear,
If he would spend his power. God save you, sir!

GENTLEMAN
And you.

HELENA
10 Sir, I have seen you in the court of France.

GENTLEMAN
I have been sometimes there.

HELENA
I do presume, sir, that you are not fallen
From the report that goes upon your goodness;
And therefore, goaded with most sharp occasions
Which lay nice manners by, I put you to
The use of your own virtues, for the which
I shall continue thankful.

GENTLEMAN   What's your will?

HELENA

  That it will please you
  To give this poor petition to the King,
  And aid me with that store of power you have   20
  To come into his presence.

GENTLEMAN

  The King's not here.

HELENA   Not here, sir?

GENTLEMAN   Not indeed.
  He hence removed last night, and with more haste
  Than is his use.

WIDOW   Lord, how we lose our pains!

HELENA

  All's well that ends well yet,
  Though time seem so adverse and means unfit.
  I do beseech you, whither is he gone?

GENTLEMAN

  Marry, as I take it, to Rossillion;
  Whither I am going.

HELENA   I do beseech you, sir,
  Since you are like to see the King before me,   30
  Commend the paper to his gracious hand,
  Which I presume shall render you no blame,
  But rather make you thank your pains for it.
  I will come after you with what good speed
  Our means will make us means.

GENTLEMAN   This I'll do for you.

HELENA

  And you shall find yourself to be well thanked,
  Whate'er falls more. We must to horse again.
  Go, go, provide.   *Exeunt*

PAROLLES Good Master Lavatch, give my Lord Lafew
this letter. I have ere now, sir, been better known to
you, when I have held familiarity with fresher clothes;
but I am now, sir, muddied in Fortune's mood, and
smell somewhat strong of her strong displeasure.

CLOWN Truly, Fortune's displeasure is but sluttish if it
smell so strongly as thou speakest of. I will henceforth
eat no fish of Fortune's buttering. Prithee, allow the
wind.

10 PAROLLES Nay, you need not to stop your nose, sir. I
spake but by a metaphor.

CLOWN Indeed, sir, if your metaphor stink I will stop my
nose, or against any man's metaphor. Prithee, get thee
further.

PAROLLES Pray you, sir, deliver me this paper.

CLOWN Foh! Prithee stand away. A paper from Fortune's
close-stool, to give to a nobleman! Look, here he comes
himself.

Enter Lafew

Here is a pur of Fortune's, sir, or of Fortune's cat, but
20 not a musk-cat, that has fallen into the unclean fishpond
of her displeasure and, as he says, is muddied withal.
Pray you, sir, use the carp as you may, for he looks like a
poor, decayed, ingenious, foolish, rascally knave. I do
pity his distress in my similes of comfort, and leave him
to your lordship. *Exit*

PAROLLES My lord, I am a man whom Fortune hath
cruelly scratched.

LAFEW And what would you have me to do? 'Tis too late
to pare her nails now. Wherein have you played the
30 knave with Fortune that she should scratch you, who of
herself is a good lady and would not have knaves thrive
long under her? There's a cardecue for you. Let the

justices make you and Fortune friends; I am for other business.

PAROLLES I beseech your honour to hear me one single word.

LAFEW You beg a single penny more. Come, you shall ha't, save your word.

PAROLLES My name, my good lord, is Parolles.

LAFEW You beg more than 'word' then. Cox my passion! 40 Give me your hand. How does your drum?

PAROLLES O my good lord, you were the first that found me.

LAFEW Was I, in sooth? And I was the first that lost thee.

PAROLLES It lies in you, my lord, to bring me in some grace, for you did bring me out.

LAFEW Out upon thee, knave! Dost thou put upon me at once both the office of God and the devil? One brings thee in grace and the other brings thee out.

Trumpets sound

The King's coming; I know by his trumpets. Sirrah, 50 inquire further after me. I had talk of you last night. Though you are a fool and a knave you shall eat. Go to, follow.

PAROLLES I praise God for you.   *Exeunt*

Flourish. Enter the King, the Countess, Lafew, the two V.3
French Lords, with attendants

KING
We lost a jewel of her, and our esteem
Was made much poorer by it; but your son,
As mad in folly, lacked the sense to know
Her estimation home.

COUNTESS   'Tis past, my liege,
And I beseech your majesty to make it

137

Natural rebellion done i'th'blade of youth,
When oil and fire, too strong for reason's force,
O'erbears it and burns on.

KING   My honoured lady,
I have forgiven and forgotten all,
Though my revenges were high bent upon him
And watched the time to shoot.

LAFEW   This I must say –
But first I beg my pardon – the young lord
Did to his majesty, his mother, and his lady
Offence of mighty note, but to himself
The greatest wrong of all. He lost a wife
Whose beauty did astonish the survey
Of richest eyes, whose words all ears took captive,
Whose dear perfection hearts that scorned to serve
Humbly called mistress.

KING   Praising what is lost
Makes the remembrance dear. Well, call him hither;
We are reconciled, and the first view shall kill
All repetition. Let him not ask your pardon;
The nature of his great offence is dead,
And deeper than oblivion we do bury
Th'incensing relics of it. Let him approach
A stranger, no offender; and inform him
So 'tis our will he should.

ATTENDANT   I shall, my liege.   *Exit*

KING
What says he to your daughter? Have you spoke?

LAFEW
All that he is hath reference to your highness.

KING
Then shall we have a match. I have letters sent me
That sets him high in fame.

    Enter Bertram

LAFEW   He looks well on't.

KING

I am not a day of season,
For thou mayst see a sunshine and a hail
In me at once. But to the brightest beams
Distracted clouds give way; so stand thou forth:
The time is fair again.

BERTRAM   My high-repented blames,
Dear sovereign, pardon to me.

KING   All is whole.
Not one word more of the consumèd time.
Let's take the instant by the forward top;
For we are old, and on our quickest decrees   40
Th'inaudible and noiseless foot of time
Steals ere we can effect them. You remember
The daughter of this lord?

BERTRAM

Admiringly, my liege. At first
I stuck my choice upon her, ere my heart
Durst make too bold a herald of my tongue;
Where, the impression of mine eye infixing,
Contempt his scornful perspective did lend me,
Which warped the line of every other favour,
Scorned a fair colour or expressed it stolen,   50
Extended or contracted all proportions
To a most hideous object. Thence it came
That she whom all men praised, and whom myself,
Since I have lost, have loved, was in mine eye
The dust that did offend it.

KING   Well excused.
That thou didst love her, strikes some scores away
From the great compt; but love that comes too late,
Like a remorseful pardon slowly carried,
To the great sender turns a sour offence,

60 Crying 'That's good that's gone'. Our rash faults
Make trivial price of serious things we have,
Not knowing them until we know their grave.
Oft our displeasures, to ourselves unjust,
Destroy our friends and after weep their dust;
Our own love waking cries to see what's done,
While shameful hate sleeps out the afternoon.
Be this sweet Helen's knell, and now forget her.
Send forth your amorous token for fair Maudlin.
The main consents are had, and here we'll stay
70 To see our widower's second marriage-day.

COUNTESS
Which better than the first, O dear heaven, bless!
Or, ere they meet, in me, O nature, cesse!

LAFEW
Come on, my son, in whom my house's name
Must be digested, give a favour from you
To sparkle in the spirits of my daughter,
That she may quickly come.

Bertram gives Lafew a ring

                                By my old beard
And every hair that's on't, Helen that's dead
Was a sweet creature; such a ring as this,
The last that e'er I took her leave at court,
80 I saw upon her finger.

BERTRAM   Hers it was not.

KING
Now pray you let me see it; for mine eye,
While I was speaking, oft was fastened to't.
This ring was mine, and when I gave it Helen
I bade her, if her fortunes ever stood
Necessitied to help, that by this token
I would relieve her. Had you that craft to reave her
Of what should stead her most?

140

BERTRAM   My gracious sovereign,
  Howe'er it pleases you to take it so,
  The ring was never hers.
COUNTESS   Son, on my life,
  I have seen her wear it, and she reckoned it   90
  At her life's rate.
LAFEW   I am sure I saw her wear it.
BERTRAM
  You are deceived, my lord, she never saw it.
  In Florence was it from a casement thrown me,
  Wrapped in a paper which contained the name
  Of her that threw it. Noble she was, and thought
  I stood ingaged; but when I had subscribed
  To mine own fortune, and informed her fully
  I could not answer in that course of honour
  As she had made the overture, she ceased
  In heavy satisfaction, and would never   100
  Receive the ring again.
KING   Plutus himself,
  That knows the tinct and multiplying medicine,
  Hath not in nature's mystery more science
  Than I have in this ring. 'Twas mine, 'twas Helen's,
  Whoever gave it you; then if you know
  That you are well acquainted with yourself,
  Confess 'twas hers, and by what rough enforcement
  You got it from her. She called the saints to surety
  That she would never put it from her finger
  Unless she gave it to yourself in bed,   110
  Where you have never come, or sent it us
  Upon her great disaster.
BERTRAM   She never saw it.
KING
  Thou speakest it falsely, as I love mine honour,
  And makest conjectural fears to come into me

141

Which I would fain shut out. If it should prove
That thou art so inhuman – 'twill not prove so,
And yet I know not; thou didst hate her deadly,
And she is dead; which nothing but to close
Her eyes myself could win me to believe,
120 More than to see this ring. Take him away.
My fore-past proofs, howe'er the matter fall,
Shall tax my fears of little vanity,
Having vainly feared too little. Away with him.
We'll sift this matter further.

BERTRAM   If you shall prove
This ring was ever hers, you shall as easy
Prove that I husbanded her bed in Florence,
Where yet she never was.   *Exit, guarded*

KING
I am wrapped in dismal thinkings.
        Enter a Gentleman (the Astringer)

GENTLEMAN   Gracious sovereign,
Whether I have been to blame or no, I know not:
130 Here's a petition from a Florentine
Who hath for four or five removes come short
To tender it herself. I undertook it,
Vanquished thereto by the fair grace and speech
Of the poor suppliant, who, by this, I know,
Is here attending. Her business looks in her
With an importing visage, and she told me,
In a sweet verbal brief, it did concern
Your highness with herself.

KING (*reading the letter*) *Upon his many protestations to*
140 *marry me when his wife was dead, I blush to say it, he*
won me. Now is the Count Rossillion a widower; his vows
are forfeited to me and my honour's paid to him. He stole
from Florence, taking no leave, and I follow him to his
country for justice. Grant it me, O King! In you it best

*lies; otherwise a seducer flourishes, and a poor maid is
undone.*
                              Diana Capilet.

LAFEW I will buy me a son-in-law in a fair, and toll for
    this. I'll none of him.

KING

    The heavens have thought well on thee, Lafew,   150
    To bring forth this discovery. Seek these suitors.
    Go speedily, and bring again the Count.
                              Exeunt some attendants
    I am afeard the life of Helen, lady,
    Was foully snatched.

COUNTESS   Now justice on the doers!
        Enter Bertram, guarded

KING

    I wonder, sir, since wives are monsters to you,
    And that you fly them as you swear them lordship,
    Yet you desire to marry.
        Enter the Widow and Diana
                              What woman's that?

DIANA

    I am, my lord, a wretched Florentine,
    Derivèd from the ancient Capilet.
    My suit, as I do understand, you know,   160
    And therefore know how far I may be pitied.

WIDOW

    I am her mother, sir, whose age and honour
    Both suffer under this complaint we bring,
    And both shall cease, without your remedy.

KING

    Come hither, Count. Do you know these women?

BERTRAM

    My lord, I neither can nor will deny
    But that I know them. Do they charge me further?

DIANA

Why do you look so strange upon your wife?

BERTRAM

She's none of mine, my lord.

DIANA   If you shall marry

170 You give away this hand, and that is mine,
You give away heaven's vows, and those are mine,
You give away myself, which is known mine;
For I by vow am so embodied yours
That she which marries you must marry me –
Either both or none.

LAFEW Your reputation comes too short for my daughter;
you are no husband for her.

BERTRAM

My lord, this is a fond and desperate creature
Whom sometime I have laughed with. Let your highness
180 Lay a more noble thought upon mine honour
Than for to think that I would sink it here.

KING

Sir, for my thoughts, you have them ill to friend
Till your deeds gain them; fairer prove your honour
Than in my thought it lies!

DIANA   Good my lord,
Ask him upon his oath if he does think
He had not my virginity.

KING

What sayst thou to her?

BERTRAM   She's impudent, my lord,
And was a common gamester to the camp.

DIANA

He does me wrong, my lord; if I were so
190 He might have bought me at a common price.
Do not believe him. O behold this ring
Whose high respect and rich validity

Did lack a parallel; yet for all that
He gave it to a commoner o'th'camp,
If I be one.

COUNTESS   He blushes and 'tis hit.
Of six preceding ancestors, that gem
Conferred by testament to th'sequent issue,
Hath it been owed and worn. This is his wife:
That ring's a thousand proofs.

KING   Methought you said
You saw one here in court could witness it.   200

DIANA
I did, my lord, but loath am to produce
So bad an instrument: his name's Parolles.

LAFEW
I saw the man today, if man he be.

KING
Find him and bring him hither.   *Exit an attendant*

BERTRAM   What of him?
He's quoted for a most perfidious slave
With all the spots o'th'world taxed and debauched,
Whose nature sickens but to speak a truth.
Am I or that or this for what he'll utter,
That will speak anything?

KING   She hath that ring of yours.

BERTRAM
I think she has. Certain it is I liked her   210
And boarded her i'th'wanton way of youth.
She knew her distance and did angle for me,
Madding my eagerness with her restraint,
As all impediments in fancy's course
Are motives of more fancy; and in fine
Her infinite cunning with her modern grace
Subdued me to her rate. She got the ring,
And I had that which any inferior might

At market-price have bought.

DIANA   I must be patient.

220   You that have turned off a first so noble wife
May justly diet me. I pray you yet –
Since you lack virtue I will lose a husband –
Send for your ring, I will return it home,
And give me mine again.

BERTRAM   I have it not.

KING

What ring was yours, I pray you?

DIANA   Sir, much like
The same upon your finger.

KING

Know you this ring? This ring was his of late.

DIANA

And this was it I gave him, being abed.

KING

The story then goes false you threw it him
230   Out of a casement?

DIANA   I have spoke the truth.

Enter Parolles

BERTRAM

My lord, I do confess the ring was hers.

KING

You boggle shrewdly; every feather starts you. –
Is this the man you speak of?

DIANA   Ay, my lord.

KING

Tell me, sirrah – but tell me true I charge you,
Not fearing the displeasure of your master,
Which on your just proceeding I'll keep off –
By him and by this woman here what know you?

PAROLLES So please your majesty, my master hath been

146

an honourable gentleman. Tricks he hath had in him, which gentlemen have. 240

KING Come, come, to th'purpose. Did he love this woman?

PAROLLES Faith, sir, he did love her; but how?

KING How, I pray you?

PAROLLES He did love her, sir, as a gentleman loves a woman.

KING How is that?

PAROLLES He loved her, sir, and loved her not.

KING As thou art a knave and no knave. What an equivocal companion is this! 250

PAROLLES I am a poor man, and at your majesty's command.

LAFEW He's a good drum, my lord, but a naughty orator.

DIANA Do you know he promised me marriage?

PAROLLES Faith, I know more than I'll speak.

KING But wilt thou not speak all thou knowest?

PAROLLES Yes, so please your majesty. I did go between them as I said; but more than that, he loved her, for indeed he was mad for her and talked of Satan and of Limbo and of furies and I know not what; yet I was in 260 that credit with them at that time that I knew of their going to bed and of other motions, as promising her marriage and things which would derive me ill will to speak of; therefore I will not speak what I know.

KING Thou hast spoken all already, unless thou canst say they are married. But thou art too fine in thy evidence – therefore, stand aside.

This ring you say was yours?

DIANA   Ay, my good lord.

KING

Where did you buy it? Or who gave it you?

DIANA

270   It was not given me, nor I did not buy it.

KING

Who lent it you?

DIANA   It was not lent me neither.

KING

Where did you find it then?

DIANA   I found it not.

KING

If it were yours by none of all these ways
How could you give it him?

DIANA   I never gave it him.

LAFEW This woman's an easy glove, my lord; she goes off
and on at pleasure.

KING

This ring was mine; I gave it his first wife.

DIANA

It might be yours or hers for aught I know.

KING

Take her away, I do not like her now.
280   To prison with her. And away with him.
Unless thou tellest me where thou hadst this ring
Thou diest within this hour.

DIANA   I'll never tell you.

KING

Take her away.

DIANA   I'll put in bail, my liege.

KING

I think thee now some common customer.

DIANA

By Jove, if ever I knew man 'twas you.

KING

Wherefore hast thou accused him all this while?

DIANA

    Because he's guilty and he is not guilty.

    He knows I am no maid, and he'll swear to't;

    I'll swear I am a maid and he knows not.

    Great king, I am no strumpet; by my life   290

    I am either maid or else this old man's wife.

KING

    She does abuse our ears. To prison with her.

DIANA

    Good mother, fetch my bail. Stay, royal sir;

                       Exit the Widow

    The jeweller that owes the ring is sent for

    And he shall surety me. But for this lord

    Who hath abused me as he knows himself,

    Though yet he never harmed me, here I quit him.

    He knows himself my bed he hath defiled,

    And at that time he got his wife with child.

    Dead though she be she feels her young one kick.   300

    So there's my riddle: one that's dead is quick.

    And now behold the meaning.

        Enter the Widow, with Helena

KING   Is there no exorcist

    Beguiles the truer office of mine eyes?

    Is't real that I see?

HELENA   No, my good lord,

    'Tis but the shadow of a wife you see,

    The name and not the thing.

BERTRAM   Both, both. O pardon!

HELENA

    O my good lord, when I was like this maid

    I found you wondrous kind. There is your ring,

    And, look you, here's your letter. This it says:

    When from my finger you can get this ring ...   310

And is by me with child, etc. This is done.
Will you be mine now you are doubly won?

BERTRAM

If she, my liege, can make me know this clearly
I'll love her dearly, ever, ever dearly.

HELENA

If it appear not plain and prove untrue
Deadly divorce step between me and you!
O my dear mother, do I see you living?

LAFEW

Mine eyes smell onions, I shall weep anon.
(*To Parolles*) Good Tom Drum, lend me a handkercher.
320 So, I thank thee. Wait on me home, I'll make sport with
thee. Let thy curtsies alone, they are scurvy ones.

KING

Let us from point to point this story know
To make the even truth in pleasure flow.
(*To Diana*) If thou beest yet a fresh uncroppèd flower
Choose thou thy husband and I'll pay thy dower;
For I can guess that by thy honest aid
Thou keptest a wife herself, thyself a maid.
Of that and all the progress more and less
Resolvèdly more leisure shall express.
330 All yet seems well, and if it end so meet,
The bitter past, more welcome is the sweet.
    Flourish

EPILOGUE

Spoken by the King

The King's a beggar, now the play is done.
All is well ended if this suit be won,
That you express content; which we will pay
With strife to please you, day exceeding day.
Ours be your patience then and yours our parts;
Your gentle hands lend us and take our hearts. *Exeunt*

COMMENTARY

THE Folio edition of Shakespeare's plays (1623) is referred to as F; only the more substantial emendations to it are discussed here. For further details and lists of variants see An Account of the Text, pages 217–29.

I.1   (stage direction) *Rossillion* (three syllables, with the accent on the second; pronounced Ross-ill-yon. The F and probably Shakespeare's spelling of Rousillon, once a province of south-western France.)
         Lafew. The name possibly means *le feu*, 'the late' – a direct enough way of referring to his age.
         all in black. The characters are in mourning for the late Count, Bertram's father; they make a strangely sombre opening tableau for a comedy.

1–2   *In delivering my son from me, I bury a second husband.* The Countess opens with a riddle matched and reversed by one very near the end: *one that's dead is quick* (V.3.301). She quibbles on *delivers*, which means 'sending away', 'freeing', and 'giving birth to', wordplay close to the heart of the play; as is her association of birth and death, and her statement of the complex relationship of youth and age.

5   *to whom I am now in ward* whose ward I am now. The death of Bertram's father makes him technically an orphan, and the King guardian of the Rossillion estates, until Bertram comes of age; his age is unclear but his wardship directs our attention to his youth.

6   *of* in the person of

7   *generally* to all men, without respect of persons

151

8   *hold his virtue* continue to be good

8–10   *whose worthiness would stir it up where it wanted, rather than lack it where there is such abundance* your merits are such as to call forth kindness even from one not usually possessed of it; you will hardly then fail to meet it in one so bountifully kind as the King

13–14   *under whose practices he hath persecuted time with hope* under whose professional attentions he has wasted his days hoping

17–18   *O that 'had', how sad a passage 'tis!* The felicity of this remark arises principally from the complex quibbles in *passage*, which includes the meanings 'expression, phrase', 'event', 'transition', and 'death'.

19   *honesty* honour, integrity

33   *fistula* (a species of ulcer)

38–44   *I have those hopes of her good . . . achieves her goodness.* The courtly diction of the Countess here makes her topic (one vital to the play) sound more difficult and unfamiliar than it is. She is talking about what we have come to call Heredity and Environment, and the Elizabethans called Nature and Nurture, and the Countess calls *dispositions [which] she inherits* and *education.*

38–40   *I have those hopes of her good, that her education promises her dispositions she inherits – which makes fair gifts fairer* I believe she may come to great good, for her upbringing has added to her inborn gifts, improving fine qualities as it so often does

40   *unclean mind* bad character (inherent, not acquired)

41   *virtuous qualities* skills and accomplishments (acquired, not inherent)

42   *they are virtues and traitors too* such skills and accomplishments prove treacherous to the self and to others when they serve evil not good

43   *simpleness* purity, unmixed quality

46   *season* preserve in salt (a domestic image frequently used by Shakespeare in metaphorical senses)

49   *livelihood*. The Countess's meaning here is halfway between two senses of the word: 'liveliness or animation', and 'means of life or nourishment'.

50   *go to* come, come

51   *affect*. The Countess uses the word in its Elizabethan sense, 'to be in love with'; Helena (in line 52) picks up the word and quibbles on it, using it in both the Countess's sense and the modern sense of 'feign'.

      have't. F reads 'haue –', which many editors emend to either 'have.' or 'have it.'. It seems unlikely that either could have been misread for the F version; yet equally unlikely that the F reading, implying that Helena interrupts the Countess, can be correct. The contracted *have't* avoids both these objections, and is perhaps supported by the large number of contractions that mark this text elsewhere.

52   *I do affect a sorrow indeed, but I have it too.* We later (lines 78–97) learn that Helena is only feigning her sorrow for her father, but feels real grief on account of Bertram. When uttered, this remark (like much that she says in this first scene) is enigmatic and riddling, which makes Helena's first appearance in the play curiously like Hamlet's in his.

55–6   *If the living be enemy to the grief, the excess makes it soon mortal* if grief is firmly resisted, it will soon wear itself out by its own violence. Lafew and the Countess are getting themselves launched into a traditional topic, the proper conduct of grief.

58   *How understand we that?* The exact significance of Lafew's remark is not clear, and some editors have altered its position or assigned it to the Countess. Lafew can hardly fail to understand the bearing of either the Countess's last remark (a language which he seemed himself very well to understand) or Bertram's simple interjection, asking for his mother's blessing so that he can leave. It may be that Shakespeare wishes to draw attention to Bertram's rudeness and abrupt

impatience to leave, and uses Lafew's surprise as a means of doing this.

60   *manners* moral behaviour
        Thy may your

61-2   *thy goodness | Share with thy birthright!* may the good-ness of behaviour you have learned share the rule of your life with the goodness of nature you have inherited!

63-4   *Be able for thine enemy | Rather in power than use* make sure you are potentially as strong as your enemy, but do not use this power

66   *taxed* blamed

69   *unseasoned* immature, unready

70-71   *He cannot want the best | That shall attend his love.* The sense of this is not clear. Lafew is probably uttering a deliberately and suitably vague phrase of courtly courtesy, meaning 'Things are bound to go splendidly for him if he is a good, loving boy'. *Want* means 'lack'.

74   *comfortable* comforting

76-7   *hold the credit of your father* maintain your father's good name

79-80   *these great tears grace his remembrance more | Than those I shed for him.* Helena's soliloquy opens with a line and a half as opaque and inward as her earlier remark to the Countess (line 52). She is here presumably speaking only of her father, as Bertram is not introduced by name until line 82. The point seems to be that her present fierce grief is not aroused by her father, but does him more honour *indirectly* (by contrasting him with the cause of it, perhaps?) than did her tears of grief directly aroused by his death. Compare Bertram on a similar subject, I.2.48-51.

82   *favour* face (with a quibble on 'love-token')

87   *collateral* parallel. Helena is talking in the language of the old astronomy: she and Bertram must move like two stars describing concentric but separated circles,

one (Bertram) above the other, and never side by side, or in one *sphere*.

93   *hawking* hawk-like, sharp

94   *table* board or other flat surface for drawing and painting on

94–5   *capable | Of* susceptible to, retentive of

95   *trick of his sweet favour* characteristic expression of his dear face

96   *fancy* love

97   (stage direction) *Parolles*. His name is the French word *paroles*, 'words', clearly in the sense of '*mere* words'; and it has been suggested that there is play also on the word 'parole', 'word of honour'. It is in three syllables, accented on the second.

100   *a great way fool, solely a coward* largely a fool and wholly a coward

102   *take place*. A disputed phrase, which seems to mean 'successfully claim first place, take precedence' (over virtue, with its *steely bones*). The image here is of Parolles, wearing his ineradicable faults (*fixed evils*) as though they were smart well-fitting new clothes, bustling forward and pushing out of his way a far more virtuous man.

102–3   *virtue's steely bones | Looks bleak in the cold wind*. This phrase seems to be based on one in Juvenal: *Probitas laudatur et alget*, 'Virtue is praised and is freezing cold' (*Satires*, I.74). (See the relevant chapter in A. P. Rossiter's *Angel with Horns*, mentioned in Further Reading, page 45.) Shakespeare's *steely* admirably fuses ideas of harshness, coldness, steadiness, and purity. Good is seen here by Helena as lacking not only the bright clothes of evil on Parolles, but even the warmth of flesh and blood.

103   *Looks*. This is the old third person plural of the verb, ending in 's', which was still sometimes used in Shakespeare's time.

      Withal besides

104   *superfluous* luxurious, overdressed

105   *Save* God save

108   *And no* and no more am I a queen (than you are a monarch)

109   *Are you meditating on virginity?* ... See Introduction, pages 24–6, for a discussion of this exchange between Parolles and Helena.

110   *stain* tinge, tincture, dash. The word usually has a pejorative sense in Shakespeare.

117   *setting down before* laying siege to

118   *blow you up.* Parolles, playing with the meanings 'explode' and 'make you pregnant', here begins a series of bawdy quibbles that utilize the old analogy between sex and warfare.

123   *be blown up* (a bawdy quibble: 'reach orgasm')

126   *rational increase.* Parolles is arguing sophistically for the 'rationality' of sexual licence by saying that the result of the sexual act is an increase in the number of rational beings.

127   *got* begotten

128   *mettle* (also carries the sense of 'metal', by analogy between child-bearing and minting)

132   *stand ... die* (bawdy quibbles)

134   *in't* for it

137–8   *He that hangs himself is a virgin; virginity murders itself* a suicide is no less and no more of a self-destroyer than a virgin who refuses to give life to children who are virgins

139   *sanctified limit* consecrated ground

141–2   *feeding his own stomach* sacrificing to its own pride

143–4   *inhibited sin in the canon* prohibited sin in the Scriptures

144   *Keep* hoard (a series of commercial metaphors follows)

145   *Out with't!* put it out to interest!

145–6   *Within ten year it will make itself two, which is a goodly increase.* Many emendations have been made of the F text, on the ground that the rate of increase quoted –

which was the allowed rate of interest at the time – does not sound like a *goodly increase*. But the mistake, if any, seems to be Shakespeare's. The F reading is therefore retained.

150 *Marry* (a mild oath, originally referring to the Virgin Mary; here meaning 'to be sure')

150–51 *ill, to like him that ne'er it likes* a virgin must do ill (if she is to lose her virginity to her liking) and must like a man who does not like virginitv

153 *vendible* saleable

155 *unsuitable* unfashionable

156 *wear not now* are not now in fashion

Your date. His primary meaning concerns the fruit, with *Your* used loosely in the verbal gesture known as 'ethic dative'; but there is a quibble on the sense 'your age', which (he argues) undesirably reveals itself in time in a withered *cheek* (line 157).

162 *Not my virginity, yet.* . . . The fact that this is a half-line, followed by what seems to many an abrupt transition of thought, has made some editors conclude that there is textual corruption at this point. A passage may have been omitted, but it is not necessary to suppose so. It is usually assumed that by *There* in line 163 Helena means the court, even though she does not mention the court until line 174; and that she is meditating anxiously on the romantic encounters which the inexperienced Bertram is likely to have there. But the transition may be less abrupt than this. The discussion of virginity has, for Helena, had bearing only on her feeling for Bertram and her possible relation to him. She may, in this speech, be continuing to pursue this train of thought: that is, she is allowing herself to imagine a romantic and consummated love between them. Certainly this is not explicit. But Helena is characterized by self-communing and elliptical disclosures, and also (at this stage of the play) by a decency which would hardly permit her to speak openly on

this subject to herself, let alone to Parolles. Interpreted in this way, the *There* of line 163 is elliptical and secretive: perhaps meaning 'in the surrendering of a woman's virginity'.

164–72 *A mother, and a mistress, and a friend....* Helena alludes to the language of contemporary love poetry.

165 *phoenix* (a unique, immortal, and fabulous bird; hence, 'a wonder')

170 *disaster* unlucky star

171–2 *fond, adoptious christendoms | That blinking Cupid gossips* foolish loving nicknames given when blind Cupid is the godfather (*gossips*) at the christening

180 *Whose baser stars* (referring to the malevolent aspect of stars at their birth, which doomed them to a 'base' or poor life)

192 *under* in a bad way, in an inferior position

194–5 *predominant . . . retrograde* in the ascendant . . . moving backward (astrological terms)

200 *composition* fusion of personal characteristics (perhaps with a quibble on the meaning 'truce', 'surrender')

201 *of a good wing* swift in flight. This is praise when applied to a bird, less so when said of a soldier. (*Wing* can also mean 'a flap on clothing', hence Helena's *wear* that follows in the same sentence, meaning 'fashion'.)

205 *naturalize* familiarize

206–7 *capable . . . understand . . . thrust . . . diest* (with bawdy quibbles). Parolles is explicitly and implicitly here reiterating his earlier advice on virginity.

209–10 *When thou hast leisure, say thy prayers; when thou hast none, remember thy friends.* The sense of this undoubtedly cynical utterance is debatable. Parolles seems to be saying that prayers are good for filling in the gaps of an empty existence, but that friends should be relied on for practical purposes.

213 *The fated sky* the sky that directs and destines us, or that we think of as doing so

218–19 *The mightiest space in fortune nature brings | To join like likes, and kiss like native things* even those immensely far apart in fortune and other such conditioning can come together quite naturally like identical things, and kiss like creatures closely related

221 *That weigh their pains in sense.* A difficult passage: each of the words *weigh, their, pains,* and *sense* carries at least two different meanings. Either 'who estimate the pains they are willing to take in terms of what they may suffer as a result', or 'who consider the difficulties (of *strange attempts*) with a commonsensical level-headedness'.

I.2 (stage direction) *Flourish* fanfare

1 *Senoys* Sienese, people of Siena
by th'ears quarrelling

3 *braving war* war of challenges

5 *cousin* (a courtesy title used by a sovereign when addressing or mentioning another)

6 *move* appeal to, urge

10 *Approved* demonstrated

11 *armed our answer* persuaded me to give a hostile answer

15 *stand on either part* serve on either side

16 *nursery* school, training-ground

16–17 *sick | For breathing and exploit.* This probably means 'longing for exercise and adventure', but it may mean 'sick for lack of exercise, etc.'.

20 *Frank* generous, open, without disguise
curious careful, skilful, and precise

26–7 *He did look far | Into the service of the time* he had penetrating insight into the art of war

27–8 *was | Discipled of the bravest.* This probably means 'had the bravest men as his pupils and followers', but it may mean 'had been taught by the bravest'.

30 *wore us out of act* wore us down into inactivity
repairs refreshes

34   *Till their own scorn return to them unnoted* until at last people cease to give their derisive remarks any attention at all, except a scornful dismissal

35   *Ere they can hide their levity in honour* sooner than they can make up for their light ways with noble actions (such as Bertram's father carried out)

36   *like a courtier*. The late Count of Rossillion was truly 'courteous'; 'gentle' in his ways as well as 'gentle' born. His son's angry concern with his standing and his rights will prove him, as his mother has said, an *unseasoned courtier* (I.1.69).

40   *Exception* disapproval

41   *His tongue obeyed his hand* as the clapper (*tongue*) of a bell rings when directed by the movement of the clock's hand, so were his words directed by his (exact and true) sense of honour
          Who those who

42   *another place* a different rank (perhaps an understated form of 'an equal or higher rank')

43–5   *And bowed his eminent top to their low ranks,* | *Making them proud of his humility,* | *In their poor praise he humbled.* An elliptical and paradoxical description of *noblesse oblige* in action. The essential point is the reciprocal activity of the late Count's humility and the poor people's pride in it. A 'which' is understood after *humility* in line 44.

50–51   *So in approof lives not his epitaph* | *As in* nothing proves the truth of his epitaph so fully as does

53   *plausive* fit to be applauded, deserving of high praise

57   *On the catastrophe and heel of pastime* at the conclusion and end of pleasure

58   *out* over, finished. (There may be a reference back to *heel* in line 57, which makes a kind of quibble out of *out*, or there may be a reference forward to the image of the *flame* in line 59, already present in Shakespeare's mind.)

59   *snuff* burnt-out part of a wick (which if not trimmed

off makes the lower part of the wick (*younger spirits* smoulder)

60   *apprehensive* quick to perceive or learn

61–2   *whose judgements are | Mere fathers of their garments* whose severest mental efforts are expended on their clothes

64   *I, after him, do after him wish too* I, surviving him, agree with him in wishing that

68   *lend it you* (*it* referring to love)

73–4   *The rest have worn me out | With several applications* (that is, each doctor has his own idea of the proper treatment for the King, who has had to endure them all)

I.3.3–4   *even your content* act to your full satisfaction, come up to your expectations

4   *calendar* record

9   *sirrah* (form of address used to inferiors)

18   *go to the world* get married

19   *do as we may* get on as well as we can (probably with a bawdy quibble on *do*)

23   *In Isbel's case* (a bawdy quibble on *case*)

23–4   *Service is no heritage.* This was a proverb, meaning that a servant's life does not give a man much to leave his children; balanced by the Clown's second wise proverb, that *barnes are blessings* (lines 25–6) or 'Children are poor men's riches'. There may be a bawdy undertone to *Service*, which could have a sexual meaning.

29–30   *he must needs go that the devil drives* (another proverb)

32–3   *holy reasons, such as they are.* The words *holy reasons* form a double bawdy quibble but the Clown is also gravely alluding to the fact that procreation is recommended in the marriage service.

36–7   *I do marry that I may repent* (alluding to another proverb, 'Marry in haste and repent at leisure')

42   *madam; e'en.* Some modern editors retain F's 'Madam

in'. This may be correct, though the phrase *shallow . . . in* is unusual and elliptical. But F (or Shakespeare) so frequently spells 'e'en' as 'in' that it seems likely that it has done so here, and 'e'en' is the true reading. The Clown is answering the Countess by doggedly laying stress on his own definition of friendship.

44-9   *He that ears my land spares my team . . . he that kisses my wife is my friend.* The Clown's ironical argument is probably traditional. Something like it is found in Shakespeare's Sonnet 42, 'That thou hast her, it is not all my grief'.

44   *ears* ploughs

45   *in* bring in, harvest
     cuckold deceived husband

50   *what they are* (that is, cuckolds)

51-4   *for young Charbon the puritan . . . they may jowl horns together like any deer i'th'herd* there is a meeting-ground for all men, however divided superficially, on the common ground of their being cuckolds (who traditionally wear horns on their heads to show their humiliation); young and old, puritan and papist (eaters of flesh – or *chair bonne* – and eaters of fish – or *poisson*) are all alike in this

54   *jowl* dash, knock

57-8   *the next way* the nearest way, directly. He is probably suggesting that, like the prophets, he is directly and divinely inspired.

62   *by kind* according to nature, by a natural instinct

63   *anon* soon

68-77   *Was this fair face the cause, quoth she . . . There's yet one good in ten.* This song or fragment of song is hardly among the best in Shakespeare's plays. It is in fact less like the beautiful lyrics usually found in the comedies than the harsh scraps of ballad quoted in *King Lear* by the Fool for the light they throw on the situation. The song is presumably prompted by the Countess's mention of *Helen*, in line 67, since Helen of Troy is the owner

of the *fair face* in the song's first line. Helen's Trojan
lover, Paris, the son of Priam, may be *King Priam's joy*
in line 71, and the subject of *quoth she* in the first line
is probably Hecuba, mother of Paris and wife of Priam.

No music seems to have survived for the song, if
indeed there is a song behind Lavatch's rhyme. He
seems throughout the play to be reciting rather than
singing his ballads.

72 *fond* foolishly

74 *sentence* maxim, wise saying

78 *corrupt the song* make the song worse than it was. The
original song must have said something like, 'If one be
bad among nine good, | There's yet one bad in ten'.
The Clown answers the Countess by saying that the
song referred to men and he is referring to women; and
to find *One good woman in ten* is, if anything, an over-
generous estimate.

82 *tithe-woman* tenth-woman. The tithe was the tenth-
part of the parish produce sent to the parson as his due.

83 *quoth 'a* says he
    An if

84 *but one.* F has 'but ore'. Mistakes involving the letter
'r' are several times found in this text; and the Clown
is likely to be repeating his rhetorically important
word *one* to create a ludicrous yet vivid image of the
rarity of female decency.

86 *pluck* draw (as from a pack of cards)

89–90 *That man should be at woman's command, and yet no
hurt done!* It is usually assumed that there is a bawdy
undertone to this remark, and that the *hurt* in question
implies a sexual encounter.

90–92 *Though honesty be no puritan, yet it will do no hurt. It
will wear the surplice of humility over the black gown of a
big heart.* The Clown may here be making a pregnant
general utterance; or referring obliquely to Helena (in
which case *honesty* means 'chastity'); or saying (perhaps with irony), of his own frank nature, that though

it has no great pretensions to virtue, yet it does no real harm – he controls his proud nature and keeps the laws. The allusion is to certain Puritan clergymen who obeyed the law by wearing the surplice, but placed it over the black Geneva gown.

98 *without other advantage* even without having accrued any interest

102 *late* lately

105–6 *touched not any stranger sense* reached no one's ears but her own

107–8 *Fortune, she said, was no goddess, that had put such difference betwixt their two estates.* The difference between people's station and place in life, or *estates*, is an accidental thing, not a matter of essential importance, and not therefore a question for divinities; so Fortune or Chance is no goddess.

109 *only* except

109–10 *where qualities were level* where two people were of the same rank

111 *knight* (any chaste devotee of Diana, of either sex)

113 *touch* pang

115 *withal* with
sithence since

120–21 *Stall this* keep this close

122 (stage direction) *Enter Helena.* Helena enters some time before the Countess actually addresses her. In performance this makes a strong visual effect which brings out the affinities and also the separateness of the two women.

124 *these* (these troubles, these difficulties)

126 *blood* natural passions

128 *impressed* (as wax by a seal)

130 *or then we thought them none* or rather things that then we did not call faults

140–41 *and choice breeds | A native slip to us from foreign seeds* we choose a cutting that has grown from seeds foreign to us, graft it on and let it grow, and it becomes native to us

146   *distempered* disturbed, inclement

147   *The many-coloured Iris*. Iris was goddess of the rainbow; Helena's tears are iridescent.

148   *That I am not*. When the Countess speaks of *daughters* and *mothers*, Helena thinks of daughters-in-law and mothers-in-law, which gives ambiguity to the whole dialogue that follows.

152   *No note upon my parents* no fame attaches to my family

157   *So that* provided that

158   *both our mothers* the mother of both of us

159   *I care no more for than I do for heaven*. A dense and difficult close to a speech uttered in a state of confused desperation. Helena is trying to say both 'I wouldn't mind (*care for*) that at all' and 'In fact I should like (*care for*) that as much as I should like heaven' and produces a statement that compresses the two together.

160   *Can't no other* can it not be otherwise

163   *shield* forbid

163–4   *'Daughter' and 'mother' | So strive upon your pulse* you seem to be so upset and nervous when a daughter or mother is mentioned. The Countess may be playing on the word *mother*, which could mean 'hysteria, nervous condition'.

165   *fondness*. The word can mean both 'foolishness' and 'love'.

167   *head* source (of a stream or river)
        gross obvious, palpable

168–9   *Invention is ashamed | Against* your capacity for making up excuses is ashamed, in the face of

174   *in their kind* in their own way, after their own fashion

176   *suspected* brought under suspicion, made doubtful

177   *you have wound a goodly clew*. This is proverbial. A *clew* is a ball of thread. Compare the well-known couplet from Scott's *Marmion*:

> Oh what a tangled web we weave,
> When first we practise to deceive!

183   *Go not about* don't be evasive

186   *appeached* informed against you

190   *friends* relatives, 'people'

192–3 *I follow him not | By any token of presumptuous suit.* This
       sounds like a general statement of intention, 'I shall
       not pursue him with signs of a presumptuous love', but
       Helena may be merely saying, as G. K. Hunter sug-
       gests in his edition, that she has not communicated
       with Bertram since he left Rossillion.

197   *this captious and intenable sieve.* The sieve is described
       by F as 'intemible', which is emended or modernized
       by most modern editors into either 'intenible' or
       'inteemable'. The word may be one difficult to do literal
       justice to, since the Elizabethans often had the same
       spelling for words of slightly different meaning. For it
       seems possible that this word is a dense pun that works
       on exactly the same ground as *captious. Captious* is
       really a Shakespearian conflation of 'captious' (mean-
       ing 'deceiving', 'sophistical', 'erroneous in argument')
       with 'capacious' (meaning 'roomy', 'all-consuming')
       so as to produce a third term meaning 'deceitfully and
       deceptively all-embracing', 'leading to large errors',
       'seeming roomier than it is' and so on. *Intenable* is a
       similarly compound pun. It means 'intenable' in both
       its literal and metaphorical senses: the thing can't 'be
       held', it is hard to hold on to, and also it is intellec-
       tually impossible, an error. *Intenable* also means 'in-
       tenible': it won't hold water, it loses whatever is put
       into it. Helena is in fact condensing into two extra-
       ordinarily dense and witty words what Orsino takes
       nearly five lines to say in *Twelfth Night* (I.1.10–14):

            notwithstanding thy capacity
          Receiveth as the sea, naught enters there,
          Of what validity and pitch soe'er,
          But falls into abatement and low price
          Even in a minute.

       sieve. The sieve, used here as an emblem of hopeless
       love, is more frequently found as an emblem of

chastity; it is so used in the portrait of Queen Elizabeth I now in Siena (reproduced in Roy Strong's *Portraits of Queen Elizabeth I*, 1963, as Plate X).

199   *lack not to lose still.* A dense phrase, expressive of a rich desperation. Helena never ceases to lose her love, and never ceases to have more love to lose.

   Indian-like. She is probably thinking of the American Indians.

203   *encounter with* have a hostile encounter with

205   *cites* is evidence of

207–8   *Wish chastely and love dearly, that your Dian | Was both herself and love.* *Wish chastely* and *love dearly* are near-paradoxes, leading to the final true paradox of the fusion of Diana, the goddess of chastity, with Venus, the goddess of love. *Wish* has the sense of 'desire', and *dearly* carries, as often, the subordinate sense of 'painfully, grievously'.

211   *that* that which, what

212   *riddle-like lives sweetly where she dies.* Helena sees herself, perhaps, as a 'wonder' of love, confounding reason, like the Phoenix in Shakespeare's own *The Phoenix and Turtle*.

218   *manifest experience* expertise that is well-known, plain to all

219   *For general sovereignty* as panaceas, universal cures

220   *In heedfullest reservation to bestow them* to put them away and keep them extremely carefully (for an emergency)

221–2   *As notes whose faculties inclusive were | More than they were in note* as prescriptions more powerful than they were generally reported to be

223   *approved* tested, tried out

225   *rendered lost* said to be dying

229   *conversation of my thoughts* active process of my thinking

236–7   *Embowelled of their doctrine, have left off | The danger to itself* emptied of all their scientific knowledge, have abandoned the deadly threat as incurable and left it to itself

239   *receipt* prescription, cure

242   *try success* test the outcome

242-3   *I'd venture | The well-lost life of mine* I would willingly risk losing my life, and think it worth it

245   *knowingly* not just believe, but know

II.1.1-2   *lords . . . lords.* Many editors emend these words to the singular. It is likely, however, that the young men are in two groups, according to which side they are to support in the war.

6   *After well-entered soldiers* (a Latin construction) after becoming experienced soldiers

9   *he owes* it·owns

12   *higher Italy.* The curious word *higher* is probably simply geographical in connotation and signifies 'northerly'; the King is referring to Tuscany.

13-14   *Those bâted that inherit but the fall | Of the last monarchy.* A difficult passage. *Bated* probably means 'excepted'; but it may mean 'abated', that is weakened, fallen off, decadent. *The last monarchy* may refer to the Holy Roman Empire or the house of the Medici.

16   *questant* seeker

21-2   *Beware of being captives | Before you serve. Captives* and *serve* are both quibbles: each word has an amatory and a military sense.

23   (stage direction) *To some attendants.* F has no stage direction here. But the *Come* in line 23 must have some force; and it must be addressed to another, or others, than Bertram, Parolles, and the two Lords, who cannot simply ignore the King. He must be terminating this passage, and moving somewhat apart to address others, continuing that conversation up stage throughout what follows; and then turns down stage again as Lafew enters to him.

27   *commanded here* ordered to stay here
     kept a coil fussed, pestered

29   *An* if

30   *the forehorse to a smock* the leader in a team of horses
     driven by a woman

31   *Creaking my shoes on the plain masonry* squeaking my
     shoes on the smooth floor

36–7 *our parting is a tortured body* separating myself from
     you is as painful as being torn apart is to a man being
     tortured. Shakespeare's depiction of 'court life' takes
     the form of some remarkably mannered speech on the
     part of the young men, of which this of Bertram's is
     one of the most striking examples.

41   *metals* (meaning both 'swords' or 'swordsmen', and
     'mettles' or 'brave hearts')

43   *Spurio.* His name is the Italian word for 'false, counter-
     feit, spurious'.
     cicatrice scar

44   *sinister* left

47   *Mars dote on you for his novices!* may the god of war
     look after you tenderly, as his pupils!

49   *Stay: the King.* F, followed by some modern editors,
     has the phrase 'Stay the King' and those who retain
     this punctuation interpret as 'Support the King'.
     Bertram's phrase is punctuated here as in the second
     Folio, and is interpreted as an advertisement that the
     King is approaching; though it could mean 'Stay, for
     reasons depending on the King'.

51   *list* the selvage of cloth; hence, 'limit', 'boundary'

53–4 *muster true gait* display the true art of dignified move-
     ment

55   *received* fashionable

56   *measure* dance

57   *dilated* extended, more lengthy

62   *sue.* F reads 'see', which is possibly correct, but makes
     a clumsy and unidiomatic phrase when followed by an
     infinitive. Most modern editors emend to 'fee'. But *sue*

has a good deal more point (and could easily have been misprinted as 'see' by attraction to *thee* following). Lafew 'sues for pardon': the King, with a ludicrous and ironical courtesy, 'sues him to get up'. A closely similar exchange occurs in *Richard II* (V.3.128–9); to King Henry's 'Good aunt, stand up', the Duchess of York replies: 'I do not sue to stand. | Pardon is all the suit I have in hand.'

66   *pate* head

67   *across.* Lafew's word is from the language of tilting, which perhaps sharpens the sense of the elderliness of the combatants engaged in this slow-motion verbal passage of arms. A blow *across* is a bad hit, almost a miss: the man is trying the easy blow of a sidewise swipe across the body instead of the point head-on through the body.

69–70   *O, will you eat | No grapes, my royal fox?* The allusion is to Aesop's fable of the fox who, being unable to reach some grapes, declared them sour. Lafew misunderstands the King's dry *No*, in line 69, which meant 'No, I shall not be cured', as 'No, I do not want to be cured'; and then suggests that the King, like the fox, does not want to be cured because he thinks it impossible.

71   *My noble grapes, and if my royal fox.* A play on words: both *noble* and *royal* are the names of coins. The first two words of the line carry the main stress.

74   *Quicken* give life to
      canary a lively Spanish dance

75–8   *whose simple touch | Is powerful ... And write to her a love-line.* There is probably a sexual allusiveness in these lines, less a matter of mere bawdy quibbles than a conjuring-up of the beauty, vitality, and potency which Helena is seen to carry with her.

75   *simple* mere (but the word is also probably suggested by its relationship to *medicine* in line 72: 'simples' are medicinal herbs)

76   *Pippen* (Pepin, the eighth-century King of France)

77   *in's* in his

82   *this my light deliverance* these my jesting words. He is presumably referring to his slightly improper remarks at lines 75–8 on the nature of Helena's medical capacity.

83   *profession* claim to have skilled knowledge

84–5   *more | Than I dare blame my weakness* in a way that I cannot merely ascribe to my partiality for her, or my elderly weakness of mind

88   *admiration* wonder

89   *take off* reduce

90   *tookest it* came to conceive it (as wonderful)
       fit satisfy

91   (stage direction) *He goes to the door*. F does not have an exit here for Lafew, nor an entry for him at line 93, where Helena there enters alone; so presumably Lafew meets her at the stage-door and leads her in.

97   *Cressid's uncle* (Pandarus, who acted as go-between for Cressida and Troilus, and became the prototypical pander)

102   *In what he did profess, well found* found to be skilled at what he professed, medicine

106–7   *as the dearest issue of his practice, | And of his old experience th'only darling* the one and only beloved pet child of years of hard work and long experience

108   *triple* third

110–11   *touched | With that malignant cause* suffering from that deadly disease

111–12   *wherein the honour | Of my dear father's gift stands chief in power* with which my beloved father's honoured gift has most power to deal

113   *tender* offer
       appliance. The word covers both the doctor's services and the means of treatment he offers.

117   *The congregated college*. This is probably a reference to the assembled College of Physicians.

118   *labouring art* the endeavours of human art and skill

120   *stain* taint

        corrupt our hope (by basing it on an irrational foundation)

122   *empirics* (accented on the first syllable) quacks

122–4   *to dissever so | Our great self and our credit, to esteem | A senseless help, when help past sense we deem* to act in a way so unlike what my reputation would lead men to expect of me, as to put trust in a cure too improbable to be believed, when it is impossible to have rational belief in a cure at all

125   *My duty* the respect I owe to and feel for you

128   *A modest one* a moderate thought. She is asking the King not to be angry with her, not to laugh at her, and not to think her immodest.

135   *set up your rest* stake your all (a gambling term)

136–7   *He that of greatest works is finisher | Oft does them by the weakest minister* (an echo of such texts as 1 Corinthians 1.27, 'God hath chosen the weak things of the world, to confound the things which are mighty' (Bishops' Bible))

138–9   *So holy writ in babes hath judgement shown, | When judges have been babes.* The best-known of the Scriptural infant judges is Daniel, who gave Susanna justice against the Elders.

139–40   *great floods have flown | From simple sources.* There is possibly an allusion here to the miracle of Moses's striking water from the rock, Exodus 17.

140–41   *great seas have dried | When miracles have by the greatest been denied.* The sea in question is probably the Red Sea, dried to permit the passage of the Israelites from Egypt; the *greatest* may refer to Pharaoh, or the whole line may have a more general and unspecific reference.

144   *fits.* F has 'shifts'. The lack of end-rhyme is strange; and if *fits* was written 'ffitts' (as it could have been) the confusibility of 'f' with the old long-tailed 's' (ſ) would explain the mistake.

147   *thanks* (that is, nothing but thanks; Helena's *pains* and *Proffers*, not being taken up and put into creative use, can earn her nothing but a polite gratitude)

148   *Inspirèd merit* grace given by the spirit (breath) of God
        breath human breath (that is, human speech)

150   *square our guess by shows* base our conjectures on appearances

155–8   *I am not an impostor, that proclaim . . . nor you past cure*
        I am not a charlatan, proclaiming my marksmanship before I take aim – I know exactly what I think – that my skill has the power of curing you

160–68   *The greatest grace lending grace . . . Health shall live free and sickness freely die.* The somewhat stiff couplets of the later exchanges between the King and Helena develop at this point into an old-fashioned fustian, which helps to express Helena's incantatory intensity.

162   *diurnal ring* daily round, daily circuit

164   *Hesperus* (the evening star)

165   *glass* hour-glass

170–74   *Tax of impudence . . . let my life be ended.* Helena's verbal style becomes strained and dense in this speech; and the oracular nature of her utterance makes it hard to be certain what Shakespeare's exact intentions were at this textually difficult point. The present text departs from the punctuation of most modern editions at lines 171, 172, and 173, following two suggestions by eighteenth-century editors, as this seems to make Helena's statements at least a little clearer.

170   *Tax* accusation

172   *Traduced* slandered

173   *Seared* branded, blighted
        ne worse of worst (an almost impossible phrase. If textually correct, it is a deliberate archaism, with *ne* meaning 'nor'; the sense of the whole phrase would be 'nor would this, a death racked by savage torture, be *worse* than those other *worst* things, shame and slander'.)

173   *extended* stretched out (as on a rack)

174   *vildest* most savage

178   *sense saves* makes sense

179   *rate* reckon, consider

180   *estimate* value

182   *prime* springtime (a metaphor for 'youth')

185   *physic* medicine

187   *flinch in property* fall short in any respect

189   *Not helping* if I do not help

191   *make it even* meet it fully

192   *heaven.* F has 'helpe'. The break in the rhyme would be obtrusive, prepared for as it is by *even*; and it is hard to see any reason for such a break. Hence the traditional emendation.

198   *branch or image.* G. K. Hunter in his edition suggests that the figure is that of a genealogical tree, with portraits or *images* of the persons involved.

204   *still* always

II.2.1–2   *put you to the height of* make you show all

3   *highly fed and lowly taught* (alluding to the proverb 'Better fed than taught', descriptive – roughly – of a rich person's spoiled child)

6   *put off* dismiss, brush aside

9   *put it off* palm it off (or perhaps 'sell it')

10   *make a leg* make obeisance (by bending one leg and drawing back the other)

16   *like a barber's chair* (proverbial)

17   *quatch-buttock.* The word *quatch* does not seem to occur elsewhere but clearly means something like 'squat', 'fat'.

20   *ten groats* (the usual fee for an attorney at this time)

21   *French crown* (a play on words that is an all too frequent joke of the time: a *crown* is a coin, a *French crown* is the balding of the head caused by syphilis, called the 'French disease')

taffety punk finely dressed prostitute

22   *rush* (ring made of rush, once exchanged in mock-marriages. There is probably an element of bawdy in the references here.)

23   *morris* country dance

24   *quean* loose woman

26   *pudding* sausage

33   *But a trifle neither* nothing but a trifle

40   *O Lord, sir!* (a smart and silly catch-phrase of the time. It is hard to know exactly how funny the passage that follows is meant to be, and whether the Countess speaks ironically or seriously in her lines 55-6.)

43   *Thick* quickly

50-51   *is very sequent to* follows (or 'would follow') very closely after

51   *answer.* The Countess is quibbling in a somewhat menacing way: her answer means both 'reply to' and 'be suited to', just as her *bound to't* in line 52 means both 'bound on oath to answer' and 'bound to a whipping-post'.

59   *present* immediate

65   *fruitfully.* The Clown picks up the Countess's *understand*, makes it bawdy, and tosses back a bawdy answer. The reference to 'standing' then suggests *legs*: the Clown means 'I am in Paris already' and also perhaps 'I understand you quicker than my legs can move'.

66   *again* back again

I.3   (stage direction) *Enter Bertram, Lafew, and Parolles.* The relationship between these three persons in the exchanges that follow is a slightly curious one. The fact that Bertram utters only one remark (and that a meek one), and that Parolles – perhaps uncharacteristically – gains the upper hand in fooling with Lafew, has worried some editors into proposing textual changes that eliminate these aspects of the action. But the characters in this play do have odd angles: the youth Bertram has his meekness, and the fool Parolles has his moments of strength.

2   *modern* everyday, commonplace

3   *causeless* outside the ordinary course of nature

4-6   *ensconcing ourselves into seeming knowledge when we should submit ourselves to an unknown fear* sheltering within the illusion of knowledge when we should give ourselves up to what we most fear, the unknown

7   *argument* topic of conversation

8   *shot out* suddenly appeared (like a comet)

10   *relinquished of the artists* abandoned by the professionals

11   *both of Galen and Paracelsus* (that is, both 'parties' of medical opinion, the former representing the Ancients, the latter, the Moderns. Galen and Paracelsus were two famous physicians, the first a Greek of the second century A.D., the second a Swiss of the sixteenth century.)

12   *authentic fellows* authorized, qualified practitioners. (This is, perhaps, like the mention of the *congregated college*, a reference to the Fellows of the Royal College of Physicians.)

21   *in showing* before your eyes, in print, in a picture

23   *A showing of a heavenly effect in an earthly actor*. Most modern editors regard this as the title of a broadsheet ballad, referred to in the *what-do-ye-call there* of Parolles and read aloud by Lafew. This may well be correct; but it is as possible that the point lies in Lafew's misunderstanding, or only half-hearing or half-listening to, what Parolles means by *showing*, and himself using the word gravely to mean 'showing-forth', 'manifestation'.

25   *dolphin* (a symbol of love and lust)

Fore me (an exclamation like 'upon my soul', 'upon my word'. Though spoken with the greatest seriousness, the context of what goes before it and what follows it on Lafew's lips makes it highly comical.)

27–8   *the brief and the tedious of it* (a mannered way of saying 'the long and the short of it')

28   *facinerious* wicked, villainous

33   *debile* weak

40   *Lustique* sportive, frolicsome, lusty
      Dutchman German

41   *a tooth in my head* a taste for the pleasures of the senses (compare 'a sweet tooth')

42   *coranto* a lively dance

43   *Mor du vinager* (a meaningless pseudo-French oath. The words sound like 'death of vinegar' and may have, like many oaths, some vague and blasphemous reference to the Crucifixion.)

44   *Fore God, I think so.* Lafew cannot be, like Parolles, surprised, since it was he who introduced Helena to the King. He may be speaking in a proud understatement, or he may be watching the King and musing happily on his recovery.

48   *repealed* called back from exile or banishment

50   (stage direction) *Enter four Lords.* F's reading '*Enter 3 or 4 Lords*' is the kind of tentative or permissive stage direction that probably derives from the author's manuscript copy: he had not yet decided – though he very soon did so – how many Lords were to speak. A copy prepared in the theatre would have had exact specifications.

51   *parcel* small group

52   *at my bestowing.* The King had the right to marry his wards to whom he pleased, provided he did not make them marry a commoner. It seems unclear whether Shakespeare wishes this latter condition to provide Bertram with grounds for recalcitrance; but he makes his King speak with an almost tyrannical rage at lines 148–65.

54   *frank election* free choice

58 *bay curtal and his furniture* my bay horse with the docked tail, and his trappings

59 *broken.* Lafew is wishing he were still young: he may be speaking literally, and wishing he had all his teeth, or metaphorically, and wishing he had not yet been 'broken to the bit', like a young horse.

60 *writ* claimed to have, laid claim to

61 (stage direction) *Helena addresses the Lords.* F reads here '*She addresses her to a Lord*', which may mean 'She moves over and stands in front of a Lord'. This is hard to make sense of, followed as it is by the plural *Gentlemen*, and it is often dropped by editors. It may be a simple survival from the author's manuscript copy, giving evidence of an uncancelled change of plan. Or the phrase may be a mere note (rather than an actual stage direction) left by Shakespeare in his manuscript at a pause in composition, to remind himself how he should proceed when he returned to it.

69 *choose, but, be refused.* F punctuates 'choose, but be refused;', and this may be only a matter of 'rhetorical' punctuation which tends to punctuate heavily after words which should be stressed or require a pause after them.

77 *ames-ace* (two aces, the lowest throw at dice. If Lafew were dicing with his life at stake, this throw would certainly lose it, unless his opponent threw the same. He must therefore be speaking with an ironical understatement, since what he means is that he would give a very great deal to be *in this choice*.)

79 *honour* (that is, the 'honour' that he appears to wish to do her, of hoping she will be his wife)

83 *No better, if you please* I wish for nothing better than your humble love

85 *Do they all deny her?* It has usually been assumed that the four young Lords' professions are sincere, and that Lafew's comment is a misunderstanding of what happens, due to his somewhat removed position on the

stage. More recently, Joseph Price (in *The Unfortunate Comedy*) has convincingly argued that Lafew, who is usually a trustworthy choric commentator, is so here: the Lords' words are no more than a frigid formality, performed in obedience to the King.

98–9   *There's one grape yet. I am sure thy father drunk wine* there's one product of a good stock left still. I am sure your father had good red blood in his veins

100   *known* (probably means 'found you out')

113   *breeding* upbringing

114–15   *Disdain|Rather corrupt me ever!* sooner (than be ruined by marriage to her) let my disdain of her ruin me (or my fortunes) for ever!

116   *title* (that is, lack of title)

117–20   *Strange is it that our bloods . . . In differences so mighty* it is strange that different men's blood would be quite indistinguishable in respect of colour, weight, and heat, if it were all poured together, and yet such great distinctions are based on the concept of 'blood'

126   *great additions swell's* great titles inflate us

127–8   *Good alone | Is good, without a name* goodness is goodness because of its own essential nature, no matter what we call it. (F has 'Good a lone, | Is good without a name?' The punctuation here is rhetorical – the comma and the question mark indicate emphasis given to the words they succeed, rather than a syntactical point.)

129–30   *The property by what it is should go, | Not by the title* the particular quality that gives a thing its essential nature should decide how we think of it, and not the mere name it happens to carry

131   *immediate heir* one who inherits directly from another (and not circuitously, as honour for instance is inherited from nature through ancestors)

132–4   *that is honour's scorn | Which challenges itself as honour's born | And is not like the sire* the truly honourable feel only contempt for one who claims to be honourable by

179

birth and yet does not act with the honour of his fore-fathers

137-40 *grave ... indeed.* F has a colon after *grave*, a full stop after *tomb* in line 139, and only a comma after *indeed* in line 140. Since this makes sense – though a simpler one – of the passage, it may be that the printer was puzzled by the complexity of the syntax here.

142 *she* (that is, all the good qualities of Helena that cannot be included in the strictly moral *Virtue*)

148 *at the stake.* When he uses this phrase, Shakespeare usually seems to be fusing the term 'at the stake' from bear-baiting, in which the animal was tied to a stake and harried by dogs, with the term 'at stake' from the language of gaming, meaning 'at hazard'.
which to defeat and to overcome this threatened danger

151 *misprision.* The word here means both 'contempt' and 'error', and may have an underlying quibbling allusion to the idea of 'false imprisonment'.

152-4 *that canst not dream | We, poising us in her defective scale, | Shall weigh thee to the beam* who cannot grasp that when once the weight of my balanced judgement is added to her case, making up for whatever deficiencies are in it, your light objections fly up and away in a moment

157 *travails* labours

158 *presently* immediately

159 *obedient right* right of obedience

162 *staggers* (literally, a horse-disease. Here, 'giddy behaviour', or possibly 'sick confusion'.)
lapse fall

165 *Without all terms of pity* without pity in any form

167 *fancy* love, amorous inclinations. (He will 'see with the King's eyes'.)

168 *dole* share, portion

174-5 *if not to thy estate, | A balance more replete.* The King means here either that he will give a counterpoise which, if it will not be the size of Bertram's estate, at least will make Helena's and Bertram's estates more equal; or, just possibly, that he will give something at least the size of Bertram's estate and perhaps rather better.

177–8 *whose ceremony | Shall seem expedient on the now-born brief.* A much-discussed passage, whose uncertainty arises from the unclear meanings of *expedient* and *brief*. The probable sense is 'and the ceremony shall follow swiftly, as is right and proper, on the slightly abridged contract we have just taken part in'.

180–81 *Shall more attend upon the coming space, | Expecting absent friends* can wait until a little time has passed, and friends now absent have joined us

182 (stage direction) *Exeunt all but Parolles and Lafew, who stay behind, commenting on this wedding.* The stage direction is closely based on that in F; it can hardly be said to afford actors any real direction, since the nature of the colloquy is immediately apparent. Like the F stage directions at lines 50 and 61 above, this helps to indicate a textual source in manuscript copy rather than in a copy prepared in the theatre; and, like *'She addresses her to a Lord'*, may represent an author's self-directed remark.

190 *bloody succeeding* bloodshed in consequence

192–3 PAROLLES *To any Count, to all Counts, to what is man.* LAFEW *To what is Count's man.* Parolles is using *man* in the sense 'manly' or even 'human'; Lafew uses *man* in the sense 'servant'.

197 *write man* call myself a man, claim manhood

199 *What I dare too well do, I dare not do* what I have only too much physical courage for, I am prevented from by moral and social restraints

200 *ordinaries* meal-times

201–2 *make tolerable vent of thy travel* tell passable traveller's tales

202 *scarfs.* It was the fashion for military men to wear scarfs as an adornment of their person.

204   *burden* capacity

204–5   *I have now found thee; when I lose thee again I care not.*
Found has the sense 'found out'; *lose* perhaps has the
sense 'forget', as well as the obvious one.

206   *taking up.* As well as the literal sense of 'picking up' –
as one picks up a dropped thing – *taking up* here
carries several hostile meanings: 'arresting', 'oppos-
ing', 'rebuking', and perhaps also 'levying as a
soldier, as cannon-fodder'.

208   *antiquity* old age

212   *window of lattice.* Parolles is easy to see through; his
drapery of scarfs is like lattice-work; and he is as
commonplace as an ale-house sign, which was a red
lattice-window.

219–20   *I will not bate thee a scruple* I will not reduce the
indignity by the minutest particle

222–3   *thou hast to pull at a smack o'th'contrary* you have
to drink down a quite different mouthful (that is,
he will have to become aware of his own lack of
wisdom)

226–7   *in the default* when you default

231   *doing.* Lafew is perhaps joking on the bawdy sense of
this word.

231–2   *as I will by thee* as I will pass by you (a neat and rapid
exit-line belying Lafew's *antiquity*)

238   *I would have of –.* The *mot juste* is always escaping this
'man of words'.
      an if if

253–4   *breathe themselves upon* take exercise on

257–8   *for picking a kernel out of a pomegranate* (even for this
ludicrous, and ludicrously small crime)

258–9   *You are a vagabond and no true traveller.* Elizabethan
travellers were required to carry a species of passport,
otherwise were mere 'vagabonds'.

260–61   *than the commission of your birth and virtue gives you*
heraldry than is warranted by your birth and virtue – in
neither of which are you a gentleman

278   *kicky-wicky*. The word, which does not occur elsewhere, obviously means 'girl-friend', and is probably bawdy.

280   *curvet* (accented on the second syllable) (a horse's leap in which all four legs are momentarily extended and off the ground)

282   *jades* broken-backed nags

290   *To* compared to
        the dark house (perhaps 'the dismal house', perhaps specifically 'the madhouse', since madmen were at this time confined in darkness)

291   *capriccio* caprice. The word probably indicates Italianate affectation on Parolles's part.

295   *these balls bound, there's noise in it* now you're talking

I.4.2   *She is not well*. The Clown picks up Helena's use of *well* in its simple sense of 'in health' and introduces play on its Elizabethan sense by which the dead were said to be *well*, in the sense of well rid of their bodies and well-off in being in heaven.

16–17   *You had my prayers to lead them on, and to keep them on have them still*. The first two uses of *them* here refer to Helena's *good fortune*, as though it were a plural word, possibly by attraction to *prayers*.

20   *did as you say*. The point of this remark must be that *did* and 'died' were pronounced so similarly as to bear quibbling on.

22–3   *you are the wiser man, for many a man's tongue shakes out his master's undoing*. The Clown, like Parolles and Lafew in the previous scene, quibbles on the double sense of *man*, meaning both 'human being' and 'servant'.

25   *title* claim to possessions or other allotment in life

29   *Before me* (an exclamation, like 'upon my word', 'upon my soul')

31   *found thee* found you out

32   *in. In* could mean both 'within' and 'by'.

32–3   *were you taught to find me? The search, sir, was profitable.* F follows *me?* with another speech prefix for the Clown. A speech from Parolles may have dropped out; or what follows may have been a later insertion, written at the margin and incorrectly added; or it may be a simple mistake of the printer, continuing after a pause.

36   *well fed* (an echo of the Clown's own *highly fed and lowly taught* at II.2.3 earlier, with the proverb 'Better fed than taught' behind it)

41   *puts it off to* delays it in accordance with

42–5   *Whose want and whose delay is strewed with sweets ... And pleasure drown the brim* (an elaborate and false-sounding figure taken from the making of perfume. *Restraint, want,* and *delay* distil *sweets,* or sweet-scented flowers, in their still, the *curbèd time.*)

49   *probable need* likely necessity

II.5.2   *valiant approof* proved valour

5–6   *I took this lark for a bunting* I under-estimated him. Lafew is drily reversing the proverb 'To take a bunting for a lark', meaning 'to over-estimate someone worthless'.

8   *accordingly* correspondingly

15   *Pray you, sir, who's his tailor?* Lafew is probably here behaving like Kent in *King Lear,* who teases Oswald by pretending to mistake him for a tailor's dummy (II.2.50–51).

27–8   *A good traveller is something at the latter end of a dinner.* Lafew continues his meditations on Parolles initiated in the previous scene, II.3.200; if not a tailor's dummy, Parolles is a mere teller of tales.

36   *made shift* contrived, managed

37   *like him that leaped into the custard.* A clown's leaping into a giant custard was a famous turn at Lord Mayor's

Feasts at this period – an early association of fools with custard pies.

38-9   *suffer question for your residence* stand being asked why you are there

41-2   *though I took him at's prayers.* Lafew picks up Bertram's *mistaken* and lets it mean 'mis-taken' or 'taken amiss': if he found Parolles praying, he would still take him amiss, or think some ill of him.

45   *I have kept of them tame* I have had some such creatures as pets

47-8   *we must do good against evil.* Compare 1 Thessalonians 5.15, 'See that none recompense evil for evil unto any man; but ever follow that which is good' (Bishops' Bible).

49   *idle* stupid, empty, crazy

50   *I think not so.* F has 'I think so', which can be explained as an essentially hesitant and doubting agreement, such as to provoke Parolles's surprised and annoyed rejoinder. But it is more likely that the *not* in the next line confused the printer into thinking the first a slip, and omitting it.

53   *Gives him a worthy pass* reputes him a good man
      clog (a cruel word. A *clog* is a block of wood tied to man or beast to stop him straying.)

58-69   *You must not marvel, Helen, at my course ... To you that know them not.* Bertram's lies emerge as conspicuously null rhetoric: his language is here quite devoid of vitality and savour.

59   *Which holds not colour with the time* which is not very well suited to the happy day (his wedding-day)

59-61   *nor does | The ministration and requirèd office | On my particular* my course of action forces me to omit my personal duties and responsibilities as a husband

66   *my respects* the circumstances which prompt me

67   *appointments* purposes

74   *observance* dutiful service, respect
      eke out add to

75   *homely stars* the fate of being born of simple, humble family

79   *owe* own

89   *Where are my other men? Monsieur, farewell.* Some editors have found it hard to believe that Helena speaks these words, and have given either the whole line or the first part of it to Bertram. This text follows F.

92   *Coragio* courage (assimilated Italian)

III.1.3-4   *Whose great decision hath much blood let forth, | And more thirsts after* deciding the great issue involved in the war has caused the spilling of much blood and will cause more

7   *cousin* (title used by one sovereign of another)

10-13   *The reasons of our state I cannot yield ... By self-unable motion* I cannot speak with authority on state policy, only give my views like a commoner who from outside the council-chamber creates an image of what great affairs go on within, out of sketchy and subjective fantasies

17   *nature* temperament, type. It is possible that this word is an error for 'nation', but *nature* makes sense as it stands.

18   *That surfeit on their ease* who find a life of ease too much for them (in the sense of sickening, and needing the *physic* or blood-letting of war to bring them back to health)

22   *When better fall, for your avails they fell* when better places become available, you shall have them

III.2.3   *troth* faith

7   *ruff.* This usually means the neck-frill of the period, or a ruffled cuff on the sleeve, but here it seems to mean the same as one meaning of 'ruffle', the cuff or turned-over portion at the top of a boot.

8   *knew*. F has 'know'. Some change is necessary in this sentence to bring 'know' and *hold* into grammatical concord. Some editors follow the third Folio and emend *hold* to 'sold', bearing in mind the proverb 'Sold for a song'. This proposes a printer's slip less frequent than the familiar 'o'/'e' misreading of 'know'/ 'knew'; and the grammatical lack of concord between 'know' and *had* gives the impression that the error lies there, not later.

9   *hold* offer as a wager

13 *old lings* salt cod (bawdy)

16 *stomach* keenness of appetite

18 *E'en*. F has 'In', which is a common spelling for 'e'en' in Shakespeare.

22 *'not'*. There is possibly a quibble on 'knot' in the sense of 'marriage-tie'.

30 *misprizing* despising

31 *For the contempt of empire* for even emperors to despise

40–41 *The danger is in standing to't; that's the loss of men, though it be the getting of children.* The contrasting effects of *standing* in a bawdy and in an orthodox military sense form a frequently treated topic in literature at this period.

49 *on the start* suddenly appearing

50 *Can woman me unto't* can make me behave in the conventional 'womanly' way, and weep

55 *passport* licence to wander on a specified route as a beggar

65 *If thou engrossest all the griefs are thine* if you monopolize all the grief that is yours

66 *moiety* share

68 *thou art all my child* only you are my child, you are my only child

    Towards heading for

72 *convenience* fitness, propriety

76 *haply* perhaps

89   *With his inducement* by his (Parolles's) misleading example, his temptation

90–91   *The fellow has a deal of that too much | Which holds him much to have* the man goes a good deal too far a good deal too often, and finds it very profitable

97   *Not so, but as we change our courtesies* only if the service is mutual (and you allow me to serve you)

101   *Rossillion.* Helena gives Bertram his formal title, which makes a dramatic point economically. She is withdrawing any private claims or any proprietary interest, and giving back to Bertram his independence and his important public status.

104   *event* outcome

110   *still* always, ever

        still-piecing. F reads 'still-peering', which makes sense, though a difficult and very debatable sense. Numerous emendations have been proposed, of which *still-piecing* is the most widely accepted. It has a sense found in several other places in Shakespeare, that winds and waters, if an attempt is made to 'wound' them, merely close or repair (*piece*) themselves again.

111   *That sings with piercing.* The whine of the bullet becomes a song sung by the air.

113   *forward* eagerly facing the enemy, in the van of the battle

114   *caitiff* wretch

117   *ravin* ravenous

119   *owes* owns

121–2   *Whence honour but of danger wins a scar, | As oft it loses all* from the battle-field, where honour survives danger with nothing but a scar to show for it, and often does not survive danger at all

126   *angels officed all* all the work was done by angels

127   *pitiful* (as taking pity on, being kind to Bertram)

129   *with the dark, poor thief, I'll steal away.* The last words of this speech make an effective close to the first movement of the play.

I.3   (stage direction) *drum and trumpets* (that is, a drummer and trumpeters)

2   *Great in our hope* with high hopes

        lay our best love and credence wager our love and faith in you

7   *helm* helmet

9   *file* ranks, army

I.4.4   *Saint Jaques. Jaques* is pronounced in two syllables. The shrine referred to here (and as *Saint Jaques le Grand* at III.5.33) is clearly that of Great St James at Compostella in north-west Spain. Since Helena is starting out from Rossillion in south-west France, it is something of a surprise to meet her next in Florence, a city which neither Shakespeare nor most of his audience can have believed to be on any direct route from the one to the other – even though the Widow, in III.5, shows no surprise at the route. There is an element of mystery here, as in the rumours of Helena's death propagated by the rector of the shrine (IV.3.46–58). Possible explanations are: Providence, chance, Helena's contrivance, or combinations of any of these. It is also possible that Shakespeare is using the romance mode (where such things need no explanation) to move the stress from the rational motivation or cause of events, on to their fruits or effects. The mystery worries few in the theatre.

5   *Ambitious love.* The phrase *ambitiosus amor* occurs in Ovid's *Amores* (II.4.48) – though the consonance may be accidental.

7   *sainted vow* a vow to a saint

9   *hie* hasten

12   *His taken labours* the labours he has undertaken

13   *despiteful Juno.* Hostile Juno imposed on Hercules his legendary twelve labours.

14   *From courtly friends, with camping foes to live.* 'Court'
and 'camp' were commonly linked at this period,
usually in opposition.

17   *Whom I myself embrace to set him free. Whom* refers to
death, *him* to Bertram; but, coming as it does as the
last line of a sonnet, the line has an epigrammatic
finality and paradoxical point that makes it sound as
though Helena were also embracing Bertram to set him
free – as, in a sense, she does.

19   *you did never lack advice so much* you were never so ill-
advised

22   *prevented* forestalled

23   *at overnight* last night, last evening

27   *her prayers.* It is just possible that this is a reference to
the intercessory prayers of the Virgin Mary, a Popish
reference which, like Helena's pilgrimage, could be
safely thrown into a play set in the world of feudal
romance. But it is more likely that the Countess is
referring to Helena, and making her sound like a saint
interceding.

30   *this unworthy husband of his wife* this husband unworthy
of his wife

III.5   (stage direction) *A tucket* (a trumpet-call signalling
someone's approach)
her daughter Diana, and Mariana. F reads here '*her
daughter, Violenta and Mariana*'. If there was ever a
separate character called Violenta, she has nothing to
say, and she has disappeared from the stage by line 96
of this scene, where there are only four characters present – Helena, Diana, the Widow, and Mariana. It may
be that the comma prefacing '*Violenta*' in F was an
error, and the name is a first idea for the Widow's
daughter, later cancelled; hence the curious stage
direction at IV.2 in F, '*Enter Bertram, and the Maide
called Diana*'. The name *Diana,* which was that of the

goddess of chastity, has an obvious appropriateness to
the girl's role in the play.

13   *honesty* chastity

16–18   *a filthy officer he is in those suggestions for the young Earl.*
This is ambiguous. It probably means 'He is a dis-
gusting go-between who leads girls astray for the young
Earl', but may mean, more simply, 'He is a horrible
soldier who is always tempting the young Earl'.

19   *engines* tricks and traps

20   *the things they go under* what they seem to be

23   *dissuade succession* prevent others from following in her
footsteps

23–4   *limed with the twigs that threatens them* caught by the
trap waiting for them, like birds on twigs spread with
bird-lime

30   *lie* lodge

34   *palmers* pilgrims. The word is here used in its ordinary
loose sense; more precisely, the word describes a pilgrim coming from the Holy Land, and bearing a palm
leaf.

35   *the Saint Francis* (that is, an inn with Saint Francis for
a sign)

    port city gate

37–9   *Ay, marry, is't. Hark you, they come this way. | If you
will tarry, holy pilgrim, | But till the troops come by.* The
curious lineation here may be the effect of verse-
speaking that is broken by stage business, noises off, etc.
Or it may be evidence of revision in the text. Or it may be
a compositor's misunderstanding of a somewhat over-
written and confused copy that should perhaps read
> Ay, marry, is't.
> Hark you, they come this way. Holy pilgrim,
> If you will tarry but till the troops come by. . . .

42   *ample* well, fully. The Widow may be quibbling
genially and also mean that the hostess and herself are
'liberal', 'generous of good things'.

50   *His face I know not.* Strictly speaking this is a lie and an

unnecessary one. Shakespeare's intention is presumably to express Helena's desire to make a fresh start: it is *as if* she had never met Bertram.

50   *Whatsome'er* whatever

51   *bravely taken* thought a very fine fellow

54   *mere the truth* absolutely true, nothing but the truth

56   *coarsely* slightingly, meanly

58   *In argument of praise or to the worth* if we are discussing her praiseworthiness or comparing it to the worth

60–61 *all her deserving | Is a reservèd honesty* her only merit is a well-guarded chastity

65   *I warrant.* F's 'I write' has been much emended. *I warrant* is excellent sense, and is supported by the fact that 'warrant' is misprinted where it occurs elsewhere.

67   *shrewd* bad, nasty

70   *brokes* bargains

81   *Yond's* that one there is

87   *Lose our drum.* Apart from the symbolic reference that Shakespeare gives to the drum by making it the particular attribute of Mars (see III.3.11), it had peculiar importance in carrying the colours of the regiment, so that the loss of the drum was a very signal loss of honour.

88   *shrewdly* intensely

91   *courtesy.* Parolles has saluted the women. The words 'curtsy' (a bow or other salute, male or female) and 'courtesy' were not distinguished in spelling, so that Mariana may be speaking of the act of courtesy in the abstract or the concrete.

      ring-carrier bawd, go-between in seductions. Presumably the ring signifies the promise of marriage.

93   *host* lodge

      enjoined penitents (those bound by oath, like Helena, to undertake a pilgrimage as an act of penance)

97–8 *the charge and thanking | Shall be for me* I shall pay for it, and thank you for coming

99   *of* on

I.6.1	*put him to't* make him show himself up utterly
3	*hilding* worthless fellow
5	*bubble* something as pretty, empty, and worthless as a bubble
8–9	*to speak of him as my kinsman* to put it kindly
11	*entertainment* patronage, attention, reception
17	*fetch off* recapture, win back
22	*hoodwink* cover, blindfold
24	*leaguer* camp
28	*intelligence* information
35	*John Drum's entertainment* a rough reception
38–9	*in any hand* in any case
40–41	*sticks sorely in your disposition* vexes you a good deal
42	*pox* plague (literally, syphilis)
46–7	*in the command of the service* on the orders given for the action
50	*our success* the way we came out of it
57	*hic jacet* (the traditional beginning to an epitaph, 'here lies' in Latin)
58	*stomach* appetite, will
59	*mystery* mastery, art, skill
61	*magnanimious* (an alternative form of 'magnanimous'; here in the sense of 'great of spirit', 'great of heart')
62	*speed* succeed, prosper
65	*syllable* (perhaps just metaphorical for 'minute quantity', perhaps an *ad hominem* joke referring to the name of Parolles)
68	*presently* immediately
69	*dilemmas* (arguments leading to a choice of two or more conclusions)
70	*my mortal preparation* (preparation either for his own death, that is, making his will and so on, or for that of another, that is, arming himself)
76	*possibility* capability
91	*probable* likely-sounding
92	*embossed him* run him down (a term from hunting: to

emboss is to drive an animal to the point of exhaustion so great that its mouth foams)

96 *case* flay

smoked exposed (like a fox driven out of its earth by smoke. But the *first* also gives the word its other sense of 'suspected', 'got wind of'.)

100 *twigs* trapping manoeuvres. Twigs spread with bird-lime were used for catching birds.

102 FIRST LORD. The speech prefix here, and those at lines 104 and 110, are in reverse in F, so that Second Lord leaves the stage and First Lord stays with Bertram. But clearly they fulfil the opposite roles in what follows (First Lord directs the ambush of Parolles, and Second Lord accompanies Bertram to Diana's house). It is therefore necessary to make such emendations in speech prefixes here as will straighten out the confusion.

107 *have i'th'wind* have got scent of, are hunting down

III.7.3 *But I shall lose the grounds I work upon* except by cutting the ground from under my own feet (that is, by revealing herself to Bertram)

7 *staining* disgraceful, dishonouring

9 *sworn counsel* private ear, on the understanding of absolute secrecy

11 *By* in regard to, as to

19 *carry* conquer, take by assault

in fine finally (or perhaps 'in short')

21 *important* importunate, demanding

22 *County* Count

26 *choice* special estimation

idle foolish, crazy

27 *will* lust, object of appetite

33 *In fine* (see note to line 19)

35 *To marry her* as a dowry to marry on

37 *persever* (accented on the second syllable)

39 *coherent* fitting, accordant
41 *To her unworthiness.* The Widow seems to be showing
    here the crisp rebuttal of romanticism that in the next
    Act reveals itself as a characteristic of her astringent
    daughter. Some editors, however, believe that the
    meaning of this phrase is that Bertram's musical
    performances are ruining Diana's reputation, and
    making her 'unworthy'.
    It nothing steads us it's of no use to us at all
44 *speed* succeed
45 *meaning* intention
45–7 *Is wicked meaning in a lawful deed . . . and yet a sinful
    fact.* The first two lines of this riddle or charade deal
    with each of the partners in the bed-trick singly, and
    the last line takes them together. Bertram intends
    adultery and accomplishes it in lawful cohabitation
    with his wife; Helena intends and accomplishes lawful
    cohabitation with her husband; both together succeed
    in making innocent an act that could have been in fact
    fornication or adultery.

.1.11 *linsey-woolsey* (a mixture of flax and wool; hence, a
    medley of words, a mish-mash language)
14–15 *strangers i'th'adversary's entertainment* foreign mer-
    cenaries on the enemy's side
15 *smack* smattering
16–19 *we must every one be a man . . . to know straight our
    purpose* every man must make up his own fantasy-
    language, so that we shan't know what we are saying to
    each other – but to *seem* to understand each other is
    what we are aiming at
19 *choughs' language* jackdaw-chat
26 *plausive* plausible
27 *smoke* suspect
39 *instance* evidence (so the phrase means 'where's the
    evidence')

40   *butter-woman's.* Presumably dairywomen were loud and frequent talkers.

41   *Bajazeth's mule.* Shakespeare elsewhere associates mules with silence, and one might therefore furnish Parolles with the tongue he needs. Why it has to be *Bajazeth's* mule is a question so hard of solution as to have driven editors to frequent and various emendations of the whole phrase. It is possible that Parolles does not know either: words do not always act as he intends them to.

47   *afford you so* give you that much, let you off that easily

48   *baring* shaving

62   (stage direction) *Alarum* call to arms

67   *Muskos* (presumably the Muscovites)

71   *discover* reveal

80   *hoodwinked* blindfolded

81   *Haply* perhaps

87   (stage direction) *A short alarum.* J. Dover Wilson in his edition suggests that this is an ironic drumroll.

89   *woodcock* (a bird noted for its stupidity)

91   *'A* he

IV.2   (stage direction) F reads '*Enter Bertram, and the Maide called Diana*'. See the second note to the opening stage direction at III.5.

1   *They told me that your name was Fontybell.* The attribution of this obtrusively romantic name to Diana suggests the callow or ingenuous nature of Bertram's romanticism.

3   *worth it, with addition!* you are worth further splendid titles also

14   *vows* (not to be a husband to Helena)

18   *our roses* our virginity

19   *You barely leave our thorns* you leave our thorns (of painful guilt and shame) bare and exposed to the

view. There is perhaps a quibble, 'You leave us nothing but the thorns'.

21–31 *'Tis not the many oaths that makes the truth ... At least in my opinion.* What Diana is saying here is important to the theme of the play as a whole, but the course of her close arguing is difficult at first sight. Bertram imagines himself (perhaps) to be passionately serious; Diana is trying to show him that real seriousness is a will-to-good-actions. She tells him first (lines 21–2) that frequency in promises is less important than sincerity; then adds (lines 23–9) that in any case sincerity is not the most important thing, if we mean by it only a subjective passionate conviction, for all men *take the highest to witness* at some time in that sense. The vital thing is to *vow true* by objective standards – to act out the love that is vowed, and to swear only the love that can be acted out.

25 *Love's.* F reads 'Ioues', with the 'I' and the 'u' that were normal usage for 'J' and 'v' at the time. The possibility of confusion between 'I' and 'l' will be obvious. When to this fact is added another, that at two earlier points where the text cites *love* as a divinity (II.3.74 and 84) a later Folio misread or emended the word to 'Jove', then it will be clear that the 'love'/'Jove' confusion suggests (what Johnson first conjectured): that the printer misread Shakespeare's *Love* (or *love*). To read *Love* here also clarifies a difficult argument, for Diana needs the verbal identity of the beloved and the sworn-by divinity for her case – that it is possible, in the name of Love, not to love one's love.

27 *love you ill* not love you, or love you with ill effect

30 *poor conditions but unsealed* a contract that is only a poor one so long as it remains one without legal ratification

32 *holy-cruel* holy by being cruel, cruel by being holy (perhaps with a quibble on 'holy'/'wholly')

35 *my sick desires.* Bertram sees his *desires* detachedly,

even coldly, as though they were a diseased acquaintance of his whom Diana must cure, as Helena cured the King.

38   *I see that men make vows in such a flame.* F reads 'I see that men make rope's in such a scarre'. Attempts have been made to defend this, but *some* degree of corruption has clearly taken place; and the line has been variously emended. The present reading adopts a nineteenth-century conjecture of *vows*. Diana must have some words to indicate that she is (supposedly) melting, and beginning to favour Bertram; and she does this by speaking – seriously to Bertram, but ironically in the understanding of the audience – the high love-language of romance that he has just been talking about and in. *Vows* is a word very obviously relevant to its context here. *Flame* has occurred twice earlier in the play in the sense of 'passionate love' (I.3.206, II.3.79) and once in the sense of 'life' (I.2.59). In secretary hand (Shakespeare's probable script) it is possible to mistake 'vowes' for 'rope's' and 'flame' for 'scarre' – particularly since the latter word seems often to have been spelt by Shakespeare 'skarre' (with the long-tailed 's' (ʃ)).

42   *honour* an object to which honour is attached

45   *honour* chastity

49   *proper* personal

56   *band* bond, obligation

65   *though there my hope be done* though this succumbing to you finishes my hopes of becoming a wife

71   *had* would have

73   *braid* (of uncertain meaning: perhaps 'loose', 'licentious', from Scots 'braid' meaning 'broad'; or perhaps 'deceitful', from the word 'braid' meaning 'plaited', 'twisted')

75   *in this disguise* in this game of deceiving

76   *cozen* deceive

.3-4   *he changed almost into another man.* If taken over-literally this suggests something for which there is no later evidence at all. The remark should probably be taken as a high-wrought and courtly way of saying that Bertram was at least shocked and shaken.

13   *perverted* seduced, corrupted

15   *fleshes his will in the spoil.* The image is from hunting: a hawk or hound was given a piece of the kill (*the spoil*) to reward it and excite it with the prospect of further occasions, and this was 'fleshing'. Bertram's lust (*will*) was to be fleshed on Diana.

16   *monumental* serving as a memento

16-17   *thinks himself made in the unchaste composition* thinks himself a made man by his dishonourable bargain

18   *delay.* Some editors have proposed emendations for F's 'delay': 'allay' and 'lay'. *Delay* may have the sense 'quench', or it may have the more frequent modern sense of 'postpone', with a colloquial idiom being used: 'total moral reformation is too much to hope for, but an improvement for the next day or so might feasibly be petitioned'.

    rebellion. This word frequently carries, in Shakespeare, a subdued sexual reference: 'the rebellion of the flesh', 'anarchic lust'.

19   *ourselves* in ourselves alone, without grace

20   *Merely* nothing but, absolutely

20-24   *as in the common course of all treasons ... in his proper stream o'erflows himself* all traitors, all the way through their treacherous plots and enterprises and up to the achievement of their wicked ends, are expressing their own true treacherous natures; even so Bertram, here destroying his own honour, does it in a way characteristic of his own peculiar energies

25   *Is it not meant damnable* is it not intended to be a mortal sin

28-9   *dieted to his hour* limited to his one hour

31 *company anatomized* companion dissected and probed into

32-3 *wherein so curiously he had set this counterfeit* in which he has given this false jewel so elaborate a setting

34-5 *him ... he ... his ... the other* Parolles ... Bertram ... Bertram's ... Parolles

41 *higher* (unclear: perhaps 'further')

47 *pretence* intention

49 *sanctimony* sanctity, holiness

53 *justified* proved, confirmed

57 *rector* (probably 'priest', possibly 'ruler')

59 *intelligence* information, news

61 *to the full arming of the verity* fully and forcibly substantiating the truth of it

71-3 *Our virtues would be proud if our faults whipped them not, and our crimes would despair if they were not cherished by our virtues.* An elusive and figurative passage, whose paradoxes are vital to the play. The rough sense is: 'Our virtuous selves would grow arrogant, were they not humiliated [into being good?] by the sense of our faults; and our criminal natures would give up hope, were they not aided and abetted by all that is best in us'.

79-80 *They shall be no more than needful there, if they were more than they can commend* even if they said more than any letter of recommendation could, they would still be no more than is needful (to reconcile the King to Bertram)

85 *By an abstract of success* (either 'to give a brief summary of my successes', or 'to summarize briefly and in order of events')

86 *congied with* taken my leave of

88 *entertained my convoy* hired my transport

89 *parcels of dispatch* items to be settled

 nicer more trivial (with a quibble on the sense 'wanton', 'lecherous')

95-6 *fearing to hear of it hereafter* (since Diana may take him at his word and claim him as her husband)

98   *counterfeit module* sham image
      has who has

101   *gallant* showy, smart

102-3 *His heels have deserved it in usurping his spurs* it is what
      he deserves, for being base when he should have been
      chivalrous

106   *shed* spilled

109   *setting* sitting

115   *Muffled* blindfolded

117-18 *Hush, hush! Hoodman comes.* These four words appear
      to be a call from the old game of Blind Man's Buff;
      Hoodman is another name for the Blind Man. F gives
      the first two words to Bertram, who so little joins in the
      playfulness of the two Lords as to make this seem to
      need emendation.

135-6 *how and which way you will.* The exact significance of
      the sacrament, and the manner of its administration
      and reception, were all of course matters crucial to the
      Reformation and at this period gave rise to great debate
      and polemic. Parolles refers helplessly here to the
      possibility of large difference of opinion on the matter,
      especially since he does not know the nationality of his
      captors, or whether they are Protestant or Catholic.

137   *All's one to him.* F adds this to the end of the last re-
      mark of Parolles. It is possible that *him* is a slip for
      'me', on the author's part rather than the com-
      positor's. But most editors have seen it as a mistake
      comparable to that in line 117, and have given it to
      Bertram, as here.

141   *theoric* theory

142   *chape* metal plate on a scabbard, covering the point of
      the dagger

150-51 *But I con him no thanks for't, in the nature he delivers it*
      but I refuse to thank him gratefully for it, when it is
      such truth as he tells

158   *live this.* Some editors emend this F reading to 'live but
      this', 'leave this', or 'die this'. It is possible that

Parolles is, in his confused condition, conflating two statements: 'as I hope to live' (see line 133 of this scene) and 'if I were to die this present hour'.

159–63 *Spurio . . . Vaumond, Bentii.* Some of the names in this passage are strange in their formation, and they make an odd assortment as a whole. G. K. Hunter in his edition suggests that Shakespeare is inventing odd names in order to give the impression of an international force.

165 *poll* head

166 *cassocks* military cloaks

176 *well-weighing* heavy (but also quibbling on the sense 'influential')

182 *botcher* clumsy patcher (that is, tailor or cobbler without much expertise)

184 *shrieve's fool.* The crown had nominal charge of insane persons – 'fools' or 'innocents' – but where their estate was of no value their care was delegated to the sheriff or *shrieve.*

187 *his brains are forfeit to the next tile that falls* he's heading straight for a sudden violent death

198 *In good sadness* honestly, to be perfectly serious

208 *advertisement* word of advice, piece of good counsel
proper decent, respectable

210 *ruttish* lustful (a derisive term: deer are 'in rut' in the mating season)

216 *fry* small fish (swallowed in huge numbers by the whale)

219 *After he scores he never pays the score* after he's hit the mark (with sexual innuendo) he never pays the bill

220 *Half-won is match well made; match, and well make it* if you get the terms of a bargain good and clear and satisfactory, you're halfway to getting your money – so draw up your terms, and make sure they're good

221 *after-debts* bills remaining unpaid after the goods are delivered

223   *mell* be involved with (but with an obvious bawdy sense here)

224   *For count of* on account of

231   *manifold linguist, and the armipotent soldier* (a mocking echo of the earlier bombastic language of Parolles. *Armipotent* means 'mighty in arms'.)

244   *an egg out of a cloister* even the most trivial thing out of even the most holy place

245   *Nessus* (the centaur who attempted to rape Deianira, the wife of Hercules. Centaurs were associated with lust.)

251   *conditions* habits, characteristics

259   *has* he has

259–60 *has led the drum before the English tragedians.* The strolling players advertised themselves by processing with a big drum at their head: and one such company, so Parolles is affirming, had one of the Dumaines for drummer.

262–3 *Mile-end* (where the London citizen militia drilled, presumably not reaching a high standard of the soldier's art)

263   *doubling of files* (a simple drill exercise in which every alternate man takes up position behind the next)

270   *cardecue* quarter of a crown or *quart d'écu* (old French silver coin of small value)
       fee-simple an estate held by its owner and his heirs absolutely and for ever

271–3 *cut th'entail from all remainders, and a perpetual succession for it perpetually* make quite sure that his heir will not inherit the interest on the estate, nor his nor any heir for ever and ever

281–2 *outruns any lackey.* A lackey at this time was a 'running footman' who went on errands and ran before the coach of his employer.

290–91 *beguile the supposition* gratify and fool the mind

323   *thing.* When applied to human beings, this word

usually means 'creature' in Shakespeare; though the meaning may extend here to cover 'object' as well.

328   *being fooled, by foolery thrive* since I have been made a fool of, I had better live and prosper by playing the fool

IV.4.6   *which gratitude* gratitude for which

9   *Marcellus* (that is, Marseilles. The spelling is one that probably records the pronunciation of 'Marseilles' at the time, and may be Shakespeare's own.)

10   *convoy* transportation

11   *breaking* disbanding, dispersing

12   *hies him* hastens

19   *brought me up* brought me to adulthood (or perhaps 'ennobled me', 'enriched my fortunes')

20   *motive.* Shakespeare is using the word here in a way which seems to be unique to him and which is paralleled in 'every joint and motive of her body' (*Troilus and Cressida*, IV.5.57); that is, to mean 'moving-agent', thing by which something moves.

23   *saucy trusting of the cozened thoughts* lecherous acceptance of the fantasies of the fooled mind

25   *for that* taking it for that

28   *death and honesty* death, if the price of chastity

29   *impositions* orders

30   *Upon your will to suffer* to face suffering if you request it
Yet yet further, still more (suffering)

31   *But with the word the time will bring on summer.* This line has generally been regarded as a 'crux', and has been much emended. The major problem seems to have been the exact reference of the phrase *But with the word*: what word? It seems likely, however, that Helena refers to the word which she has just uttered twice – the word *Yet*, with all its complex and quibbling senses. Helena is breaking it to Diana and the

widow, after their involvement in the bed-trick, that
there is *yet* another ordeal for them still (*yet*) to suffer.
Yet she has a comfort for them. Their journeyings and
sufferings *will* bring them to a happy ending, just as
time, saying *Yet* (both 'nevertheless' and 'yet a little
longer to wait'), *brings on summer*, like the presenter
leading on one of the characters in a Masque of the
Seasons. It is in this sense that (as she says in line 34)
time revives us, making things new, and bringing hope.

34   *revives* refreshes (but also with its literal sense pro-
minent: time 'gives life to us again')

35   *the fine's* the end is

36   *the renown* the part that makes us famous

IV.5.1–2   *snipped-taffeta* slashed-silk (a cut both at Parolles's
fancifully pretty clothes and at his somewhat double
personality)

2   *saffron*. Saffron was used as a starch at this time, hence
the link with the clothes of Parolles; it was also used to
colour pastry, hence the *unbaked and doughy youth* of
line 3.

6   *red-tailed humble-bee*. Noise and uncreativity make the
point of the comparison between Parolles and a
bumblebee.

10   *dearest* full of both love and pain

13   *sallets* salads

15   *herb of grace* rue

16–17   *They are not herbs, you knave, they are nose-herbs*. The
distinction here is between herbs for salad, called
simply *herbs*, and sweet-scented plants, called *nose-
herbs*.

18   *Nabuchadnezzar* (the King of Babylon who is said in
his insanity to have eaten grass: Daniel 4.28–37)

19   *grass* (with a quibble on 'grace', which is what F reads
at this point)

20   *Whether* which

22 *service*. This word frequently gives occasion for a sexual innuendo, or for an actual bawdy quibble, and does so here.

28 *bauble* rod of office carried by a court fool (a bawdy quibble)

37 *name*. F reads 'maine' here. It is just possible that this is correct and that the word means 'meinie', or 'household servants'. There is a stronger probability that 'maine' was a misreading of the usual emendation of it, *name* – a probability supported by the wordplay which some find between *name* and *fisnomy* (fis*namy*) meaning 'physiognomy'.

38 *more hotter*. The Clown is playing with two ideas: that the Black Prince, who fought wars in France, was therefore more choleric and heated there; that he must also have had syphilis, 'the French disease'.

43 *suggest* tempt

47 *the prince of the world*. Compare 'Now is the judgement of this world: now shall the prince of this world be cast out', John 12.31 (Bishops' Bible).

48–53 *I am for the house with the narrow gate ... the broad gate and the great fire*. Compare 'Enter ye in at the strait gate: for wide is the gate, and broad is the way, that leadeth to destruction, and many there be that go in thereat: Because strait is the gate, and narrow is the way, which leadeth unto life ...', Matthew 7.14–15 (Bishops' Bible).

51 *chill and tender* faint-hearted and fond of comfort, cool and sensitive

59 *jades' tricks*. The Clown's joke depends on a simultaneous reference to the literal and metaphorical usage of this phrase, which then comes to mean 'the kind of vicious practices you expect from ill-tempered, broken-down nags, or from clowns'.

61 *A shrewd knave and an unhappy* a sharp-tongued, discontented fellow. Some editors understand *unhappy* to mean 'mischievous' and would gloss *shrewd* with a

harsher word than 'sharp-tongued'; but there seems
no linguistic evidence for this.

65   *pace* (the temperate, obedient movement of a trained
horse)

71   *self-gracious remembrance* an act of recollection owed to
his own gracious self (and not to someone's reminder)

78   *post* at express speed

81   *intelligence* information, news

83–90   *I shall beseech your lordship to remain with me ... I
thank my God, it holds yet.* In a mannered, courtly
diction which utilizes legal metaphors (*privilege*,
charter), and with the utmost politeness, the Countess
is inviting Lafew to stay at her castle until the meeting
of the King and her son, and Lafew is pleased to
accept.

91–2   *patch of velvet* (such as might cover either a battle-scar
or the marks of surgery for syphilis)

95   *is worn bare* has no patch on it, reveals bare skin

98   *carbonadoed* slashed (with cuts by a surgeon, treating
syphilitic ulcers)

.1.1   *exceeding posting* extreme haste

4   *wear* tire

5   *bold* confident
     requital debt

6   (stage direction) *Enter a Gentleman, Astringer to the
King.* F's stage direction, '*Enter a gentle Astringer*', has
been emended by editors to '*Enter a Gentleman*',
'*Enter a Gentleman Usher*', and '*Enter a Gentleman, a
stranger*' (in the last of these, the presumption is that
Shakespeare is reminding himself or others that this
'Gentleman' is not one of those who have appeared
earlier). The main difficulty about F's '*Astringer*' is
the question of how his profession, that of a keeper of
hawks – for that is what the term means – could have
been made clear to an audience. The opening stage

direction of *2 Henry VI*, II.1, contains '*Falconers halloing*', but their occupation is explained by the dialogue which follows. Otherwise, there is no intrinsic unlikelihood of Shakespeare's so denominating a minor character in this courtly and often socially realistic play.

6   *In happy time!* just at the right moment!

15   *Which lay nice manners by* which cause us to put aside delicate politeness

26   *adverse* (accented on the second syllable)

35   *Our means will make us means* our resources will allow us

V.2.1   *Lavatch.* There seem to be various discrediting suggestions behind Lavatch's name. One is *la vache*, 'cow', but colloquially meaning something like 'trollop'; another is *lavage* (or the Italian form of the same word, *lavaccio*) meaning 'slop'.

4   *muddied in Fortune's mood. Mood* means 'anger', 'displeasure'. The word carries a quibble that explains the lengthy lavatorial wordplay that follows. *Muddied* and *mood* echo the now obsolete word 'mute', which is the correct term for an animal's or more specifically a bird's droppings. Once Parolles, with his high-flown phrase, has fallen into this trap, the Clown eagerly – indeed incessantly – reiterates it in subdued puns in *buttering*, line 8 ('butt' means 'bottom' or 'buttocks'), *metaphor*, lines 12–13 ('mute' again), *close-stool*, line 17 (an early form of lavatory), and *pur* (line 19) which means 'animal excrement'.

8–9   *allow the wind* go down-wind

19   *pur.* Apart from the sense referred to in the note to line 4, this word quibbles on 'purr', hence the transition to *Fortune's cat.* The word has a third sense, that of the knave in a card game of the time, and this sense is picked up in Lafew's next speech (lines 30–31).

20   *not a musk-cat.* A type, not of cat but of deer, from which the scent musk is obtained. The Clown means that Parolles is far from sweetly scented.

21   *withal* with it

22   *carp* (a last lavatorial insult, as carp are, it seems, bred in manured fish-ponds; with a quibble also on the word for a 'carper', or 'talking fellow')

23   *ingenious.* This word, the reading of F, has a somewhat random appearance in the Clown's list. It has been explained as meaning 'un-genious', that is, stupid, on the analogy of Shakespeare's use elsewhere of 'illustrious' to mean 'unlustrous'; it has also been emended by editors to 'ingenerous' and 'ingenuous'. The Clown is perhaps merely using the word ironically, as 'clever' might well be used now.

24   *similes of comfort.* F reads 'smiles of comfort', which may just be correct, and mean 'invigorating, fortifying jokes'. There are, however, two separate points which support emendation. The first is that *similes* picks up the wordplay with *metaphor* at lines 12 and 13. The second is that the phrase 'similes, comfortable and profitable' occurs elsewhere in this period, the word 'similes' in it appearing to mean 'instructive sayings or parables', and such a meaning may be present here.

33   *justices.* After 1601 Justices of the Peace were in charge of the very poor and could relieve those who they felt deserved it.

40   *more than 'word' then.* He refers to the name Parolles, or 'words'.
     Cox my passion! (an oath produced by euphemistic distortion from 'God's my passion', that is, 'by the suffering of God')

42-3 *found me.* This and Lafew's *lost thee* in the next line repeat the wordplay of II.3.204-5, by which *found* quibbles on 'found out', and 'lost' contains the meanings 'dropped' and 'forgot'.

V.3.1   *of* in
          esteem value in absolute terms, worth (repeated in
          estimation, line 4)

4   *home* to the heart, fully

5   *make it* consider it

6   *blade* (the green part of a plant before the ear appears.
          The word is emended to 'blaze' by some editors, be-
          cause of the felt lack of congruence with the 'oil'
          metaphor; but this is unnecessary.)

10   *high bent* fully, strongly bent, like a taut bow

12   *first I beg my pardon.* With nervous punctiliousness
          Lafew, the true courtier, apologizes for being about to
          express a different opinion from the King's. Compare
          his equally nervous apology for bringing a new doctor
          to the King, at II.1.61.

17   *richest* most experienced

21-2   *kill | All repetition* put an end to any discussion of the
          past

23   *The nature of his great offence is dead* I have forgotten
          even what the nature of his great offence was

25   *incensing relics* memories arousing anger

29   *hath reference to* exists only in relation to

32   *not a day of season* not seasonable (meaning 'not con-
          forming to the conventional idea of a summer day, that
          is all sunshine, or a winter day, that is all hail')

36   *high-repented blames* bitterly repented faults, sins

37   *All is whole* all is well

38   *consumèd* past

39   *take the instant by the forward top* take time by the fore-
          lock

45-52   *ere my heart ... To a most hideous object.* Bertram's
          language is so abstract and generalized here that it is
          impossible to know whether he is talking about Helena
          or the lady later named as Maudlin. The main current
          of meaning seems to be that he fell in love with
          Maudlin *At first*, but did not dare to propose to her, or
          did not dare to tell the King and company that he had

fallen in love with her; once his eye was fixed on her, he felt *Contempt* for every other face, especially Helena's. But he may mean that he loved Maudlin before that moment when he spoke all too boldly to the King, and when contempt fixed his eye and made Helena seem hideous.

48 *perspective* (accented on the first syllable) (an optical instrument or device that distorts)

49 *favour* face

57 *the great compt* the great reckoning. The phrase sounds as though it must mean 'the day of judgement', but may mean only 'the long account of your sins in this matter'.

58 *remorseful.* The word may mean 'compassionate', or may reflect more on Bertram's situation than on its own metaphorical context, and carry its more modern meaning of 'guilty', 'regretful', 'sorry'.

59 *turns a sour offence* (like milk sent too dilatorily to a starving man: it turns sour, and is merely offensive, and is seen as merely offensive by the would-be-great sender)

66 *shameful hate sleeps out the afternoon* to our shame, hatred sleeps a sweet after-dinner sleep without regrets (having *Destroyed our friends* and left torpid love to wake and weep them uselessly)

68 *Maudlin.* The name may well be yet another of the play's significant proper names. It is a common English form of (Mary) Magdalen, the Saint of Penitence ('the Weeper'). Maudlin's name suggests that she is a proper match for a young man who is nominally penitent.

71–2 *Which better than the first, O dear heaven, bless! | Or, ere they meet, in me, O nature, cesse!* F assigns these two lines to the King, but they are clearly more appropriate to the Countess, and are usually so assigned.

72 *cesse* cease

74 *digested* swallowed up
   favour token, present

75–6 *To sparkle in the spirits of my daughter, | That she may quickly come* that the jewel may give its own brilliant brightness to my daughter's present thoughts of you, and make her come to you happily and soon

79 *The last that e'er I took her leave at court* the last time I ever took leave of her at court

85 *Necessitied* in need of

86 *reave* rob, deprive

87 *stead* help, benefit

96 *ingaged*. The word may mean either 'engaged to her' or 'unengaged to anyone else'.

96–7 *subscribed | To* admitted, acknowledged

100 *In heavy satisfaction* in sad acceptance of the facts

101 *Plutus* (the god of wealth and gold. Logically enough, he is shown here as the greatest of alchemists, having huge *science* or expertise in *nature's mystery*, the art of turning base metals into gold and multiplying gold itself, by means of the *tinct* or *elixir*.)

105–7 *then if you know | That you are well acquainted with yourself, | Confess 'twas hers.* This is somewhat obscure, but the King seems to mean 'admit it was hers, a truth which is as clear as the fact that you know you are yourself'.

115–20 *If it should prove | That thou art so inhuman . . . More than to see this ring.* The disjointed movement of this sentence echoes the disturbed, wretched, and finally conclusive movement of the King's mind.

121–3 *My fore-past proofs, howe'er the matter fall, | Shall tax my fears of little vanity, | Having vainly feared too little* however the affair turns out, the proofs which have already accumulated show that my fears are anything but vain; the vanity or folly has rather been in fearing too little

131–2 *Who hath for four or five removes come short | To tender it herself* who has tried to catch up with you (to present her petition herself) but has just missed doing so, on the last four or five stages of your journey from one stopping-place to the next (*removes*)

136   *importing* full of significance (or perhaps 'urgent')

137   *verbal brief* a summary by word of mouth

148–9 *toll for this* enter this one as 'for sale' in the toll-book
       of a market

151   *suitors* petitioners

156   *as you swear them lordship* as soon as you swear to be
       their lord and marry them

157   (stage direction) *Enter the Widow and Diana*. F brings
       on Parolles with the Widow and Diana here, although
       there is a separate entry for him at line 230.

164   *both shall cease* (both her ageing life and her honour
       will come to an end with grief and shame if Bertram is
       not made to marry Diana)

170   *this hand*. She presumably points to Bertram's left hand.

178   *fond* foolish

183   *them; fairer*. F reads 'them fairer:', which has been
       emended by editors to the punctuation as here given.

188   *gamester* prostitute

192   *high respect and rich validity* great honour and high
       value

195   *'tis hit* she has got him there, she has hit the mark.
       Some editors emend to ''tis it', on the ground that *hit*
       in F represents merely the old emphatic form of 'it'
       and should therefore be modernized.

197   *sequent issue* next heir

198   *owed* owned

199–200 *Methought you said | You saw one here in court could wit-
       ness it*. Diana has not in fact said this so far. Either
       Shakespeare is using a dramatic shorthand to cut down
       tedious complications, or this is a rewriting of the
       possible earlier idea for this scene in which Diana and
       Parolles entered in company (see note for stage
       direction, line 157).

205   *quoted for* regarded as, spoken of as

206   *With all the spots o'th'world taxed and debauched*
       accused (*taxed*) of being corrupted with all the dis-
       graceful crimes in the world

213

208 *Am I or that or this for what he'll utter* am I to be written down a 'this' or a 'that' on *his* evidence

211 *boarded* accosted

212 *She knew her distance* she knew how to keep just far enough off (to madden and attract me more)

214–15 *in fancy's course | Are motives of more fancy* in the way of passionate desire only serve to increase that desire

215 *in fine* 'at last' or 'to be brief'

216 *Her infinite cunning with her modern grace* her immense, timeless artfulness and her commonplace charm. F reads 'insuite comming' for the first phrase. It is just possible that 'insuite' is correct and is an anglicization of a Latin word for 'unusual'; but orthographical evidence strongly supports the supposition of misreading.

217 *rate* price

221 *diet me* restrain me, limit my pleasures

232 *boggle shrewdly* startle and shy away from things violently

every feather starts you a mere feather makes you jump. This remark, like that which immediately precedes it, is of course ironical; it has taken a good deal of battering to make Bertram admit this much.

237 *By him and by this woman* concerning him and this woman

245–6 *as a gentleman loves a woman.* The social difference in these two terms makes the point of the answer here.

248 *He loved her, sir, and loved her not* he loved her person, but not *her*

249–50 *equivocal companion* equivocating, quibbling fellow

253 *He's a good drum, my lord, but a naughty orator.* Lafew's surface meaning is that Parolles is a good drummer but a poor – or wicked – orator; but he uses *drum* quibblingly so that an apparently kind and even protective remark becomes rather harsher, and means 'He's good at making noise when beaten, and can boom out notes invented by someone better than him-

self, but as more than a mere instrument he's worthless
or worse'.

262   *other motions* proposals, offers (but probably with a
      bawdy quibble)

266   *fine* subtle

284   *customer* prostitute

294   *owes* owns

297   *quit.* The main sense here is 'acquit', but there is also
      a wordplay, on the sense 'am quits with, have my
      revenge on', and also 'leave'.

301   *quick* alive (but also with a quibble on 'pregnant')

302   *exorcist* one who summons and lays spirits

303   *truer office* (that is, to see real things)

305   *shadow* (a word whose many meanings contribute
      much to the moment: a *shadow* may be a ghost, an
      image or imitation, a reflection, or an actor)

307   *like* in the place of

308   *kind.* In Shakespeare's day this word held more, and
      more complex, meanings than it does now. Helena's
      intended meaning is 'kind' in the modern sense:
      Bertram has been humane and generous. But the whole
      situation to which she alludes reminds a reader of the
      rich ground for irony and double meaning which the
      potentially disparate other senses of the word afforded.
      A major sense at this period was 'natural': a 'kind'
      person is one who acts after his 'kind' or his nature. A
      subordinate sense was 'sexually responsive, willing to
      make love'. It is Helena's triumph that she has
      achieved, even if only momentarily, the unification of
      these meanings, and is able to suggest that Bertram's
      sexual instincts are not only natural but humane and
      generous.

310–11   *When from my finger you can get this ring . . . | And is by
      me with child.* Compare the earlier form of the letter,
      at III.2.56–9.

323   *even* exact, precise

329   *Resolvèdly* so that uncertainty is removed

EPILOGUE

1   *a beggar* (in asking for applause; and in being only the 'shadow' of a king, until the audience confirm him by applause)

4   *strife* striving

5   *Ours be your patience then and yours our parts* we shall patiently wait while you 'act out' applause as you patiently waited while we acted out the play

6   *Your gentle hands lend us and take our hearts* your kind and civilized applause will win our love

AN ACCOUNT OF THE TEXT

OUR only authoritative text of *All's Well That Ends Well* was published in 1623 – seven years after Shakespeare's death – in the volume now known as the first Folio. The plays included in the first Folio present many different kinds of textual problem, and the first question to be considered with each is its provenance. It has to be remembered that the text of a Shakespeare play once existed in a number of forms, among which there might be interrelationship. There were two major forms. One source was 'foul papers', the name given to the author's own draft or drafts of a play, before they were regularized for use in the theatre. This is a class of text that is regarded as distinctively authentic and indicative of authorial intention. The second source was 'prompt-copy', the manuscript of the play as used in the theatre by actors – a source for a text that would be likely to give a version 'cleaner', more coherent, and more regular than the former.

There is a fair consensus of opinion that the text of *All's Well That Ends Well* is based on foul papers or authorial manuscript, and may even record quite early stages of composition, during which the author was still working things out. Some signs of authorial indecisiveness are as follows. There are a good many cases of inconsistent speech prefixes (for example, in the course of the play the Countess appears as *Coun.*, *Old Coun.*, *Mo.*, and *La.*, for *Countess*, *Old Countess*, *Mother*, and *Lady*) which may reflect the way in which various attributes of a character would, scene by scene, present themselves to the author. Such inconsistency would necessarily prove inconvenient in prompt-copy, and would have been regularized. Similar evidence of foul papers is the fact that certain characters in the play start off by being named according to their type (for example, the Widow, the Clown, the Steward, the French Lords) and only acquire their individual names at a later stage in the action (when they become Widow Capilet, Lavatch, Rynaldo, the brothers Dumaine). The last named, the brothers Dumaine, form a textual problem in themselves. In the Folio text there appear to be (at least) *two* sets of paired Lords: one pair, who are attached to the French King, Shakespeare refers to as 'E' and 'G', while the other pair, who are attached to the Duke of Florence, he calls '1' and '2'. It looks as though, at some point in his work, Shakespeare decided to fuse these two pairs (who would probably have been played by the same actors) into one pair. In the process of fusion certain mistakes seem to have occurred so that, for example, there is uncertainty about which Lord helps Bertram woo Diana and which one helps him to fool Parolles. Modern editors have to simplify the situation and eliminate the inconsistency. There are other signs of foul papers. Certain stage directions in the Folio text seem to suggest an attitude of permissiveness on the part of the author, where prompt-copy would probably have been more specific: for example, *Enter 3 or 4 Lords* (II.3.50). There are other stage directions in the Folio text which are equally hard to assign to prompt-copy: for example, that at II.3.61, *She addresses her to a Lord* (whereupon she in fact says *Gentlemen . . .*), or that at II.3.182, *Parolles and Lafew stay behind, commenting of this wedding* (where the nature of the two men's talk is made immediately apparent by what they say). It has been suggested that these are not true stage directions at all: they are in fact some kind of author's note or reminder, perhaps left on breaking off composition, such as would have no place in prompt-copy.

The textual situation can be summarized, then, by saying that the compositors of the Folio text were almost certainly working on foul papers, which perhaps incorporated quite early drafts of the play. In so far as they reproduced their manuscript, their text deserves high respect for its authenticity. On the other hand, there is also evidence that the manuscript was not at all clear and easy to read. The Folio text of *All's Well That Ends*

Well is not, in short, a very good one. Minor errors are frequent; punctuation is poor; major cruces are (for this type of textual situation, where there is only one authoritative text) unusually high in number. It may be that the printer, faced by bad handwriting or confused copy, sometimes found the play too difficult and too original for his guesses: the complex syntax baffled him, and the striking turns of phrase left him behind.

Whatever the reasons for it, a modern edition must depart in a good many ways from the Folio text. Such departures are listed below in the tables of Collations. The Collations include only major departures, such as affect the sense of the text. They do not include such minor details as obvious misprints, mislineations, and so on, nor do they list any details of the modernization of spelling and punctuation – except those which affect the sense of the text. As part of such modernization, *and* meaning 'if' is reduced to *an* throughout, and contracted second person singular endings and superlatives are in general extended to their fuller form.

The names of persons and places have *not* been modernized, since this might obscure their pronunciation. Also, since even those editions which do modernize names always retain the form *Parolles* (which should, strictly, be modernized to 'Paroles'), it seems preferable to retain the old forms throughout: *Lafew* not 'Lafeu', *Lavatch* not 'Lavache', and so on. This applies also to place names: *Rossillion* not 'Rousillon', and *Marcellus* not 'Marseilles'.

COLLATIONS

I

Text

Below are listed major departures in the present text from that of the first Folio (F), whose readings are given – unmodernized except for the 'long s' (ſ) – on the right of the square bracket. A few of these alterations were made in one of the seventeenth-century reprints of F (F2, F3, and F4) and are so indicated.

Most of the others were made by eighteenth- and nineteenth-century editors. Those made by recent editors of the play are acknowledged (see also Further Reading).

THE CHARACTERS IN THE PLAY] *not in* F
I.1.   1   COUNTESS] *Mother*.
        3, 31, 34,   BERTRAM] *Ros*.
              57
              51   have't.] (*this editor*); haue –
              73   BERTRAM] *Ro*.
              86   me.] me
             156   wear] were
I.2.   3, 9, 18   FIRST LORD] 1.*Lo.G*.
          15, 67   SECOND LORD] 2.*Lo.E*.
              18   Rossillion] *Rosignoll*
I.3.   42   madam; e'en] Madam in
              84   but one] but ore
             110   level; Dian no queen] leuell, Queene
             166   loneliness] louelinesse
             172   it t'one to th'other] it 'ton tooth to th'other
             197   intenable] (*C. J. Sisson, 1956*); intemible
II.1   3   gain all,] gaine, all
              15   wed it. When] wed it, when
              16   shrinks, find] shrinkes: finde
              18   FIRST LORD] *L.G*.
        24, 34, 38   FIRST LORD] 1.*Lo.G*.
        25, 35, 39   SECOND LORD] 2.*Lo.E*.
              43   with his cicatrice, an emblem] his sicatrice, with an Embleme
              46   FIRST LORD] *Lo.G*.
              49   Stay: the King] (F2); Stay the King
              62   sue] see
             109   two, more dear; I] two: more dear I
             144   fits] shifts
             155   impostor] (F3); Impostrue
             171   shame;] shame

172 ballads my maiden's name;] (*this editor*); ballads: my maidens name

173 worst, extended] (*C. J. Sisson, 1956*); worst
extended

192 heaven] helpe

II.2.   1 COUNTESS] *Lady* (*Lady or La. throughout
scene*)

37 could!] could:

58 An end, sir! To] And end sir to

II.3.   1 LAFEW] *Ol. Laf.* (*so to line* 183; *except lines* 37,
58, 92: *Old Laf.*; *line* 98: *Ol. Lord*)

69 but, be refused,] but be refused;

95 HELENA] *La.*

124 place when] place, whence

128 good, without a name: vileness] good without a
name? Vilenesse

137 grave] graue:

139–40 tomb | Of ... indeed. What] Tombe. | Of ...
indeed, what

167 eyes. When] eies, when

169 it,] it:

200 ordinaries to] (F3); ordinaries: to

290 detested] detected

II.4.   33 find me? The] finde me? *Clo.* The

II.5.   26 End] And

50 not so] so

III.1.   9 SECOND LORD] *French E.*

17 FIRST LORD] *Fren. G.*

III.2.   8 knew] know

10, 17 COUNTESS] *Lad.* (*La. throughout scene, except
line* 64: *Old La.*)

18 E'en] In

44 FIRST LORD] *French E.* (*so throughout scene,
except line* 62: *1.G.*)

46 SECOND LORD] *French G.* (*so throughout scene*)

110 still-piecing] still-peering

III.4.   18 COUNTESS] *not in* F

III.5.   33 le] (F3); la
          65 I warrant] I write

III.6.   1 FIRST LORD] *Cap. E. (so to line* 102)
           3 SECOND LORD] *Cap. G. (so to line* 102)
          33 his] this
          34 ore] ours
          58 stomach, to't, monsieur! If] stomacke, too't
             Monsieur: if
         102 FIRST LORD As't ... lordship. I'll ... you.]
             Cap. G. As't ... lordship, Ile ... you.
  104, 110 SECOND LORD] *Cap. E.*

III.7.   19 Resolved] Resolue
          34 After,] (*G. K. Hunter, 1959*); after

IV.1.   1 FIRST LORD] *1. Lord E. (so — Lor. E., Lo.E.,
             L.E. — throughout scene*)
          66 FIRST SOLDIER] *Inter. (so throughout scene,
             except lines* 72, 79: *Int.*)
          67 Muskos'] *Muskos*
          87 art] (F3); are

IV.2.   25 Love's] Ioues
          30 words, and poor conditions] (*G. K. Hunter,
             1959*); words and poore conditions,
          38 make vows ... flame] (*this editor*); make rope's
             ... scarre

IV.3.   1 FIRST LORD] *Cap. G. (so throughout scene*)
           2 SECOND LORD] *Cap. E. (so throughout scene,
             except lines* 305, 307: *Lo.E*)
          43 counsel] councell
          75 MESSENGER] *Ser.*
          81 FIRST LORD] *Ber.*
      117–18 me. FIRST LORD (*aside to Bertram*) Hush,
             hush! Hoodman] me: hush, hush. *Cap.
             G.* Hoodman
         119 FIRST SOLDIER] *Inter. (so — Int., Interp. —
             throughout scene*)
       136–7 will. BERTRAM All's ... him. What] will: all's
             ... him. *Ber.* What

	192	lordship] Lord
	234	the] (F3); your
	257	him!] (*P. Alexander, 1951*); him
	259	has] ha's
IV.4.	3	fore] (F2); for
	9	Marcellus] (*G. K. Hunter, 1959*); *Marcellæ*
	16	you] (F4); your
IV.5.	19	grass] grace
	37	name] maine
V.2.	1	Master] Mr
	19	Here] *Clo.* Heere
	20	musk-cat] Muscat
	24	similes] smiles
	32	under her] (F2); vnder
V.3.	27	ATTENDANT] *Gent.*
	44	Admiringly, my liege.] Admiringly my Liege,
	71	COUNTESS Which] Which
	155	sir, since] sir, sir,
	183	them; fairer] them fairer.
	207	truth.] truth,
	216	infinite cunning] insuite comming

Act and scene divisions

Act divisions are marked in F, but of scene divisions there is only '*Actus primus. Scœna Prima*' at the opening of the play. The present text follows the traditional scene numberings used by editors.

Stage directions

Stage directions in the present edition are based on those in F. Emendations and additions have been made where necessary to clarify the action. Indications of persons to whom speeches are addressed, and such directives as *aside* and *aloud* have been silently added to the text. The forms of name by which the hero and heroine appear in stage directions in F (*Bertram, Rossillion,* and *Count Rossillion, Helena* and *Hellen*) have been regularized

223

to the more traditional usage in each case: *Bertram* and *Helena*. Other significant departures from, or additions to, F stage directions are listed below. The reading of the present edition is to the left of the square bracket.

I.1.	72	*Exit*] (F2); *not in* F
	77	*Exeunt Bertram and Lafew*] *not in* F
	184	*Exit*] *not in* F
	211	*Exit*] (F2); *not in* F
I.2.	76	*Exeunt*] *Exit*
I.3.	0	*Enter the Countess, Rynaldo her Steward, and Lavatch her Clown*] *Enter Countesse, Steward, and Clowne.*
II.1.	0	*Enter the King . . . Bertram and Parolles; attendants.*] *Enter the King . . . Count, Rosse, and Parrolles.*
	23	*To some attendants*] *not in* F
		He withdraws] *not in* F
	46	*Exeunt the Lords*] *not in* F
	60	*The King comes forward*] (G. K. Hunter, *1959*); *not in* F
	61	*kneeling*] *not in* F
	91	*He goes to the door*] (G. K. Hunter, *1959*); *not in* F
	210	*Exeunt*] *Exit*
II.3.	45	*Exit an attendant*] *not in* F
	50	*Enter four Lords*] *Enter 3 or 4 Lords*
	61	*Helena addresses the Lords*] *She addresses her to a Lord.*
	182	*Exeunt all but Parolles and Lafew, who stay behind, commenting on this wedding*] *Exeunt* | *Parolles and Lafew stay behind, commenting of this wedding.*
II.4.	54	*Exeunt*] *Exit*
II.5.	48	*Exit*] *not in* F
	69	*He gives Helena a letter*] *not in* F
	92	*Exeunt*] *not in* F

III.1.　　o *Florence, and the two French Lords, with*]
　　　　　Florence, the two Frenchmen, with

　　　　23 *Flourish. Exeunt*] *Flourish.*

III.2.　 19 *reading the letter aloud*] *A Letter.*

　　　　43 *Exit*] *not in* F
　　　　　Enter Helena and the two French Lords] *Enter*
　　　　　Hellen and two Gentlemen.

　　　　55 *She reads the letter aloud*] *not in* F

　　　　74 *reading*] *not in* F

　　　　98 *Exeunt the Countess and the Lords*] *Exit.*

III.3.　 11 *Exeunt*] *Exeunt omnes*

III.4.　　4 STEWARD (*reading*)] *Letter.*

III.5.　　o *her daughter Diana, and Mariana, with other*
　　　　　citizens] *her daughter, Violenta and Mariana,*
　　　　　with other Citizens.

　　　　 7 *Tucket*] *not in* F

　　　　91 *Exeunt Bertram, Parolles, and the army*] *Exit.*

III.6.　　o *Enter Bertram and the two French Lords*] *Enter*
　　　　　Count Rossillion and the Frenchmen, as at first.

　　　 102 *Exit*] *not in* F

III.7.　 48 *Exeunt*] *not in* F

IV.1.　　o *Enter the First French Lord*] *Enter one of the*
　　　　　Frenchmen

　 64, 65 *They seize him . . . They blindfold him*] (G. K.
　　　　　Hunter, 1959); *not in* F

　　　　87 *Exit with Parolles guarded*] *Exit*

　　　　94 *Exeunt*] *Exit*

IV.2.　　o *Enter Bertram and Diana*] *Enter Bertram, and*
　　　　　the Maide called Diana.

　　　　66 *Exit*] *not in* F

IV.3.　　o *Enter the two French Lords, and two or three*
　　　　　soldiers] *Enter the two French Captaines, and*
　　　　　some two or three Souldiours.

　　　 100 *Exeunt the Soldiers*] *not in* F

　　　 114 *Enter Parolles guarded, with the First Soldier as*
　　　　　his interpreter] *Enter Parolles with his Inter-*
　　　　　preter.

225

IV.3. 128, 156,   *reading*] *not in* F
    172, 206

      218   FIRST SOLDIER (*reading*)] *Int. Let.*

      302   *He removes the blindfold*] *not in* F

      312   *Exeunt Bertram and the Lords*] *Exeunt.*

      319   *Exeunt the Soldiers*] *Exit*

IV.5.   0   *Enter the Countess, Lafew, and the Clown*] *Enter Clowne, old Lady, and Lafew.*

V.1.   6   *Enter a Gentleman, Astringer to the King*] *Enter a gentle Astringer.*

      38   *Exeunt*] *not in* F

V.2.   25   *Exit*] *not in* F

      49   *Trumpets sound*] *not in* F

      54   *Exeunt*] *not in* F

V.3.   0   *Enter the King, the Countess*] *Enter King, old Lady*

      27   *Exit*] *not in* F

      76   *Bertram gives Lafew a ring*] *not in* F

     127   *Exit, guarded*] *not in* F

     128   *Enter a Gentleman (the Astringer)*] *Enter a Gentleman.*

     139   KING (*reading the letter*)] *A Letter.*

     152   *Exeunt some attendants*] *not in* F

     154   *Enter Bertram, guarded*] *Enter Bertram.* (*after line* 152)

     157   *Enter the Widow and Diana*] *Enter Widdow, Diana, and Parrolles.* (*after* 'that')

     204   *Exit an attendant*] *not in* F

     293   *Exit the Widow*] *not in* F

Epilogue   6   *Exeunt*] *Exeunt omn.*

2

The following are some of the more interesting and important variant readings and proposed emendations *not* accepted in the present text. They derive from F2, F3, and F4, or have been made or conjectured in other editions of the play. To the left of the square brackets are the readings of the present text, and to the right of them the suggested emendations. Where there are several citations, they are separated by semi-colons.

I.1.   55–8   COUNTESS If ... mortal. BERTRAM Madam
                ... wishes. LAFEW How ... that?] COUNTESS
                If ... mortal. LAFEW How ... that? BERTRAM
                Madam ... wishes; COUNTESS How ... that?
                If ... mortal. BERTRAM Madam ... wishes

        114–15 valiant, in the defence] valiant in the defence,

        145   ten year ... two] the year ... two; two years
                ... two; ten months ... two; one year ... two

I.3.   84   but one] but or; but o'er; but for; before

        244   day, an] day, and (F3)

II.1.   62   sue] fee

        76   Pippen] Pepin

        162   torcher] coacher

        164   her] his

        173   Seared otherwise, ne worse of] Seard otherwise,
                no worse of (F2); Sear'd otherwise; nay, worse
                of; Sear'd otherwise; nay worse – of; Seared;
                otherwise – ne worse of
                worst, extended] worst extended,

II.2.   37   could!] could,

        58   An end, sir! To] And end; sir to; An end, Sir;
                to

II.3.   7–9   PAROLLES Why ... times. BERTRAM And so
                'tis] Why ... times. PAROLLES And so 'tis

        11–12   PAROLLES So ... Paracelsus. LAFEW Of all]
                PAROLLES So I say. LAFEW Both ... Paracel-
                sus. PAROLLES So I say. LAFEW Of all

        22   what-do-ye-call there] what-do-ye-call't there;
                what-do-ye-call't here; what do you call these

        23   A showing ... actor] *A showing ... actor*

        32–7   LAFEW In ... weak – PAROLLES And ... be –
                LAFEW Generally thankful] LAFEW In ...
                weak – PAROLLES Ay, so I say. LAFEW And

		debile . . . as to be (*after a pause*) generally thankful; LAFEW In . . . weak and debile . . . King, as to be generally thankful
II.3.	128	good, without a name: vileness] good, without a name vileness
II.4.	33	find me? The] find me? PAROLLES In myself. CLOWN The; find me? (*Parolles shakes his head*) The; find me? . . . The
II.5.	89	Where . . . men? Monsieur, farewell] BERTRAM Where . . . men, Monsieur? – farewell; BERTRAM Where . . . men? HELENA Monsieur, farewell
III.1.	17	nature] Nation
III.2.	9	hold] sold
	110	still-piecing] still-piercing; still-'pearing; still-pairing
III.5.	65	I warrant] I right (F2); Ah! right; A right; I weet
III.6.	102	FIRST LORD As't . . . lordship. I'll . . . you] SECOND LORD As't . . . Lordship, I'll . . . you; FRENCH GENTLEMAN As't . . . lordship. FRENCH ENVOY I'll . . . you
	104, 110	SECOND LORD] FIRST LORD
III.7.	34	After,] after this
IV.1.	41	Bajazeth's mule] Bajazet's mute; Balaam's mule; Bajazet's mate
IV.2.	25	Love's] God's
	28, 29	him] Him
	30	words, and poor conditions] words and poor, conditions
	38	make vows in such a flame] make Hopes . . . Affairs; make hopes . . . scene; make rapes . . . scour; may grope's . . . scarre; may cope's . . . stir; may rope's . . . snare
IV.3.	18	delay] allay; lay
	158	live] die; leave
		this] but this

IV.4.   9 Marcellus] Marseilles

30–31 pray you. | But with the word the] pray you, |
Bear with the word: the; pay you | But with the
word; the; pray you ... | But with the word,
that; pray you; | But with the word: 'the

IV.5. 16 not herbs] not Sallet-Herbs; knot-herbs

78 Marcellus] Marseilles

V.2.   1 Master] Monsieur

4 mood] moat

23 ingenious] ingenuous; ingenerous

V.3.   6 blade] blaze

96 ingaged] engag'd; ungag'd

195 hit] his; it

FOR THE BEST IN PAPERBACKS, LOOK FOR THE

In every corner of the world, on every subject under the sun, Penguin represents quality and variety – the very best in publishing today.

For complete information about books available from Penguin – including Pelicans, Puffins, Peregrines and Penguin Classics – and how to order them, write to us at the appropriate address below. Please note that for copyright reasons the selection of books varies from country to country.

In the United Kingdom: For a complete list of books available from Penguin in the U.K., please write to *Dept E.P., Penguin Books Ltd, Harmondsworth, Middlesex, UB7 0DA*

In the United States: For a complete list of books available from Penguin in the U.S., please write to *Dept BA, Penguin, 299 Murray Hill Parkway, East Rutherford, New Jersey 07073*

In Canada: For a complete list of books available from Penguin in Canada, please write to *Penguin Books Canada Ltd, 2801 John Street, Markham, Ontario L3R 1B4*

In Australia: For a complete list of books available from Penguin in Australia, please write to the *Marketing Department, Penguin Books Australia Ltd, P.O. Box 257, Ringwood, Victoria 3134*

In New Zealand: For a complete list of books available from Penguin in New Zealand, please write to the *Marketing Department, Penguin Books (NZ) Ltd, Private Bag, Takapuna, Auckland 9*

In India: For a complete list of books available from Penguin, please write to *Penguin Overseas Ltd, 706 Eros Apartments, 56 Nehru Place, New Delhi, 110019*

In Holland: For a complete list of books available from Penguin in Holland, please write to *Penguin Books Nederland B.V., Postbus 195, NL–1380AD Weesp, Netherlands*

In Germany: For a complete list of books available from Penguin, please write to *Penguin Books Ltd, Friedrichstrasse 10 – 12, D–6000 Frankfurt Main 1, Federal Republic of Germany*

In Spain: For a complete list of books available from Penguin in Spain, please write to *Longman Penguin España, Calle San Nicolas 15, E–28013 Madrid, Spain*

'It should be acknowledged now that the present RSC is a national treasure' —*The Times*

Since its formation in 1960 the Royal Shakespeare Company has become one of the best-known theatre companies in the world. Its central concern is Shakespeare and in its five theatres – the Royal Shakespeare Theatre, the Swan Theatre and The Other Place in Stratford, the Barbican Theatre and The Pit in London – the Company performs more Shakespeare each year than any other theatre company. It is highly appropriate, therefore, that the company performing Shakespeare more frequently than anyone else should get together with this country's largest publisher of his plays.

Find out more about the RSC and its activities by joining the Company's mailing list. Not only will you receive booking information for all five theatres but also priority booking, the exclusive RSC News, special ticket offers and special offers on RSC publications.

If you would like to receive details and an application form for the RSC's mailing list please write, enclosing a stamped addressed envelope, to: Mailing List Organizer, Royal Shakespeare Theatre, Stratford-upon-Avon, Warwickshire CV37 6BB

THE AGE OF SHAKESPEARE

Edited by Boris Ford

This volume of *The Pelican Guide to English Literature* covers the period of Shakespeare's own lifetime. It contains a long general survey of the English literary renaissance, and also an account of the social context of literature in the period. Then there follow a number of essays which consider in detail the work and importance of individual dramatists and poets and prose-writers, but above all the dramatists, for this was their age: five of the essays are devoted to Shakespeare's plays alone. Finally, this volume contains an appendix giving short author-biographies and, in each case, standard editions of authors' works, critical commentaries, and lists of books for further study and reference.

There are nine further volumes in *The New Pelican Guide to English Literature*

MEDIEVAL LITERATURE (2 parts)
FROM DONNE TO MARVELL
FROM DRYDEN TO JOHNSON
FROM BLAKE TO BYRON
FROM DICKENS TO HARDY
FROM JAMES TO ELIOT
THE PRESENT
A GUIDE FOR READERS

SHAKESPEARE'S TRAGEDIES
An Anthology of Modern Criticism

Edited by Laurence Lerner

Shakespeare's tragedies have always been fertile areas for comment and criticism. The same dramas which inspired Keats to write poetry appealed to A. C. Bradley – or to Ernest Jones, the psycho-analyst – as studies of character; and where the New Criticism has been principally interested in language and imagery, other critics in America have seen the plays as superb examples of plot and structure. Most of Aristotle's elements of tragedy have found their backers, and as the editor points out in his introduction these varying approaches to Shakespeare are by no means incompatible.

In what *The Times Literary Supplement* described as an 'excellent collection' Laurence Lerner has assembled the best examples of the modern schools of Shakespearean criticism and arranged them to throw light on individual plays and on tragedy in general.

THE ELIZABETHAN WORLD PICTURE
B. M. W. Tillyard

In this short study Dr Tillyard not only elucidates such fairly familiar – though often mystifying concepts as the four elements, the celestial harmony of 'the nine enfolded Sphears', or macrocosm and microcosm: he also shows how this world picture was variously regarded as a chain of being, a network of correspondences, and a cosmic dance. Such concepts were commonplace to the Elizabethans. By expounding them the author has rendered plain, and not merely picturesque, a host of contemporary passages.

THREE JACOBEAN TRAGEDIES

Edited by Gāmini Salgādo

Renaissance humanism had reached a crisis by the early seventeenth century. It was followed by a period of mental unrest, a sense of moral corruption and ambiguity which provoked the Jacobean dramatists to embittered satire and images of tragic retribution.

John Webster (c. 1570–1625) in *The White Devil* paints a sinister and merciless world ruled by all the refinements of cunning and intrigue, whilst in *The Revenger's Tragedy*, one of the most powerful of the Jacobean tragedies, Cyril Tourneur (c. 1570–1626) displays in a macabre ballet the emotional conflicts and vices typical of the age. *The Changeling* is perhaps the supreme achievement of Thomas Middleton (1580–1627) – a masterpiece of brooding intensity.

FOUR JACOBEAN CITY COMEDIES

Edited by Gāmini Salgādo

The idiom of these Jacobean comedies is everywhere that of the bustling and bawdy metropolis; and the gulling of dupes and the seduction of women and the activities of sharpers and rogues are presented with irresistible vivacity. London and its court appeared to these dramatists as a striking and comprehensive image of human appetite and folly. However, though satire may dominate, the moralist's censure is often tempered by an affection for the richness and variety of city life.

Only Massinger in *A New Way To Pay Old Debts*, his finest play, explicitly condemns human weakness. Both Marston and Jonson, in expansive mood, remind us that man is also an animal, and that he forgets this at his peril, while in Middleton's *A Mad World, My Masters* we find an unambiguous celebration of the virtuosity of its villain-heroes.

Sir Philip Sidney
ARCADIA
Edited by Maurice Evans

For more than 200 years after its first publication in 1593, *The Countess*
Pembroke's Arcadia was the most read, best-selling story in the language *t*
great English popular classic and one of the most influential.

As much a work of entertainment and wit as of instruction, it affords pe
haps the best insight we have into the tastes and standards of the Elizabethan
Sidney became to his contemporaries the *beau idéal* of the Renaissance courti
and his *Arcadia* embodies the highest literary aspirations of the age. Here w
have a gladiatorial display of rhetoric which outshines anything achieved
English before and possibly since.

Thomas Nashe
THE UNFORTUNATE TRAVELLER
AND OTHER WORKS
Edited by J. B. Steane

Thomas Nashe, a contemporary of Shakespeare, was a pamphleteer, poe
story-teller, satirist, scholar, moralist and jester. His work epitomizes every
thing that comes to mind when we think of the character of the Elizabethan
their shameless minglings of devoutness and bawdy, scholarship and slang, th
inexhaustible fluency of their language, their strictly *ad personam* controversie
their relish for life and their constant awareness of the imminence of death.

This volume offers the modern reader a selection of those of his work
whose interest is perennial. As well as *The Unfortunate Traveller* it contain
Piers Penniless, Terrors of the Night, Lenten Stuff and *A Choice of Valentine*
and extracts from *Christ's Tears over Jerusalem, The Anatomy of Absurdity* an
other works.

CHRISTOPHER MARLOWE
THE COMPLETE PLAYS

Edited by J. B. Steane

In recent years there has been a widening of opinion about Marlowe; at one extreme he is considered an atheist rebel and at the other a Christian traditionalist. There is as much divergence in Marlowe's seven plays and, as J. B. Steane says in his introduction, that a man's work should encompass the extremes of *Tamburlaine* and *Edward the Second* is one of the most absorbingly interesting facts of literature; the range of Marlowe's small body of work covers such amazingly unlike pieces as *Doctor Faustus* and *The Jew of Malta*. Controlled and purposeful, these plays contain a poetry which enchants and lodges in the mind.

BEN JONSON
THREE COMEDIES
VOLPONE/THE ALCHEMIST
BARTHOLOMEW FAIR

Edited by Michael Jamieson

As Shakespeare's nearest rival on the English stage, Ben Jonson has both gained and suffered. Productions of recent years have, as it were, rediscovered him as a comic dramatist of genius and a master of language. This volume contains his best-known comedies.

Volpone, which is perhaps his greatest, and *The Alchemist* are both *tours de force* of brilliant knavery, unflagging in wit and comic invention. *Bartholomew Fair*, an earthier work, portrays Jonson's fellow Londoners in festive mood – bawdy, energetic, and never at a loss for words.

NEW PENGUIN SHAKESPEARE

General Editor: T. J. B. Spencer